D0003788

The King in the Tree

THREE NOVELLAS

CONTRA COSTA COUNTY LIBRARY

STEVEN MILLHAUSER

VINTAGE CONTEMPORARIES

Vintage Books

A Division of Random House, Inc.

3 1901 03611 1799

FIRST VINTAGE CONTEMPORARIES EDITION, JULY 2004

Copyright © 2003 by Steven Millhauser

All rights reserved under International and Pan-American Copyright Conventions.
Published in the United States by Vintage Books, a division of Random House,
Inc., New York, and simultaneously in Canada by Random House of Canada
Limited, Toronto. Originally published in hardcover in the United States by
Alfred A. Knopf, a division of Random House, Inc., New York, in 2003.

Vintage and colophon are registered trademarks and
Vintage Contemporaries is a trademark of Random House, Inc.

"Revenge" previously appeared in *Harper's Magazine* (July 2001).

The Library of Congress has cataloged the Knopf edition as follows:
Millhauser, Steven.
The king in the tree : three novellas / Steven Millhauser.—1st ed.
p. cm.
1. Triangles (Interpersonal relations)—Fiction.
2. Don Juan (Legendary character)—Fiction.
3. Tristan (Legendary character)—Fiction.
4. Iseult (Legendary character)—Fiction.
5. Historical fiction, American.
6. Love stories, American. I. Title.
PS3563.I422 K46 2003
813'.54—dc21   2002072956

Vintage ISBN: 1-4000-3173-7

Book design by Virginia Tan

www.vintagebooks.com

Printed in the United States of America
10 9 8 7 6 5 4 3 2 1

WITHDRAWN

Acclaim for Steven Millhauser's

The King in the Tree

"An ingenious geometer of love triangles, Millhauser tinkers with tested formulas in these three novellas, while giving full rein to his taste for the fantastical. . . . [His] shrewd sense of psychology makes his characters' impulses toward romantic excess manifestly believable."　　　　*—The New Yorker*

"Coursing through these novellas are such literary ghosts as Byron, Wagner-as-librettist, Matthew Arnold and Alfred Lord Tennyson. . . . But when Millhauser is plumbing the mysteries of the human heart, there's no question that he is writing after, not before, Sigmund Freud—and Kate Chopin, and John Updike and the sexual revolution. . . . *The King in the Tree* is a moving, melancholy book about the unlovely toll exacted by love on those it has abandoned."
　　　　　　　　　　　　　　　　　　　—Los Angeles Times

"Ever finish a book that was so good you ached to grab the collar of the next passer-by and shout in his unsuspecting face, 'Read this! You have got to read this!'? Steven Millhauser writes that kind of book."　　*—The San Diego Union-Tribune*

"Among [Millhauser's] best. . . . *The King in the Tree* is a flawless retelling of the story of Tristan and Iseult. . . . Astonishingly, Millhauser creates a version that though modern reads like a newly discovered medieval tale. . . . His story will live with the older versions, and Richard Wagner's, as part of the myth."　　　　　　　　　　　　*—The Boston Globe*

"Reading a book by Steven Millhauser is like tumbling down Alice's rabbit hole. In the Millhauser Wonderland, time reels backward, life is but a fairy tale, and figures of mythology rule the universe. . . . All three of the novellas that make up *The King in the Tree* inhabit eerie realms of the imagination. Here men and women yearn for love, but it's a poison more often than a tonic." —*Newsday*

"These three tales, each in different ways, confirm Millhauser's reputation as a master stylist." —*The Star-Ledger* (Newark)

"Millhauser is our most brilliant practicing romantic, for whom surface reality is merely an uninteresting illusion, and ultimate reality is always artifice." —*Milwaukee Journal Sentinel*

"All three of the novellas have Millhauser's gifted storytelling voice going for them—a voice that grabs the reader by the ear and makes him pay attention." —*Rocky Mountain News*

"Millhauser's characters are poignantly likable. They hurt, long and love like the rest of us. . . . Sentence by sentence, Millhauser displays awesome control." —*Minneapolis Star Tribune*

"Millhauser's three novellas are marvels of craftmanship and inventiveness . . . a storytelling tour de force and an emotional rollercoaster ride." —*Richmond Times-Dispatch*

STEVEN MILLHAUSER

The King in the Tree

Steven Millhauser received the Pulitzer Prize for *Martin Dressler*. He is the author of nine other books, including *Edwin Mullhouse*, *Enchanted Night*, and *The Knife Thrower and Other Stories*. He teaches at Skidmore College and lives with his wife and two children in Saratoga Springs, New York.

ALSO BY STEVEN MILLHAUSER

Enchanted Night

The Knife Thrower and Other Stories

Martin Dressler

Little Kingdoms

The Barnum Museum

From the Realm of Morpheus

In the Penny Arcade

Portrait of a Romantic

Edwin Mullhouse

The King
in the Tree

To Marc Chénetier

Contents

Revenge

FRONT HALL

This is the hall. It isn't much of a one, but it does the job. Boots here, umbrellas there. I hate those awful houses, don't you, where the door opens right into the living room. Don't you? It's like being introduced to some man at a party who right away throws his arm around your shoulders. No, give me a little distance, thank you, a little formality. I'm all for the slow buildup, the gradual introduction. Of course you have to imagine it without the bookcase. There isn't a room in the house without a bookcase.

May I take your coat? Oh, I like it. It's perfect. And light as a feather. Wher*ever* did you find it? It's so hard to know what to wear this time of year, warm one day cold the next. I worry about my jonquils. They came out last week and then wouldn't you know it: snow. Luckily it didn't stick. It's a miracle they didn't die. I'll just hang it right here, next to mine. It must look very empty to you, all those hangers side by side. Those are my late husband's hats. Funny. One day I cleared out all the coats, all the shoes and galoshes—it just seemed pointless. But I left the hats. I couldn't touch the hats.

LIVING ROOM

This used to be my favorite room. Listen to me! *Used* to be. But that's the way it is, you know. I don't have a favorite room anymore. Still, I spend most of my time here. Where else would I go? I'm so glad you like it. One thing we always agreed on, my husband and I, was furniture: it had to be comfortable. As Robert put it, no matter how new it was, it had to look *sat* in. And of course the piano—what's a living room without a piano, I'd like to know. Not that *I* ever touched it. No, I gave up piano at twelve. Don't know why, really. It's the sort of thing you later think you regret, without really regretting it. But Robert, now. He quit lessons at fifteen but kept on practicing. He never did like to give anything up.

It's a warm room too. When we bought the place it was a little drafty in winter, but first we insulated and then we replaced those drafty old windows that Robert had to put up every fall. Triple-track: it made a difference, let me tell you. When you close the curtains, in cold weather, it's just as if you're sealing yourself in. I'd sit on the couch with my feet tucked under, reading, while Robert sat in the chair there, by the bookcase, reading and marking passages. Or we'd talk— you know, thoughts drifting up, turning into words, like, I don't know, like a way of breathing. Sometimes he made a fire in the fireplace—excellent draft. I meant to tell you I had the chimney cleaned only last month. Was *that* ever a job. You wouldn't believe what was in there. I almost fell over when I saw the bill. But hey, can you blame the poor guy? *Any*way. When the fire was going, I'd move to that end of the couch, to be near it. I could feel the heat all along my right side. Some- times Robert would go over to the piano, if the mood struck him. He never played for anyone except me. This wasn't exactly as romantic as it sounds. He called himself an *amateur*—harsh word for Robert—said he refused to destroy beautiful things in public. Robert never liked to make mistakes. It upset him. He played for me because he knew I wouldn't mind an occasional wrong note. Or you could say he played for himself and allowed me to overhear him. But I loved to hear him play, especially his Chopin nocturnes. He was crazy about Chopin, said he was the greatest composer—not ever, but of piano music. Second was Mozart. He'd play those Mozart sonatas over and over—every single one of them. Do you know what he'd do? He'd begin with any sonata and play right through the book, in order, till all of a sudden—right in the middle of a movement—the middle of a phrase—he stopped. "That's enough of *that!*" he'd say, as though he were angry at himself, or . . . or disappointed. Robert was hard on himself. You had to know when to soothe him and when to leave him alone. Men are harder on themselves that way than women, don't you think? Or am I wrong? But when he played, he was able to lose himself for a while, in the music. So imagine a fire going— wood snapping the way it does when it's a little green—the wind rattling the windows behind the curtains—and one of those Chopin melodies that feel like sorrow and ecstasy all mixed together pouring from the keys—and you have my idea of happiness. Or just reading, reading and lamplight, the sound of pages turning. And so you dare to be happy. You do that thing. You dare.

I hope you don't mind these little . . . anecdotes of mine. We can just breeze on through the house if you'd rather. Then it's all right to continue?

Well. I don't want you to think of me sitting on that couch for twenty-two years with a look of blissful idiocy on my face.

You know, the adoring wife and the happy hubby. Twenty-two years! That was how long Robert and I were married: twenty-two years. Things are bound to be a little imperfect, in twenty-two years. I met him when I was twenty-four, working in a bookstore in Vermont. Robert was thirty. Even back then he had that gloomy kind of handsomeness that just . . . slayed me. A handsome moody man. Doomed, as he was fond of saying. Difficult, was what it boiled down to. Robert was difficult. But you work your way through. Besides, I was a handful myself, back then. Demanding. Temperamental. Robert was very patient. Impatient with himself and others, patient with me. We . . . fell in love, as they say. And stayed there. That was the thing. And I knew him: God, did I know him. I was a student of his expressions, a scholar of his moods. I don't know when it was, exactly, that I felt something was wrong. It was last year—spring was further along, half my forsythias dead. You remember that late frost. I was sitting on the couch with a book, after dinner, and Robert was sitting in his chair, with a book facedown on his leg, thinking. Brooding, you could say. For no particular reason I asked myself: Am I happy? And I felt a little pause, a little—oh, breath of hesitation, before I answered: Well, yes, of course I'm happy. Of course I am. Happy.

What stayed with me was that blink of hesitation. Robert had been acting a little strange lately. I'd noticed it without noticing it, the way you do. His work wasn't going well again, he was—I mean, all this was nothing new. But there was a new element, something I was suddenly aware of. Robert was very good at giving you his full attention. I've never known anyone who was so good at giving you their full attention that way. He would listen with a kind of . . . a kind of alertness, and whatever he said would be at the center of what you were talking about. I realized that I'd missed this for a while—that his deepest attention was elsewhere. Now, listen. There was no question of unfaithfulness between Robert and me. I knew Robert. It wasn't the sort of thing he *did*. Not that he didn't notice a pretty woman. He *liked* pretty women. He liked *me*, didn't he? Was always talking about how pretty I was and all that; I didn't deny it. And of course women were always noticing him. But noticing's one thing, and Robert . . . it wasn't his way. It just wasn't in the bounds of possibility. Besides, we were happy. Weren't we? But I found myself thinking, on the couch—or not really thinking, it was more like the shadow of a thought: could it be that Robert . . . ? I immediately felt embarrassed, almost . . . ashamed, as if I'd been caught in some unpleasant act. But there it was. The little thought-shadow.

This mantelpiece came with the house. I can show it to you in the original plan. Solid marble. Nice, if you like that sort of thing.

Listen. I'll tell you a story.

Once upon a time there was a woman—just like me. She grew up in a small New England town, just like me. She was well loved and cheerful and fond of reading, just like me. She was good at school but not brilliant and went to a small college in Vermont, and at the age of twenty-four she fell in love—just like me. She married the next year, and she and her husband moved into a comfortable old house. The years passed. She was happy. Then one day, do you know what happened? Listen: I'll tell you what happened. Nothing happened. She was happy, life was worth living, she liked the summer, and the fall, and the winter, and the spring, and she liked all the days of the week. And this woman was not like me, not like me at all.

That's my story. Did you like it?

But—good lord—can you believe it? All along I've been holding this envelope. You must have been wondering. Why didn't you *say* something? It's the appraisal. As I said on the phone, I'm selling the house myself. I have no use for realtors—or reelators, as everybody says these days. God, how Robert hated that. Put some water in the perculator for the reelator. Then we can discuss nucular war. Anyway, I had the place appraised, and here's the report. I won't ask a penny more, but I also won't take a penny less. That keeps it nice and simple.

Now if we step around this way.... Door to the cellar. Back porch. I want to show you the back porch. But first the kitchen. *That* door?

DOWNSTAIRS BATH

The downstairs bath. Half bath—tub and no shower—newish WC—everything in fine working order. Please note the bookcase. I promised you a bookcase in every room and, by God, girl—as my grandpa used to say to my grandma—you'll get a bookcase in every room! I mean, what with Robert's books and mine. Will you just *look* at these things. A real mishmash. *Wealth of Nations. Jane Eyre. Wizard of Oz.* We knew where everything was, it just wasn't in any particular order, except of course in Robert's study. *The Guermantes Way. Psychopathology of Everyday Life.* Now there's a title I've always liked. Screw's coming out of that towel rack. The paint's cracking over there; you'd want it redone. When I ordered the new toilet—I was the one who took care of things like that—the man said they came in two sizes: a short one, and a longer one. So I ask him what the difference is. He looks embarrassed, lowers his eyes. "Well, ma'am," he says, "the longer one is . . . sometimes it's more comfortable for . . . the gentleman." Can you believe it? I practically bit my tongue off, not to laugh. "More comfortable for . . . the gentleman." Robert and I howled over it. Of course I ordered the larger one. We called it The Gentleman. Permit me to introduce you. Lady: Gentleman. Ahm right proud to make your acquaintance, ma'am. *To the Lighthouse. Tristes Tropiques.* Good God. I spent one night lying on the floor of this room, right here on this old linoleum. Can you imagine? It's hard to see how anyone could fit.

KITCHEN

Lots of sun through those windows. Kitchens should be bright, don't you think? You ought to see the light coming through the window onto the table, on a good summer morning. Of course it's terribly old-fashioned. Not nearly enough cabinet space. I know, I know. And I'm the only woman in America without a dishwasher. But really, where would you put it? I refuse to give up my sunny table. I could put one there—and cramp up the whole room. No, let it go. Besides, what would my friends do if they couldn't say: Oh, you poor *thing*! You've just *got* to redecorate. Of course I understand a new kitchen's a selling point. But I've told you about that. I'm sticking to the appraisal, no matter what.

You see up there? On top of the cabinets? Complete works of James Fenimore Cooper. Library sale. They were practically giving it away.

I could use a cup of tea. Would you care to join me? Oh, good. Good. I've been talking a blue streak, haven't I? And that's strange, because I'm known as a more or less quiet person. I calmed down after a few years of marriage. As I say, I was happy. It quiets you down. So: Robert's quiet wife. And now, isn't it odd, I have a desire to talk. Of course I don't talk to just anyone. But there's something about you . . . a sympathy, I think. I could sense it when you first entered the house.

Milk? Sugar? I'm afraid I've only got whole. I can't stand that two-percent stuff. Tastes like bad water, if you ask me. They say it isn't much different from whole anyway, you have to have *one* percent to accomplish anything. Accomplish *what*, I'd like to know. Of course someone with your figure doesn't have to worry. But I suppose it's always the ones who don't have to worry who do. No milk? I hadn't thought of that. Solves the problem nicely, doesn't it?

Mmm, that's good. That's very good. Tea calms me. Selling this house rattles me—it's like stirring a pile of leaves with a stick—you never know what's going to come slithering out— but tea, now. Tea calms me. Especially on an afternoon like this, the sun in and out—a little on the cool side. I do worry about my jonquils. Last year I lost half my forsythias. Just look at those clouds. Well. After that evening I told you about—the evening when a doubt crossed my mind—things continued as usual—except that they weren't as usual. I knew something was wrong. Believe me, I knew. Robert was withholding something from me. You have to understand that Robert was a secretive man. I mean, he was a combination of secretiveness and . . . openness. It's one of the things you get to know about a man. But this withholding, this, this awkwardness—well. It was new. Something had changed. It upset me. He knew it did. I still thought it was the book that was harming him. He'd taken a semester off, he was putting tremendous pressure on himself, and it wasn't going well. He told me very little about it. Typical Robert: bottle it up, fight it alone. Be a man! I knew it had to do with *things*, American things—I think he was even plan-

ning to call it *American Things*—familiar household objects
that were supposed to reveal something about American life in
the late nineteenth century. Robert taught history and American studies at the community college. Have I mentioned
it? They paid him nothing. It was a crime. Anyway: things.
Fountain pens, tin cans, bottle caps—he kept reading about
these things, searching for something deep. He wanted everything to *mean* something. So of course I thought it was that. I
wanted it to be that. I could hear him scraping back the chair
in the study, pacing around. Sometimes he left the house on
long walks, or rode to the supermarket late at night, where
he'd spend hours studying boxes, cans—or so he said. I felt
estranged from him. And, funny as it sounds, I began drinking
a lot of tea. I liked the ritual, I suppose. One evening last summer I was sitting right here at this table, alone, drinking tea.
Iced tea, it was, with a slice of lemon. I heard Robert's footsteps coming down the stairs. He came through the dining
room into the kitchen and sat down, right where you're sitting
now. He had his sad, doomed look but also something else, a
tension, an energy. I had the impression of a dangerous electri-
cal wire—touch it and you're dead. In a clipped, haughty way,
angry and cold but weary, broken—oh, who knew *what* it
was—he told me. He confessed. It was a withheld kind of outpouring, a strangled eruption. But he confessed. He'd been seeing someone. You won't believe this, but I thought he meant a
therapist. A shrink. Robert? But of course he meant a woman.

More tea?

Now this, too, may surprise you. My first thought was: Oh,
no! Poor Robert! Not *him!* I mean, *Robert,* whose harshest word
after *amateur* was ba*nal*—accent on the last syllable, to give it
the true French stink. I could hear him mocking it all, in that
way of his. *Adultery,* for Chrissake, in *suburbia,* for Chrissake.

Doesn't the poor sap have a sense of style? Pure kitsch, kiddo. Right up there with busts of Beethoven and bookmarks with Emily Dickinson poems printed on them. And so forth. Poor Robert! What a sad falling off. And so, creature of habit that I was, I wanted to *comfort* him, the poor man. I mean there he was, sitting all doomed and sort of crumpled and . . . and ba*nal,* so of course the only thing you want to do is reassure your husband, while at the same time it's dawning on you what he's actually said, and there's a panic starting somewhere because this handsome man with his doomed look has gone and done something bad to you, if only you could stop comforting him and start concentrating long enough to figure out just what it unbearably *is.*

I suppose I should have told you the house is haunted. Well, of *course.* All houses are haunted. It's just that some are more haunted than others. Robert's ghost is sitting right there, where you're sitting now, and my ghost is sitting here, listening to his strangled confession. The air is full of ghosts. At night you can hear them: sifting through the house, like sand.

I said nothing. I think he wanted me to say something—to scream at him, to burst into tears. I felt he wanted drama. I lowered my eyes. I could tell I was disappointing him. At the same time I felt threads of fire shooting through me, a wondrous fiery piercing, a kind of . . . a kind of exhilaration of misery. I thought I might die, and that dying might be a strange, exciting thing to do. And you know, I felt almost soothed, almost comforted in my private fire, because it protected me from him, from the words he had spoken.

I think I exasperated him. The poor man needed something from me, blame or forgiveness or . . . *drama,* and there I sat, exalted in misery, a saint of suffering. Who knows? When the living have become the dead, who shall speak? There was too much silence in the room. The kitchen was no longer large enough to contain all that silence. It was pushing against the walls, cracking the plaster. I don't think he intended to say more, but the silence was choking him. He spat out some words, the way you do when someone's hands are around your neck. He told me things. I said nothing. He told me her name. That's when I learned it was you.

You seem upset. Of course you ought to be. Of course Robert would have sworn eternal secrecy. I wouldn't be surprised if he made you prick your finger with a needle and sign a document in blood. Secret love! What could be better? What you failed to understand was Robert's loyalty. It's true that by taking you as his—do you mind the word *mistress*?—he had been disloyal to me. That's what confused you. Your mistake was to assume that there were two separate facts: a disloyalty, to me, and a new loyalty, to you. No, whatever his feelings might have been for you, his disloyalty to me simply stirred up and even strengthened the old loyalty. He confessed to me because he was loyal and couldn't do anything about it. He was stuck with it. Robert betrayed you. I want you to know that. It's something we have in common.

Do you know what else he told me? He told me you were nothing to him. Don't you say anything. He told me you were a body, just a body. If he was trying to soothe me, he was failing brilliantly. But I want you to know what he said, sitting right there. Just a body. Men can be a little thoughtless sometimes, don't you think? Of course you can choose not to believe me, if it makes you feel better. Or you can believe that Robert was lying. A good man, lying to spare the feelings of his wife.

But let's adjourn to the porch, shall we? There's so much more to tell.

BACK PORCH

This was all open, when we bought the place. I used to hang a line between these two posts: I remember Robert's socks dripping onto the handrail. On Robert's salary and the little I picked up part-time at the library, we had to be careful—a dryer was the last thing we considered necessary. It was the mosquitoes that finally drove us to screen it in. I don't think it's too chilly out here, do you? We can sit a little. Sit, why don't you. I just loved it out here, summer evenings. I'd come out with a book and sit with it facedown in my lap. You can hear a lot of sounds in the summer, and I liked all of them: children's voices all woven together, a car radio suddenly loud and then fading away, a basketball hitting a driveway with that smacking sound, grackles in the trees—and the crickets, always the crickets, and always the lawn mowers. I used to think of the evening lawn mowers as big summer insects—a sort of bee. Robert never lasted long out here. I think it made him restless. But he always sat for a while, in the summer, to keep me company. Sometimes we'd talk about converting it to a full-time room—windows, heat, I imagined myself sitting out here feeling warm in winter—but my heart wasn't in it. A porch needs to be open. You need to feel the air and hear the sounds. Don't you think? The whole idea is to be outside and inside at the same time. That's what a porch *is*.

After Robert's confession, I came out here. Sat right there where you're sitting now. Who knows what I was thinking? It's hard to remember things, even the most important things in your life. All you know is that they happened. I sat down. I felt dead. At the same time my mind was very sharp and alert. And this might strike you as odd, but I was in a state of—of surprise. Robert had killed me, a quick stab to the heart, and I'd come out on the porch to watch myself die. Why wasn't I dead? It did surprise me. Or maybe the dead have their thoughts, as well as the living. Do you think so? My mind, as I said, was very alert. I heard Robert's words, the words that I knew were going to change my life, and already I was judging them. You see, I heard in his confession a certain—well, a certain pride. He had said his piece—had come to terms with his conscience—he'd acted like a *good man*. He had performed well. I almost felt like standing up and applauding. Bravo, Robert! Now it was my turn—to act like a *good woman*. All I had to do was forgive him.

I don't know how long I sat out here. I remember noticing it had grown dark: a peaceful summer night. At one point I heard Robert's footsteps in the kitchen. They stopped at the door of the porch, and I knew he was standing there in the dark kitchen, looking at me through that window. Then he went away.

When I first met Robert, when I was twenty-four and he was thirty, he used to come into the bookstore where I was working. He wore jeans and work boots and flannel shirts. He looked like a skinny lumberjack. I thought he was my age—a student, maybe. Even then he was an interesting man. A teacher who hated teachers, an intellectual who made fun of intellectuals, a Jew with no ties to Judaism—unless you count the piano. Robert liked to say that all pianos are Jews. He didn't sit comfortably in his skin. It's one of the things that most attracted me to him.

I thought about that time in a dim, puzzled way, as if I'd read about it in some book I could no longer remember.

Then I recalled something that happened once at a party. A loud man was talking to Robert, a little way off. "Good old

Robert," I heard him say, with a friendly laugh. I saw Robert's face tighten behind his little smile. Later I asked what *that* was all about. "Oh, he's a fool," Robert said. "But even so, he has no right to call me *good.*" At the time I thought he was just being—you know, being *Robert.* But now I wondered about it. Was it possible he wasn't a good man? Of course I never thought he was a saint. I couldn't have stood that. Robert was difficult. But I knew him—I knew him. Didn't I?

That's what I asked myself, sitting right there where you are.

What do you do when you're dead-alive and your husband is a ghost? What do you do? You go up to bed. I went up to bed. I felt sluggish with weariness, but at the same time feverishly tense, as though I might explode. There was no question of sleeping in the same bed as Robert. But when I looked into the dark room and saw the bed empty, I felt . . . I wanted to . . . I mean, Jesus, to think that he'd gone to her—to that *body*—to *you*—well, it was too much. Then it all came rushing into me, a black wind. Do you know it, the black wind? It's the wind after the first wind. It's the wind that comes rushing in when you think the worst is over, sweeping you clean, till you feel like a room without furniture. I realized then that I wasn't going to be spared. Not even a little. At that moment I heard a creak and realized that Robert had gone to sleep on the couch in his study. I felt grateful to him for removing himself from our bed—Robert was always *sensitive,* a very *sensitive* man— and fell with relief into a sort of half sleep.

That was how it was for the next few weeks. I slept without sleeping, woke without waking. I ran a low fever. I felt . . . bruised all over, as if I'd been beaten up. Robert worried over me, without coming too close. He tried to show me that he wanted to take care of me but that he understood my desire to be left alone. A sensitive man, as I said. And you too—a sensitive woman. I can see that. I can feel that. Two sensitive people, giving off flames of hell. As for Robert and me, we barely spoke, though I didn't shut him out. I think he thought I was punishing him. But I wasn't *doing* something to Robert. I just—it was like—listen. Robert had *gone away*. Do you understand that? In his place was this—this *man*, a polite stranger, who hung around the house, making sure I didn't . . . die, I guess. Or hurt myself. You can hurt yourself, in a house. I was very weak. Once I even fell down the stairs. Can you imagine? Falling down the stairs out of sheer unhappiness? Nothing got broken, but I think it alarmed him, this man who was always in the house, imitating my dead husband.

Where was I? Sleep. Of course I didn't only sleep. I moved about. I felt heavy, draggy—and light, very light, as if at any second I'd float right up to the ceiling. I lost my color; my skin was sickly white, like one of those old dinner plates you see glimmering out at you in a dark corner of an antique shop. I felt feverish and dead. Robert was—as I said, he was very good to me. I mean, what else could he *be*? He wanted me to see a doctor. Can you imagine that? Doctor, Doctor, my husband is *seeing another woman.* Do you have a pill for that, Doc? Maybe a shot in the behind? No, I'd never be able to keep a straight face. Besides, wasn't Robert thinking of himself, as well as of his poor zombified wreck of a wife? Much better for *him* if she's a happy, perky little wifey-wife. Thaaat's all right, dear. Boys will be boys. A little *fun* never hurt anybody, for gosh sakes. All's forgiven! Really! Not only that, you can bring her over here! Sure, why not? We have a big bed—there's room for one more. I'll make punch and sandwiches. Bring my binoculars. Well. Don't get me going on that. If I was sick, if I was depressed, at least my sickness was mine. I wasn't going to let him take *that* away too.

But, as I said, I wasn't thinking a whole lot about Robert, at that time. I was actually thinking about . . . you. Does that surprise you? It shouldn't. It's a natural thing. Up to that point, there had really been only the two of us—Robert and me. Now there were three. People say that about having a baby, you know: go in two, come out three. Well, we had *you.* There was Mommy, and Daddy, and cute li'l cuddly-wuddly you. So of course I *thought* about you. God, did I think about you. I thought about you all day long. I even thought about you that night I spent lying on the floor of the bathroom. Dizzy spell—lay there all night long, after coming downstairs at two in the morning. Do you know what it feels like, lying on the linoleum in the bathroom thinking about your husband's cutie pie? Sometimes I imagined you as a big blond slut in a tight red dress. Other times you were a slim business-type in a snazzy skirt suit—you know, one of those jackets with a notched lapel and a trim skirt that zips up the side. Zip zip. Oh, *darn,* my zipper's stuck. Would you mind giving me a hand, Robert? Of course it wasn't *you* I thought about, exactly. Just: that woman. And so I thought about her. I became obsessed by her: by you. I tried to imagine you as Robert would: a desirable body. I . . . undressed you, in my mind. I looked at you. I . . . did things to you. Or rather, I did things to her, to them, to all women—no one was safe from me, in my mind. I've always thought of myself as a—a *modest* woman, but I wasn't modest as I tried to find my way to the heart of Robert's need. I imagined the friends of friends, women I didn't know by name, wondering if she was the one. I unhooked their bras, I pulled down their underpants—the way I imagined Robert would. Just a body. What was a body? I had one, but it wasn't the right one. Which one was that? Maybe a *young* one?—sophomore?—a no-bra, T-shirt kind of a girl—one of those hipless wonders, legs like a nutcracker. Could be. Who knew? Not me. There was one woman—a colleague of his. Someone without a name. Miss Colleague. I'd met her a few times, one of those touchy-feely types, always putting her fingers on everybody's arm, as if she were afraid she wouldn't be noticed unless she stabbed you to death with her nails. You know the type. Eyes too bright, chin too sharp, bra too pointy. Was she the one? Why not? What did they have, these phantom-women, that I didn't have? I tried to picture things I'd never . . . well, I won't say *never*. But they never concerned me, especially, the things other women did in bed. Why should they? Things were fine between us, in that department. I mean, weren't they? Of course things weren't exactly the way they used to be—not after twenty-two years. You get used to each other. You don't feel *crazy* anymore. It's actually a *good* feeling. But I mean . . . but I'm losing the thread. And so I made women naked in my mind. I tore off their clothes. I looked at their bodies. I turned myself into a man. My hips shrank. My arms grew hard. I was a lovely man; tense, dangerous. I was a lean teenager, mean and cool, prowling the suburban streets till dawn.

Women's bodies! They were out there, millions of them, and men wanted them. It was just that I had the wrong body. A shame, really. I'd always figured I had the right body, but it turned out I'd gotten the wrong one by mistake. A shipping error. Sorry, lady, no refunds. Earlier, we'd been friends, my body and me—at worst I'd treated it with a kind of skeptical affec-tion. Now I became ruthless. I judged it mercilessly. Upstairs in the hall there's an old mirror—framed in mahogany—shaped like a shield. It's one of the pieces of furniture we inherited from Robert's grandmother. One day I took the hand mirror from my dresser and stood in front of the hall mirror, in my underpants. I turned around and studied my figure in the hand mirror. I put my weight first on one leg, then the other. I tried to desire myself, I tried to imagine myself an object of desire. And as I stood there, studying myself coldly but feverishly too, it came over me that what was upsetting wasn't so much the harsh judgment I passed on my body as the knowledge that I was entering willingly into a world of humiliation.

Finally I couldn't bear it any longer—I mean, not knowing what you looked like. And so one night I paid you a little visit. Oh, Robert neglected to mention that? How careless of him.

It must have been toward the end of July, the second or third week after Robert's famous little confession. I was still in a strange state, drifting through the house, never really sleeping, never really awake. Ghosts are like that, I imagine. Do you think ghosts are like that? I remember it was a hot night: a hot summer night, the kind I had always liked, back in the days when I was among the living. Robert was asleep in the study; I came down and sat here, on the porch. I was still running a low fever. I was dressed, I remember that, jeans I think and a blouse, and I tried to listen to the sounds of the night, but I was too restless for that. It was impossible to breathe, and I thought I'd go out and take a little walk.

I was struck by the peacefulness of the night, and I thought maybe—just maybe the peace would enter me and calm me a little. And I was struck, you know, by how much it looked like a summer night. I could feel myself smiling, the way you do when something is so much itself that it seems a little . . . contrived. Somebody'd put a big white moon up there in the sky, and for some reason it reminded me of the round white top of a Dixie cup, the underside—the way the ice cream sticks to it and makes little patterns like mountain ranges—and you could see the shadows of chimneys slanting along roofs and the shadows of trees thrown up against the fronts of houses. I could smell things very sharply: the leaves of a big Norway maple, fresh tar from a driveway, wet grass and gravel under a sprinkler. Of course I knew where I was going. Robert had told me your name, and one night I'd looked it up in the phone book. Right here in town! How fortunate for both of you.

I knew it was on the other side of town, out past the cemetery. I wasn't exactly sure where. It seemed to me that I'd been walking for hours; it may be that I lost my way. But when you have a fever, when you're walking in a waking dream, through a summer night made up of nifty stage props—streetlight, moon, tree—then what does it matter whether you get there sooner or later or never or always, your husband asleep in the study, your front door open, your mind disordered, your heart opening and closing like a fist, the hair of a dead woman streaming from a tree—or was it a kite string, a ball of unraveling twine, rope of a hanged man; not for me to say. Then I was there, in front of her house—your house—the house of the wicked witch. Go awaaay, my voices sang in me. Oh staaay, my voices echoed. I took in the front porch—wicker sofa, the two plants hanging like . . . oh, like anchors . . . and shutters . . . with those little grooves in them. I went around the side toward the back. Two garbage pails with little wheels, tomato sticks with nothing growing, one of those grills that look like a diving bell. Magnolia in back yard. Round glass table, metal chairs. Two doors! The back door at the top of the steps: locked. But the cellar door—really, people ought to be more careful, why only the other day . . . It opened so easily, as if you'd been expecting me. Were you? Up the little stairs. Moonlight in the kitchen. So tired! I was, you know: tired, I mean. Everything was strange. The edges of the plates in the dish rack caught the moonlight. I realized that I was in an enchanted cave. Clock ticking like a stick knocking. Bick bock. Bick bock. Knife handles sticking out of a block of wood, as though the knives had been thrown at a target. But where was the knife thrower, where was the woman on the turning wheel? I took one out—the sort of thing you do, in a fever-dream. The hall led to three doors, all open. Three: just like a fairy tale. I looked in the first. Empty! Looked in the second. Empty! Of course! I wanted to shout: Oh, *I* know where you're hiding! Can't fool *me*! Through the third door I could see you lying in your bed. I went in—just like that—and stood over the bed, looking at you. I was surprised to see a knife in my hand. Where had it come from? I felt that I was on a stage, and people were watching: the crazy lady with the knife, bent over the sleeping witch. You had stolen my husband. Broken my heart. Ruined my life. Why shouldn't you die? I felt the moon turn suddenly red, bleeding great red drops into the sky. I was exalted. I was an angel: wrathful. I looked at you. Robert didn't tell you this? Your face was on the pillow, turned a little to one side, your hair loose, flowing. You were younger than I was, but not *young,* not the way I had imagined. Light hair, straw not blond. The covers were partway down, sheet turned over the spread to form a border. Your hand on the edge of the sheet, as though you were stroking it. Your bare throat, your nightgown. Not the silky clingy thing I'd expected, but a cottony smocky sort of thing. I could see you were an attractive woman, handsome not beautiful, not drop-dead gorgeous, nothing little-girly about you—character in the mouth. I stood there. I stood there. What came over me then . . . it was . . . I had a sense that all this . . . the moonlight in the room, the stillness, the hair on the pillow . . . it was as if I'd crept into the room of a sleeping child, or . . . something along those lines. Call me a sucker for cheap effects. But suddenly I was the wicked witch and you were . . . only you. A woman sleeping. I looked at you. I tried to make you dream me. I saw something in my hand. I left the room and never looked back.

That was our first meeting.

And when I got home, it was the strangest thing. Robert was there in the doorway, waiting for me. Isn't that just too much? He looked worried to death, poor man. So I told him— where I'd been, I mean. I left out the part about the knife. Then I went up to bed.

But, good lord, listen to me!—nattering on and on. You'd think a person had nothing better to do all day than sit and listen to stories. You can stay a bit longer, can't you? I'm *so* glad. I haven't even shown you the upstairs. But first the dining room. This way, this way.

DINING ROOM

I promised you bookcases. Well, take a look. *Uno. Due.* And please observe the top shelf of the hutch. Book junkies, both of us. I started reading at five and forgot to give it up the way I gave up everything else—my tutu, my ballet slippers—so long, piano music, goodbye, ice skates, Ginnie doll, tennis racket . . . I can remember in sixth grade sitting holding *Anne of Avonlea* open on my lap, pretending to memorize the products of Central America. Chicle. Or was that *South* America? I had bangs back then—down to my eyebrows, like a helmet. I kept reading in high school, and college—where I majored in guess what—and then came the bookstore, and Robert, and good old marriage—still turning those pages. Do you think people can read too much? I'm grateful for it, myself, but you know what? I haven't opened a book for nearly a year. One day I simply stopped. That's right. Just when you'd think I needed it most, reading deserted me. Books just didn't like me anymore. Betrayed by literature! But really, among so many betrayals, what's one more?

This table is also from Robert's grandmother. Solid mahogany—and will you look at the carving on those legs. Still, there's a heaviness, don't you think? We ate breakfast and lunch in the kitchen, dinner always here. Robert complained about the table at first—said it made him think he was eating roast pig with Queen Victoria—though really there's nothing actually Victorian about the thing. But it was too fine a piece just to let go. It always got on his nerves a little. I kept it covered with a cheerful tablecloth, which helped.

There's a secret about this table—two secrets. But first I have to tell you about tough girls and golden girls.

Just sit. Pull out a chair.

In high school I was never aware of any special unhappiness. You look surprised. But no, really. Oh, I had my bad days, my rotten days, but they were basically exceptions. The truth is, adolescent angst bored the hell out of me. At fourteen, fifteen, sixteen, I was never a morbid type, never broody or gloomy or crazy-restless. All that was like some dumb style of hat I wouldn't be caught dead in. There were girls in my school—I could tell you stories. Girls who wore long black dresses with lots of rattly beads, stared at you with big sorrowful eyes, and looked like they started each day bright and early by slitting their wrists in the bathtub. Who needed it? Really, who needed it? I had a few good friends, I got on all right with my classmates. I fit in well enough, without fitting in completely—which was fine with me. But right from the start I was aware of two kinds of girls whose very existence made me uneasy. I would see girls walking down the halls in pairs, wearing tight skirts and sweaters, swinging their hips—girls who laughed loud, brassy laughs, wore too much lipstick, talked dirty at the lockers, and had sudden fits of anger. These were the tough girls, who'd give you a hard look if you met their eyes. What was it about them that seemed to make me doubt myself? And then there were the golden girls. . . . Ah, those golden high-school girls! Beautiful—really *gifted* with beauty—slightly languorous, clean-smelling, friendly but somehow untouchable. There they were, the golden girls, sashaying down the halls with their long hair swaying, giving off a kind of light, as if whenever you saw them they'd just spent the entire day at the beach . . . oh, they were as far as possible from the tough girls with their black leather jackets and cheap pocketbooks. But I saw that they shared a secret, the tough girls and the golden girls, a secret I wasn't allowed to know. It was the way they walked. Yes, they were at ease in their bodies, they inhabited their bodies—while I, don't you see, I stood a little outside my own body, I didn't fit myself. I was like one of those color comics where the color doesn't fit the outlines but leaves a space on one side and spills out the other. Don't misunderstand me. I wasn't ashamed of my body. It was a pretty good body, as bodies went. No, I wasn't morbidly self-conscious—that came much later. That was *your* gift. But I was estranged from my body—in a not unpleasant way.

The grand thing about Robert is that he made the color fit the outline. In college I'd had two lovers—to call them that—strange name for the loveless—who taught me something about pleasure—and anger. But it was as if my body had its own life, and I myself another. But with Robert—well, he liked to tell me I was *good in the sack,* and all that jazz, but what thrilled me was how I no longer . . . I mean . . . it's difficult to say. But the color fit the outline. I somehow got into my own skin. Do you see what I mean?

But I was telling you about the table. Here was this heavy, serious, deeply *solemn* piece of furniture, sitting right there where we had to eat our dinner. Robert said we ought to paint it yellow, or maybe put up a Ping-Pong net. Or else we ought to eat on the floor, he said, underneath the table. One night after dinner we both stood looking at it, the grandmother table—gleaming, solid, unmovable—all too depressingly *there*. We looked at each other. And we knew; we knew how to break the spell. And so we made love on the table. After clearing away the dishes, of course. Right over there, near that end. "That'll give her something to think about," Robert said later. I never knew whether he meant the table, or his grandmother, or Queen Victoria.

It was our little joke—our secret—our little protest against gravity. We ate in the dining room without trouble, after that.

We were lighthearted, Robert and I. Can you understand that?

I don't know exactly what I hoped for, after the night of my visit to you. If it was peace I was looking for, an end to night madness, I found none of it. Instead of imagining all women, I confined myself to just you—but you grew to be a giantess, you were all women, you were more than all women. You were my obsession, my . . . demon. I imagined Robert making love to you, over and over again, until my head felt battered. I wondered what you did in bed exactly, what you did to draw him to you. I'd seen your plain nightgown, but I imagined you had fancy things, just for him: black lace underpants, for example. Robert had once pointed to a pair of black lace underpants on a mannequin and said, "Do you think she's trying to tell me something?" And speaking of a colleague's wife he said, "She's a white cotton underwear sort of woman"—curled lip, little dismissive wave of the fingers. "Like me," I said. "Oh, you're different," Robert said with a laugh. And it's true that I like yellow, and blue, as well as white. But I thought of that mannequin, when I imagined Robert in your room. Black lace underpants. Was that your secret? I imagined him tearing them off with his teeth. It wasn't—you realize—simply a matter of black lace underwear. It was that I thought I might have misunderstood something about Robert, that my whole life might have been wrong.

So: black lace underpants. But that was only the beginning. I imagined you owned more specialized things, things you ordered from expensive catalogs—maybe a sheer pink bra embroidered with flowers, or one of those male-fantasy things that hook up the back and come with garters to go with your lace-top thigh-highs and your spike heels. Or say a nice black nylon spandex slip with lace hem over your pale-peach bikini panties. Oh, I imagined you could teach Victoria a secret or two! Unless the trick was simpler than that. Under a tight skirt that showed off your legs—look, Robert!—no underpants.

There was no stopping you now. You'd do anything—anything. I saw you in a little-girl Sunday frock—ironed and pink—sitting with your knees pressed together—your long-lashed eyes blinking innocently—a nice pink bow in your hair—your legs in black fishnet stockings. And of course there was your classic chambermaid routine: short black dress, white apron, little white cap, lowered eyes—oh *yes*, sir, oh *no*, sir, very *well*, sir—reaching higher, higher, higher with that cute feather duster as your skirt hiked up.

I imagined Robert standing behind you, burying his teeth in your shoulder.

Or you as calendar pinup in six-inch heels and black top hat—your back to Robert and me—black-gloved hand on hip—white dress shirt not quite covering your perfect behind—as you glance over your shoulder at us—well, hel*lo* there—with bee-stung lips—in a darling little sulky pout.

But maybe that wasn't it at all, maybe there was some other trick you used, to get him into that room of yours. One summer Robert and I traveled to Paris. Our hotel room was small, but we faced a courtyard, which seemed to me exotic. On the first night I was startled by a loud cry, a terrible anguished groan that made me think someone was being murdered. I ran to the window, but Robert pulled me away, laughing. I realized that what I was hearing was the sound of a woman screaming in orgasm. I was uneasy, thinking of my own much quieter sounds. "I imagine he's completely deaf by now," Robert said, in that way of his. But now I wondered: Is that what men liked? Were you a screamer? I imagined you letting everything go, filling the room with murderous cries, with shouts of ecstasy bordering on pain.

I watched the two of you *making love*—is that what you called it?—in your moonlit love nest on the other side of town—while I lay alone in my big big bed and Robert creaked in his study. Sometimes I felt myself turning into you, a high-class whore in fancy lingerie, seducing my husband away from his boring wife. And he would make love to us fanatically—insanely—in the cheap motel room of my mind—till we hurt between the legs.

Is this what's called jealousy? I guess. Who knows? For me it was also a kind of—I don't know, a kind of exploration. As though I wanted to push past whatever I thought I was, into regions of unknown pain, frontiers of humiliation. Look at me!—the cowgirl of sorrow.

Sometimes I thought of beaches: Robert and me at the beach, sun shining on sandbars—another life. Robert leaning back on his elbows, his skinny-muscly legs crossed at the ankles, images of sky and water in his dark glasses. Dream-women walking in the sand, walking right there in his sunglasses—he always did like a pair of long legs on a woman. Like yours. At the beach he would look at them admiringly. I never minded—well, maybe a little. More than a little. And both of us liked to look people over, it was a thing we did well together. "Your type," I'd say, nodding toward some leggy bimbo in a string bikini. Robert would laugh. Sometimes I worried about my legs, that they weren't long enough. "Long enough for what?" he said once. Typical Robert.

Was it your legs? Was it that simple? Two inches taller and a girl gets it all? Maybe there was something you *did* with your legs, some special way of walking across a room, or . . . or something. A technique you practiced: a secret craft. That was it. Or maybe it was your body itself that had a secret—some special feature—some unusual development—that no man could resist. I liked the idea of a secret—something hidden—because then you were lifted into the realm of magic, where you defeated me unfairly—where nothing was my fault.

Or maybe your nasty little secret was that you talked a different way in bed—talked *dirty,* as they say. Is that what golden girls do? I imagined the words coming from your mouth, words I never used because to me they were sharp stones flung at bodies. And Robert would never. . . . In the night I whispered them aloud: Cunt. Cock. Fuck. I was oddly soothed by them, as I said them over and over again: Cunt. Cock. Fuck. Fuck me, Robert, I imagined you saying. Come on, Robert. Fuck me. That's what it comes down to, I said. Cunt. Cock. Fuck. I spoke them louder and louder. They thrilled me and hurt me. I had the confused sense that I was saying goodbye to something. My childhood? But I was a forty-seven-year-old woman! I felt tears on my face.

Late that same night I put on my robe and prowled around downstairs, exhausted and awake. I sat on the porch, but the sound of crickets was like a burn on my skin. In the kitchen I filled a glass with ice cubes and pressed it to my forehead. I walked into the dining room. That afternoon Robert had tightened a screw in a drawer pull. The screwdriver was lying on the hutch. I picked it up and went over to the table.

Here it is, under the cloth. An ugly mark, don't you think? Like a scar. As I gouged the mahogany with that screwdriver, I thought of many things—the time, long ago, when Robert and I made love on the table, the time when we were happy and lighthearted—but most of all I thought of you. I imagined the table was your face.

You look shocked. You shouldn't be. It's only a table, after all. Besides, these little expressions of yours—shock, dismay—I'm sure they're very appealing to *men*—who like to be shocking—but when you're talking to me, you really ought to drop it. It just doesn't do you a bit of good.

Robert was terribly upset, the first time he saw the mark. He wanted to know *why*.

Why, Robert? Why? He might as well have asked me to walk down the street with him holding hands.

Now I eat my meals in the kitchen. I don't like this room anymore. Oh, let's get on with it, shall we? I haven't even shown you the upstairs.

STAIRS

I like this old stairpost, don't you, with this whatchamajigger on top: a bowling ball, it looks like to me, though Robert said it reminded him of the top of a barber pole—or a bald old professor. Just follow me. The handrail's a little nicked; nothing a bit of furniture polish won't fix. Those three photographs were taken by my father—Mexico—photography was his passion, though he sold insurance. Here's the step where I stumbled. Second from the landing. This one right here. Fell right down all those steps and landed on the floor at the foot of the stairs, down there by the hall closet. I could've broken my neck; Robert was impressed. Have you ever fallen down a flight of stairs, out of sheer—I suppose it was sorrow. A sorrowful fall. I remember everything: a feeling of just letting everything go, that sense of release, it was almost exhilarating, like floating up in the air, except that my head was banging against the banister and my body was a big awkward lump with arms and legs sticking out all over the place. At the bottom I lay there thinking: so *that's* what it's like, falling down stairs. One leg was bent in a funny way and my skirt was partway up. I wondered if anyone could see my underpants. Vanity!—take it from me, even half dead we're stuck with it. So there I was, lying with my skirt up, aware of looking like some woman trying to seduce some man. Then I tried to remember the last time I'd made love to Robert. It seemed a long time ago. But was it really that long? And then out of nowhere I thought of Tom Conway. It's astonishing what a person will think of, lying at the bottom of a stairway. Tom Conway. I'll tell you about Tom Conway. But not now. Just three more steps after the landing. Robert said we ought to buy a statue and put it right there in the corner. A statue in magnificently bad taste—you know, white marble nymph emerging from bath, one hand modestly covering her pudendum. Instead: tah-dah! Emerson's *Essays. Murder on the Orient Express. Animal Architecture.* Can you believe it?

UPSTAIRS BATH

This is the shower. We had a new head installed five–six years ago, walls and ceiling painted. I ought to spray the damn walls to stop that speckling, but I never do. Those tiles are original with the house; a little grout wouldn't hurt over there.

At some point after Robert's confession—it must have been late summer? early fall?—I began to take lots of showers. I'd stay under till the hot water ran out, sometimes three times a day. If I wasn't going to die—and I realized, with astonishment—and disappointment—and a kind of outrage—that I was *not* going to die—then at least I was determined to be clean. It was as if by *seeing* you—as Robert so charmingly put it—he had made me dirty. Explain it any way you like: I needed to be clean, shining; a temple virgin; a little girl. Sometimes I took a long bath, and showered right after.

That medicine cabinet came with the house—one of the many home improvements we never made. You see the filigree work on the mirror. And here's something funny: funny *peculiar,* as a particularly obnoxious colleague of Robert's used to say, not funny *ha ha.* Every time I stepped out of the tub, I would see myself in that mirror. Of course I'd always seen myself in that mirror, but it struck me for the first time how I saw only my top half. It was a mermaid mirror. Yes, I was a mermaid—nothing below my waist. Of course by this time Robert and I were no longer *making love,* as the saying goes. So it made a weird kind of sense that when I looked at myself naked in the mirror, after stepping out of the tub, I had no lower half. That was one of your cruelest thefts: stealing my bottom half. I suppose it was just as well, since nothing any longer pleased me about my body. And this was strange, because—but haven't we spoken of this already? You've really got to excuse me if I repeat myself. So many things in my head, going round and round! But you see, I'd always been easy enough, in my mind, about my body. I mean, I always did fill out a sweater pretty well—that kind of thing. Of course my *legs*—but that's another story. Still, all in all. Not that I ever loved my body, for God sakes—or *sake,* as Robert would say. God's. Pause. Sake. It was just that I accepted it, the way I accepted my—oh, I don't know, my nose. There it is: a nose. Look at it as long as you like, it's still just a nose. Hey there, nose! You know, there are people who spend their entire lives doing nothing, I mean *nothing,* but worrying about their noses. Then they die, and go to a heaven full of angels with perfect angel-noses, and for all eternity they do nothing but worry about their noses. That was never my way. But now, thanks to you, I found myself worrying about my body. It was wrong in every way, an immense . . . wrongness. Too this. Too that. Too—oh, everything. I hated it all. For the first time in my life, at the tender age of forty-seven, I became an adolescent.

Do you know what I wanted? What I really wanted? What I wanted, the thing I wanted—it was to become a little girl again, in saddle shoes, with a dab of Mercurochrome on my knee.

Yup, you got it, sister. To start over. . . .

Oh and by the way. I was wrong. No bookcase here. But the ghosts of books—from Robert's time. See? One on the radiator—one on the floor—and there, on the edge of the tub.

You know, when you hate your body, then you think continually about your body, and when you think continually about your body, then you become nothing but a body. You become a disgusting little materialist. You become a secret sensualist, a sort of—a sort of hangdog sensualist. Oh, I like that. Hangdog sensualist. I do have a way with words sometimes, you *will* grant me that. "You have a way with words," Robert once said, and then he paused, thinking it over, and *then* he said: "Sometimes. I grant you that." So. Let us grant me that. But here's the thing: I hated my body. I hated my body because it wasn't your body. You look as if you're about to maul me with a compliment. Please refrain. Besides, I didn't hate only *my* body. I also hated *your* body. Why don't we change the subject?

STUDY

Robert's study. Wall-to-wall books, arranged by historical period. And listen to this. Within each period?—alphabetical by author. Is that order, or what? All summer long I seemed to hear him pacing. Scrape the chair back, pace, scrape the chair forward. Scrape it back. Pace, scrape, pace, scrape. God. Why no rug? Sometimes I blame his book for everything. Of course that's too easy, it lets everyone off the hook: you, Robert, and li'l ol' me. Besides, a man set on betraying his wife is bound to find an excuse. Bound to. Still! That awful book. Robert was too self-critical ever to write a book. A book for him was pure torture. He should never have taken that leave. Poor Robert. And there you were, waiting for him in that little house, with your long legs practically sticking out the window. You must have seemed—the solution. Of course he needed *consoling*. Those long walks he used to take that spring! That was the time, you know, when I felt something was a little wrong between us, a little . . . off. Later I realized he must have met you on one of those walks—unless he'd met you before, and was simply walking straight to your bedroom. What drove him crazy wasn't the knowledge that he wasn't going to finish his book. It was the knowledge that he wasn't going to begin it. He took notes, billions of notes, typed up parts of a chapter, fragments—never good enough. Scrape, pace, scrape, pace. A body in a bed was something he could count on. Makes a man feel young again, m'boy. Nothing like greasing the old engine. Of course you got something out of it, too. A *needy* man. A man wanting to be *rescued*. What could be better than that?

Did I fail Robert? Was there something I didn't understand? Of course I brooded over that too. Because if your heart is broken, if I may use that dear old expression, famous in song and legend, then the time comes, sooner or later, when you begin to wonder . . . at first only for a second or two, then for longer periods of time . . . whether you *deserved* to have it broken . . . if I may continue to make use of these time-honored phrases. Because surely it wouldn't just *happen* to you, something like that, for no reason.

So maybe Robert's little infidelity was the very sign that was supposed to alert me to my own lack of something. It was supposed to show me the way. And I misread the sign. Imagine! A bad reader, after all.

Oh my. I do hope I'm not sounding *histrionic*. That's what

he called me once: *histrionic*. It was a way of showing he disapproved of my sadness. Robert's *histrionic* wife. I just *love* the theater, darlin'—don't you? All those *histrionic* people.

I don't know when I began to suspect he hadn't stopped seeing you. After my . . . breakdown, I somehow imagined . . . But you see how naive I was! I thought a sense of decency—a sense of respect . . . Even *you*, I thought . . . But no. He must really've liked those black lace undies. And you must have enjoyed showing them to him. That fall he began teaching again, three days a week, but he'd always rush right home. Make sure nothing had happened to the crazy wife. A girl can fall down the stairs, you know. She can get dizzy in the bathroom. She can fall out a window and break her pretty neck. Razor blades have been known to cause trouble in the most well-regulated families. A house is a dangerous place: kitchen knives, deadly hammers, sleeping pills, gas stoves. . . . Ours is electric, but I've always preferred gas, at least for disposing of unwanted wives. Rope. Gasoline. Matches. No wonder he hurried home, the poor man. He'd find me lying in bed, in my nightie, or else in the shower. But I was already getting better! I was eating a little. I felt like a house that had burned down, leaving the charred foundation and half a chimney. Of course, I was still a burned-down house. It's just that I wasn't burning down any*more*.

Besides, what was all the fuss about? Men have affairs every day. It's chic—it's cool—and good *for* you too. Keeps down that bad cholesterol. And great for your lower back. The numbers say it all. According to the most recent survey, ninety-nine point eight percent of all American husbands have been unfaithful to their wives at least twice in the last year. Did you know that? Also, and this may surprise you, ninety-two point four percent of all American men have slept with their own mothers. Sad but true. But here's the good news. Ninety-four point six percent of men with erectile dysfunction say that it doesn't really matter—they never enjoyed it anyway. I found these facts in women's magazines. I was beginning to eat, as I mentioned, and I was starting to go out a little in the car: CVS, Grand Union, you name it. Wherever I went, women's magazines sprang out at me. Sleek, insolent panther-women looking at me with jungle eyes. Cheekbones like ski slopes. Thumbs hooked in bikini underpants, like a guy wearing jeans. Forty-three Ways to Snag Your Man. One Hundred Sixty-three Ways to Drive Him Insane with Lust. All over America, housewives were reading this stuff. Was I the only one who wasn't in on the secret? I bought a few and read them sitting in the car. Eat All You Want and Get Thin. Twelve Sizzling New Positions. Apparently the thing to do was find his E spot. When you found it, you pressed it. Then he raped you. Your marriage was saved. The trouble with the E spot was that it was very hard to locate; it was somewhere near the abdomen, or the pancreas. You could waste a lot of time looking for it, and meanwhile your man might fall insanely in love with someone else— someone thinner than you. I think I'm talking too fast. Am I talking too fast? I feel that I'm talking a little rapidly and I am going to make a conscious effort to control myself.

There.

One evening after returning from the Grand Union—I liked to walk up and down the long aisles pushing my basket, how it soothed me—I took a drive to your house. I parked almost across the street and watched the front windows. In the living room the blinds were down but the lights were on. Your bedroom was dark. After a while I saw the light go on in your bedroom. The blinds were closed and lowered halfway. I saw you move toward the window and lower the blinds some more, as if to keep me from spying. I could see only part of you, from a little above the waist to about mid-thigh. You were wearing an Indian-print skirt with a wide red belt. I thought of my bathroom mirror: I was the woman without a bottom half, and you—you were nothing but a bottom half. Then I imagined you were a mermaid in reverse, legs below and fish scales above, and the idea struck me as so absolutely incredibly hysterical that really I nearly died laughing.

GUEST ROOM

Bed. Bookcase. No one's stayed here in nearly a year. And yet, at one time, practically everyone stayed here: my mother, my father, Robert's mother, Robert's grandmother, for God sakes, his unmarried sister—let us please not forget Robert's unmarried sister—the sort of woman who does you a little favor, like picking you up a quart of milk at the corner store, and says with a bright little laugh, "You owe me one," meant to show her brave girlish humor in the face of life's burdens—and Robert's old roommate the failed painter, who backed me up against the refrigerator and instead of kissing me asked me the recipe for my ratatouille, and Robert's old friend Lydia, who is *so* relieved to get away from Manhattan and *so* happy to be up here where you can actually see the stars at night . . . and many more . . . scads of colorful folks . . . all of them right here, in this room. And sometimes I think of it as *your* room, if you know what I—in the sense that *that* would have been one solution. To the problem, I mean. Because you really *were* a problem, you know, a great big problem that didn't seem to have a solution, or had only difficult solutions that themselves were problems without solutions. You could have died of cancer, for example—but you were too *healthy* for that—or I could have killed you that night—or Robert could have given you up. The poor man was suffering so. We talked a little, now and then. I would come down for my late breakfast, and Robert would materialize from somewhere or other and stand by the table, looking proud and sad and doomed.

"I need to know what you're going to do."

"Going to do?"

"About us."

"Us, Robert?"

"Stop *echoing* me, will you? Just stop *echoing* me."

And then he would disappear; it was very strange. Poof! Gone. A sad, angry ghost. And so in certain moods I would think: Oh, for heaven sakes. Come *on,* girl. Grow *up.* There's no reason to be so *childish* about this. Why am I being so self-ish? It's all *me me me.* Why don't I ever think of *his* needs? Then of course I would think that you might as well move into the house—into the guest room. If I loved Robert, then I wanted him to be happy, didn't I? I saw myself tucking the two of you in at night, sitting on the side of the bed—oh, the adorable lit-tle rascals!—telling a bedtime story. And they allll lived *hap* pilyeverafter. Nighty-night! Don't let the bedbugs bite! I would be a sister, a saint. And if any little problem came up between you two, why, I'd be right there, in the house. I could serve you meals. I could bathe you. Gosh, I could do your nails: red hot, or a nice minty green, or black as witches. I could even dress you in the mornings, after your strenuous nights. As I say, it was one solution . . . to the problem. Look, the sun's gone in. Or is it getting dark? I'm feeling a little tired. I'll just sit for a minute on the side of the bed. If you don't mind. You sit on that side. No, go right ahead. There was something I wanted to tell you. . . . You know: when I was lying at the foot of the stairs? Oh, now I remember.

In high school, senior year, I had a crush on a boy called Tom Conway. He was a good-looking, clean-cut sort of boy, not my type really, very shy, a little awkward, as if he'd grown into a body he didn't know what to do with—all those arms and shoulders and elbows and things. I don't know when I realized I had a crush on him. I liked being around him; it was like turning a corner and finding yourself on a street with shady maples and front porches. This wasn't crazy teenage love, with wildfire burning in your stomach, but something else, something . . . restful. Somehow we began taking walks together, that spring. We held hands. And that was it: no kissing, no hugging, no touching except for hands. We walked all over town, along tree-lined streets, with sun flickering on us through the leaves, up into the wooded section where the roads were curvy and there were no sidewalks and the big houses were set far back from the road. One day he took me to his house to meet his mother. She was a friendly woman, standing in the kitchen wearing an apron embroidered with apple branches. Right off the kitchen was a small room, with white curtains—a guest room, where his grandmother used to stay. Somehow we ended up lying on the bed in that room. We lay on our backs, on the green spread, holding hands. I remember it was late afternoon, and the sun coming through the windows had a very orange cast to it. Everything in the room was glowing in the orange light. I lay there entirely peaceful, entirely happy—I was without desire. Or let's say the kind of desire I had for Tom Conway was completely satisfied by lying there on his grandmother's bed, in the orange light, holding hands, while his mother moved around in the kitchen. That summer his family moved to Arizona. I never saw him again. I don't know that I had time to miss him much, what with college starting and all the rest. But every once in a while, for no reason, when I'm walking along a familiar street, or coming up the back steps with a bag of groceries, or lying there at the foot of the stairs, I think of that room, with the white curtains, and the orange sunlight coming in.

You look tired. We're almost done.

BEDROOM

Our room. No, come in. I want you to come in. I said: Come in. You know, I admire that hesitation. It shows you have a certain . . . decency. Or are you afraid of something? Good heavens! Nothing to be afraid of in here. Look: another bookcase. And permit me to introduce you to the, um, conjugal bed. Or have you two already met? Ha ha: my little joke. We used to read ourselves to sleep . . . in the old days. We made love every night, just about. Maybe not *every* night, but a lot—we didn't have to count. People count, you know. Twice a week. Once a decade. Then they look it up and compare themselves to the national average. That's what I find so . . . I mean, if we had grown distant or. . . . Of course sometimes we were tired, or not exactly in the mood. But then the next night . . . or the night after. . . . And sometimes there were longer gaps, when we both, for no reason . . . I mean, twenty-two years. It's a long time. I'm going to lie down here, I'm feeling a little . . . You lie down, too. I want you to. No, please: lie down. You're tired, I can tell. We can have a nice pillow talk, like girlfriends in junior high. Of course I never had them, those nice pillow talks in junior high, but still. Oh, don't you just *adore* that dreamy new math teacher? And Todd Andrews. He's soooo cute. That's how girlfriends talk, you know. At least I think they do. I used to imagine having talks like this with a girlfriend, but they weren't about boys, those talks, they were about . . . oh, books, and . . . and things. Take my hand. All right, then I'll take yours. Sisters! We've been through a lot together, we two. Listen. This is where I was lying when the call came about Robert's accident. That was in January. He'd been very upset, you know. We'd had an argument, a week earlier. Oh, a bad one. Do you know what we were arguing about? We were arguing about making the bed. Isn't that the strangest thing? The man on the phone kept saying something about black ice. The words seemed weird and scary, as if he were talking about some disease. The Black Ice Plague. Black ice in your carotid artery. Sharp splinters of black ice piercing the left ventricle. Robert was what? Was dead? He was *angry*, for God sakes, how can you die when you're . . . ? Killed by black ice. The black ice of his black-hearted icy wife.

Isn't it fun talking like this, just the two of us? Here's a secret. Don't tell anybody. When Robert and I fell in love, when I was twenty-four and he was thirty, it was all very passionate and so forth, but for a while there . . . he couldn't make love to me. It drove him wild. He swore that never, never before. . . . He was ready to kill himself. But you know something? I didn't care. I was so in love with him that even if . . . It came right, soon enough. He was so grateful to me, as if I'd endured the impossible—fought some heroic battle. He swore I was an angel, a goddess. How I hated that. What he couldn't understand is that I was so happy that I didn't care about . . . about anything on earth. I was demented with happiness. They should've carted me off to the loony bin. And then, when we started making love, I don't know if you'll understand this, but it became absorbed into the happiness I was already feeling.

I asked him about you once. Only once. I asked him if you were married. I don't know why, but it seemed the one thing I had to know. He was shocked. His "No!" was almost violent. He looked at me—a sad, raging man. A man *misunderstood*. "I'd never break up a marriage." That's what he said to me. Proud pose: shoulders back, defiant look.

But what about *my* marriage, Robert?

Here's another secret. You won't tell, will you? Come closer: I have to lower my voice so no one will hear. I know that you've slept in this bed. With my husband, of course. Don't you pull away from me. We're having a nice little pillow talk—just the two of us. Of course it must be unpleasant for you to know that I know. I understand that. I mean, that I've known all along. It must be upsetting. Even embarrassing, for some people. But once you start sharing secrets. . . . I admit it changed my idea of you. I hadn't thought you would be so . . . what *is* the word I want? Bold? Cruel? I'll even tell you how I found out. Robert told me! Wasn't that sweet of him? Of course he had no choice. He knew I was on to something. That was in December, just after Christmas, when I went to visit my mother for a few days. At the time I'd begun to think that maybe we could somehow survive, Robert and I, the way a ruin survives. You can preserve a ruin, you know. It's artful, expensive work. And I thought: I'll stay in the house, and he'll stay in the house, and together we'll be a ruined monument, with ivy on the walls. People can come and admire us. We can charge admission. Of course you were still at the other end of town, pulling down shades, crossing and uncrossing those legs of yours. When I came home from my mother's I went up to my room to lie down. Robert had never moved back from the study. I saw right away that the bed had been made up wrong. Robert has absolutely no sense of such things. He was a domestic idiot, in some ways. I screamed; we had it out. He confessed. How many times can you confess to someone before you start wanting them dead? Or before you start wanting to be dead yourself? I remember one thing he said. He said he didn't think I loved him anymore. I believe he meant it, poor man, but it was also very clever. Because I broke your heart, dear, and because you're a cold-hearted bitch who won't forgive me one little bit for breaking your heart, I have the God-given right to screw somebody else in our bed. Like it or lump it, baby.

They say murderers always return to the scene of the crime. And look: here you are! Now all we need is a judge—and an executioner. Come on, sister! I'm almost done showing the house.

ATTIC

Look: my old cradle.

Sometimes I think everything in my life is up here. If I could just find it, if I could just put it in order, then I could reconstruct my entire life, day by day, minute by minute. . . . Bookcases. Over there too. One of them used to be in the living room . . . years ago. People talk about *finishing* their attics, but how can you *finish* an attic? Things keep accumulating. That's the whole point of attics. They're never finished. That's why houses are different from ancient civilizations—the oldest layer is always on top. We did have it insulated, about five years ago. It was supposed to save on heating bills, but I don't think it saved all that much. I don't remember. That's what you get for trying to be practical. You would never call us worldly people, Robert and me. It was one of the good things about us. Intermittently worldly, at best. Half in, half out. Of the world, I mean. Every summer I mount an exhaust fan in that window. It gets blazing up here in the summer. You wouldn't believe how hot it gets. My old dollhouse. My red parasol. I used to stand by a window with the sun coming in and watch my forearm turn brilliant red under my parasol. Robert's eighth-grade science project: optical illusions. You know: is that a vase, or is it two profiles? Hoarders, both of us. You see that beam? Scene of my suicide. Did I mention that I committed suicide up here? Well. I came up here with a rope. It was after Robert's accident—a few days after the phone call. I kept trying to *talk* to him. That's one thing about the dead: they don't talk to you. They listen, but they don't talk back. It can make you angry. I found the rope in the cellar and brought it up here. I had some confused idea, from the movies . . . I didn't even know how to make a slipknot. So you might say I didn't kill myself, after all. Still, when you come up to your attic carrying a rope, when you try to swing it over a beam, when you have every intention, then can't it be said that actually . . . in a real sense . . . despite appearances. . . . And here I stand before you, a living dead woman, come back to tell the tale. A creepy place, really. You can hear things moving around in the dark. Wings. Weensy little feet. Children are right. Stay out of the attic. It's like walking around in the head of a madwoman.

CELLAR

Personally I've always preferred cellars. Careful, this rail's a little wobbly. There's something about going *down* to a place, don't you think? Watch your head. Robert used to clonk himself all the time. It's a lot like falling, really—you can feel a sort of tug, and you hang on just to keep from tumbling head over heels. And another thing is knowing you're headed under the ground, like a . . . like a rodent. Of course, cellars can be creepy too. In my parents' house there were these big barrels under the stairs, full of who knew what. Rats. Bats. Dead men's bones. That's what I used to say, on the way down. Rats, bats, dead men's bones. Rats, bats, dead men's bones. Even here, things can surprise you. Once I reached into that pile of wood over there and a mouse ran over my hand. Do you know what it feels like, having a mouse run over your hand? It feels like you're being nibbled by lots of tiny mouths. That would be a good punishment, don't you think? Tie a person up and let mice run over them. Look: bookcases. Five, no less. Robert would sometimes talk about building a room down here to hold all the books in the house—a cellar library. He might as well have talked about building a subway station in the back yard. That's practically a new furnace. The old one broke down two years ago. It's got one of those automatic whatsits— you know, to regulate the water level. Copper water pipes. Washer/dryer hookup. Heck, we've got it all. Sink. Old bicycle. Dead refrigerator. Look at this clothesline, will you? It must be forty years old. Over here's where I murdered you. Oh yes: many times. Attics for suicide, cellars for murder. It makes sense. A quick blow to the head with a shovel or hammer. Cellars are full of hiding places, you know. Your head's in that trunk, eyes wide open. Your legs are in that metal cabinet, leaning up like oars. You stay right here. I'm not done with you. Don't play Little Miss Innocent with me. Haven't you ever murdered anyone? We all do it, you know. Lure them into cellars, hack off their limbs, stab those evil people until tears of joy pour down my face. See that cabinet? Your head again, hanging on a hook. Lovely she was, even in death. I buried you here, under the floor. Under that ratty rug. And don't look in the woodpile. This place is nothing but a graveyard, and all the corpses are you. Look! Over there. Over there. And there. But you know, a time comes when it doesn't really work anymore . . . the shovel too heavy . . . the ax handle broken . . . the voices quiet . . . the cellar empty. Do you know what I think? I think you lack imagination. I've always thought that about you. You don't murder people, you don't think about things. Did you ever imagine me? Did you? The irritating little wife left at home? Of course it was all a secret. You didn't want to *hurt* anyone. Above all, Robert, I don't want to *hurt* anyone. That's why Robert never told you he told me. He knew that at the first sign of trouble you'd head for the hills. The arrangement must have struck you as perfect. A perfect adultery: no pain. Safe for everyone. The golden-girl special.

That's the old Ping-Pong table. We used to play quite a lot, in the old days. Ping. Pong. Ping. Pong. A ridiculous game, really. My only sport. Robert took it very seriously, the way he took most things. His backhand was so-so, but he had a very good forehand smash. Did you know that about Robert? A very good forehand smash.

Oh and another thing about you. Another thing. You don't like it when I use *coarse* words—I can see it in your face—your mouth—but you also don't like it when I go the other way—use words that are way up there, like—oh, like *ecstasy.* It bothers you. I can see it does. Do you want to know something? You live in the flatlands of language. No dizzy mountain views, no hellish undergrounds—just: flat. The Kansas of things. No attic or cellar in your house of words.

How often I lured you down here and accused you of your crimes! Because you broke my heart, you must surely die. Because you turned my husband into a ghost, you must surely die. Because you stole my body from me, you must surely die. Because you lack imagination, you must surely die. Heartwrecker! Wifekiller! Manslayer! Then I cracked open your head with that shovel, stabbed you with those gardening shears, strangled you with my own hands . . . the sweet feel of your neck crushed under my thumbs. You have to hate very hard to do that. Have you ever hated anyone hard enough to want to kill them? I thought about it a lot, my hatred. Love, for me, turned out to have a limit: Robert's faithfulness. But my hatred for you breathed the pure air of infinity.

The trouble with hatred is that it doesn't really take you very far. It takes you quickly to a certain point, and then you can't get beyond it. Do you know why that is? I can tell you. It's because when you hate someone, when you really hate someone, you always turn them into a caricature. The Lady in Black Lace Underpants. The Girl with the Golden . . . but *you* fill in the missing blank. Even as I hated you I knew—I knew—that I wasn't really seeing you—at all. I was guilty of *your* crime: lack of imagination. I knew I had to be calm—calmer. I had to get at you a different way. And so, little by little, I began to make an effort, a painful effort. I began to imagine you.

Don't misunderstand me. It was never a matter of being fair to you—of being *nice*. It was simply a question of getting a more accurate picture. So that I would know what to do.

My insight—my stroke of genius—because I'd become

brilliant through hatred, brilliant—was this: to imagine that you weren't so different from me, after all. Not different from me! You! Of course I struggled violently against it. It wasn't bearable. You! And there were dangers—serious dangers. If you weren't all that different from me, if you weren't *just a body,* then I might be threatened from a new direction, one that I— but it was a risk worth taking. Slowly I gave way to it—I welcomed it—I abandoned myself to it completely. Imagining you! Yes, that was the stroke, the liberating blow! That was my deepest revenge! Because once you were like me, once you were more or less human, then you were capable of—well, of whatever I was capable of. Suffering, for example. Suffering! Unhappiness like fire! Maybe you weren't a witch. Maybe you were—oh, who knew, lonely, bereft, at the end of your rope. An unhappy woman. Sure, why not? *In love*: that, too. Fine! Wonderful! A woman in love. A woman in love would be capable of . . . feelings. Sympathies. She might even be capable of imagining *me.*

That's when I decided to put my house up for sale. There was a chance you would come. . . . You *had* to come. Because really, how could you resist? A guided tour—and what a guide!—of those unreal rooms . . . in the haunted mansion. . . . Of course you'd already invaded the house and rolled around in my sheets. Did you like it? Was it thrilling? I cut up the sheets the next day, tore them to shreds. The appalling *brashness* of that visit—whatever else it said about you—suggested a taste for . . . shall we call it *adventure*? It told me you might jump at a chance to break in again. And maybe you hadn't had time to look around, on that occasion. I imagined Robert leading you through the dark to keep you from attracting attention, as you held his hand and moved through dream landscapes of foglike furniture flashing out at you here and there in the light of a streetlamp. You were returning *my* visit, though you didn't know it at the time. And of course you never did get to see *her*—the famous wife—me. So there was that. To attract you. It must be—oh, it must be an almost irresistible pleasure, I imagined, to see the wife of your lover: to sympathize with the poor woman, as I felt you beautifully would, while secretly triumphing over her. To say nothing of comparing your body to hers, as you'd surely want to do. Robert's wife. That's his *wife*. Why didn't he just kill her? But maybe you were searching for higher pleasures—the pleasure of guilt . . . the thrill of remorse . . . and other sophisticated pleasures of that kind. Because I think we can agree, you and I, that you are a woman who likes her little *pleasures*. Of course there was a pleasure in it for me too. Your visit would tell me something I desperately had to know: whether or not Robert had told you about his confession to me. Because if he *had* told you, then you would never come. But I knew you would come. I wanted you to come. I was banking on it. I would advertise—like a spider—and you would come—like a fly. And I would show you my house. I would tell you my story. Then, when you'd seen everything, when you'd understood what you'd done— you, a woman of *feeling*, a woman like *me*—then you would know what to do. You would do the right thing.

Oh, you wouldn't do it at once, that very day. But one day, or say one night, at three in the morning, when you wake up for no reason and can't fall back to sleep, when every little thing in your life feels wrong, when you look into your heart and see rats, bats, and dead men's bones, when your soul is nothing but a lump of black ice, then, if you listen closely, you will hear my voice whispering in your ear. Then you'll get up your courage. It isn't difficult, you know. So many ways! In every room a sharp instrument, a blunt object, dangerous devices of all kinds. Pills in the cabinet, poison in the basement, knives in the kitchen drawer. A rope. A high window. Simple as ABC. Easy as pie. Did you know there's a gun shop in town? A woman like you would have no trouble. The temple. The mouth. The heart. The smooth place between the eyes. Think of it! Your arm outstretched on the bed, your head flung back, your hair strewn across the pillow. Very becoming, very . . . romantic. You do like to think of yourself that way, don't you? I mean, a *romantic* woman. A woman in a movie—windswept hair, dress blown against your legs. But no—no—now that I think of it, maybe other endings are more your style. Here's one. The ice on the road, the sudden curve, the wildly turning wheel. Is that a good one? Do you like it? That was no accident, you know. Did you really think it was an accident? An accident? Come on. You know what it was? It was Robert's way of solving the problem. Yes! If it hadn't been for you. . . . Yes! You! Murderer! You! Coming to my house! And that awful telephone. Robert's *what*? He's *what*? Black ice? I hate telephones . . . voices without faces . . . ghosts in dead houses . . . talking to you in the dark. Whispering. Shhh. I knew you'd come back. I knew you would. Did you know I knew? About you and Robert? Deep down did you know? I think you knew. I think you did. Or peaceful scenes . . . on the rug beside the fire, the small brown bottle beside you . . . or slumped in a favorite chair. Peace, at long last. Because you'll never have it any other way, you know. I'll never have it any other way. You did wrong, my dear. I'm afraid so. Of course you never meant to *hurt* anyone. Of course not. You were very, very considerate. But there you have it: Robert dead, and me . . . as you find me. I'm afraid you made a real mess of it. There's no escaping it. So you might as well get it over with. I think so. Do it.

Do it. Do it. Why don't you? Of course you can probably get by, for a while. There are crossword puzzles, and mystery novels with nice big blood drops on the cover, and men with . . . oh, what's that word . . . it's on the tip of my . . . oh, I have it. Desire. But sooner or later. One day or another. Somewhere down the line. That sudden uneasiness as you look out a window. That moment of panic as you climb the stairs. What will you do? How can you live? Where will you go? There's nowhere to go. There's nothing to do. No one to see. Don't you know? Why go on? And always the little voice whispering in my ear, always the sad ghost rustling in the dark. That is why I wanted to show you my house. To tell you who we are. So that we would know. What to do.

And now my story's done. I never dreamed I'd be so tired! But I wanted us to hear it. People don't get to hear stories much anymore, and that's a shame. Mine even has a moral, just the way a story should.

Tired . . . I really am, you know. It takes it out of you, showing a house to strangers. And planning to go . . . to some faraway place. A journey . . . out of here. That would be nice. Peaceful, and . . . nice. Don't you think? I feel as if I haven't slept for a long time. I haven't, you know. I haven't slept for nearly a year.

Remind me to show you the heating bills. I've got them all in some folder somewhere, going back ten years.

Here's a question for you. If you were a ghost, if you were a ghost in this house, if you were dead and came to live in this house, where would you hide? In the attic? Or in the cellar?

Watch it. Watch your head.

TOP OF THE STAIRS

Back from the dead. Oh, look: it's dark out. Imagine.

FRONT HALL

Your coat. Have I said how much I admire it? I need a new spring coat myself, mine's practically a rag. I'll just put the porch light on for you. They say the weather's going to be a little warmer tomorrow: sun mixed with clouds. Last time they said that, it rained for two days. I'm hoping my jonquils will pull through. I ought to tell you that someone's coming to see the house tomorrow at four, or is it four-thirty: just for you to know. You think it over. Think over what we talked about, down there. I'm sure you'll make the right decision. And I meant what I said about the appraisal: I won't budge. Not a penny less, not a penny more. You let me know. I've lived here a long time, and now I don't want to live here anymore. You let me know. You just let me know.

An Adventure of
Don Juan

I

A time came when Don Juan could no longer bear his life. He was thirty years old, hot-blooded and handsome as a god, fiercely healthy except for a dueling scar on his left shoulder that troubled him a little in damp weather; when he walked the streets or the marble halls of still another city, the great plumes on his broad-brimmed hat trembled, his cape lifted behind him, and the jeweled hilt of his sword swinging in its scabbard against his leg seemed ready to leap out at the end of a blade of fire. He was an expert swordsman, a skilled horseman, a strong swimmer who once on a dare swam across the Ebro, where he ravished a handsome washerwoman before swimming back to complete the seduction of a countess. In his brief life he had bedded more than two thousand women and killed fourteen men—five in duels, eight in self-defense, and one by mistake, through a curtain at which he was thrusting in sheer high spirits. He feared no man, mocked the machinery of heaven, and was heard to say that the devil was a puppet invented by a bishop to frighten children in the nursery. Men envied him, women of stainless virtue stood in the window to watch him ride by. And yet this man, who walked the earth like an immortal, who did whatever was pleasing to him and who satisfied his every desire, felt that a darkness had fallen across his spirit.

Sometimes Don Juan had the sensation that every drop of his bright blood was being replaced by thick, dark smoke. Sometimes he felt tired in an unfamiliar way. He had had moments of tiredness before, the kind of bone-deep tiredness that comes after weeks of excess; then he would withdraw to his rooms, admitting no one but a devoted servant, only to emerge in two or three days, filled with energy and ferocious with desire, as if he wished to seize the world in his fist for breakfast. But this was no fit of sensual exhaustion, no temporary lull in the rush of his vigor. It was something else, something akin to tiredness that wasn't tiredness—as if a little crack, like a tiny flaw in crystal, had appeared deep within him and begun to spread. He was not bored. Don Juan didn't know whether he loved women, but he knew that he loved the pursuit and conquest of women, loved the feeling that he was following pleasure to the farthest edges of his nature. No, he felt restless in some other way, dissatisfied deep in his blood; and he began to feel that he was looking for something, though he didn't know what it was, exactly, or where he might find it.

He had planned to stay in Venice for a week or two, but he had remained for nearly a year. What bound him was the shimmer of the place, the sense of a world given over to duplication and dissolution: the stone steps going down into the water and joining their own reflection seemed to invite you down into a watery kingdom of forbidden desires, while the water trembling in ripples of light on the stone facades and the arches of ancient bridges turned the solid world into nothing but air and light, an illusion, a wizard's spell. It was a fragile, trembling world that might vanish at any moment—and perhaps that was the secret of the feverish life that began at night, when women wearing the masks of wolves and birds of prey beckoned from passing gondolas, while torchlight rippled in the black water and dark figures disappeared into doorways. Venetian women were out for pleasure, and Don Juan had bedded so many of them that he sometimes had the sense that Venice was an immense brothel composed of watery corridors and floating bedrooms hung with murky mirrors and paintings of swooning women ravished by centaurs. At other times, leaning back against the cushions of his gondola, gliding under stone balconies along narrow, sinister canals that suddenly opened into broad waterways alive with crowds on bridges, pleasure parties in gondolas, the tremor of jewels in torchlight, laughter and music everywhere, and now and then an ambiguous cry, perhaps of a young girl being thrown down in a doorway or a man being stabbed in a crooked alley, it seemed to Don Juan that he knew exactly where he was: he was on the black, fiery lake he had seen one day in a church fresco, a priestly vision of the damned that he, Don Juan Tenorio, who in a moment would step into the gondola of a woman wearing the mask of a leering satyr, preferred to call A Vision of Paradise.

Here conquest had been easy—perhaps too easy. Although not every Venetian woman was by profession a whore, the kinds of resistance he had encountered were, with a few refreshing exceptions, entirely conventional and perfunctory. A married woman who set out with the intention of giving herself to the notorious Don Juan would lower her eyes, turn her face to one side to avoid a full kiss, and push away the hand resting on her carefully half-bared breasts; sometimes tears of remorse would form in eyes already clouding over with desire. Under such easygoing conditions Don Juan, who liked nothing better than overcoming a fierce resistance, by force if necessary, found

himself contriving difficulties that Venetian society failed sufficiently to provide. He would abduct a woman and lead her
blindfolded and weeping to a room so dark that she could not
see his face; he would frighten willing victims with a show of
rage, so that their bodies stiffened and he had to possess them
brutally. Sometimes he disguised himself as a gondolier, or a
humble glassblower, or a Greek sailor in a red cap. In order to
animate the game, he occupied not only a fashionable palazzo
on the Grand Canal, but also a modest set of rooms in a mean
alley, in always shifting decors intended to support the role he
happened to be playing. That sense of playing a part began to
exasperate him, and deepened his mood of discontent; even
when he reverted to Don Juan, his legend trailed after him like
a heavy velvet cloak. One black-eyed beauty had asked him
whether it was true that a famous street in Seville was popu-
lated entirely by women who had given birth to his bastards.
Don Juan, confirming it with a bow, wondered if it might be
true.

A recent escapade continued to disturb him. He had passed
a brilliantly successful night, making separate assignations with
the handsome wife of a spice merchant and her beautiful
daughter, and ravishing each of them an hour apart in his private gondola, which had been fitted with a small cabin hung
with blood-red curtains. He had then followed a dark, narrow
canal that led to an unfamiliar part of the city, where he
climbed a flight of watery steps to a maze of high chambers
and marble stairways rising to the third-floor bedroom of a silk
draper's wife. She awaited him in her curtained bed with an
anxious face and a transparent nightgown. In the candlelight
her dark-ringed nipples resembled the open mouths and
thrust-out tongues of a pair of gargoyles he had glimpsed that
morning as he glided past a church. She protested that the hour

was late, that her husband would return at any moment, that she was a respectable woman, the mother of a beautiful little boy; Don Juan disrobed without answering her chatter, and her protests had changed to cries of pleasure when there was a sound of heavy footsteps on the stairs. Don Juan considered remaining on top of the wife and killing the husband when he drew aside the curtain. He changed his mind and began to dress without haste as the footsteps grew closer. He had just fastened his sword belt and placed his great hat on his head when the door handle began to turn. Juan removed his hat and bowed to his inamorata, sweeping his plumes across the stone floor. As the door burst open to reveal the silk merchant wearing the mask of a weeping clown, Don Juan turned to the man and bowed again, a long, slow, insolently calm bow, then sprang to the window. It was a warm night—a good night for a swim. The weeping clown drew his sword, shouted "Thief! Murderer!" and rushed forward as Juan leaped from the window. As he plunged through the night air toward the canal, where his gondolier waited some twenty feet away, Don Juan saw everything very distinctly: he saw an orange peel floating on the moonlit black water, he saw a blue satin slipper on a stone step lapped by ripples, he saw, in a window across the canal, a figure in the mask of a haughty queen fondling the naked breast of a woman in the mask of a grimacing monkey, and at the same time he saw, in his mind, the merchant's wife with her eyes widening in terror, a vein in the neck of the silk merchant as he came into the glow of the candle, the big sapphire glittering on his finger, and he saw himself, falling as if slowly through the night, holding on to his plumed hat with one hand—and it seemed to him that he had seen these images before, and that he was nothing but a third-rate actor in a provincial troupe traveling from small town to small town with a play called *Don Juan Tenorio*—and a sorrow came over him as he understood that he had finished with Venice, that he must change his life.

Like many men who prey on women, Don Juan had occasional fantasies of a different life. Sometimes he imagined himself a stern, pale scholar bent over a volume of Aristotle in his library, while the brilliant blue light coming through the tall windows changed to plum blue to dove gray to black. At other times he was a humble monk, hoeing a row of peas in the monastery garden. These idle fancies lasted no longer than the next sight of a pretty girl—or an ugly girl with an interesting walk. Don Juan had no illusions about his nature: he craved pleasure, intense pleasure, and the most extreme of all pleasures was to be found in the bodies of women. If he felt a darkness lying across his life, a dissatisfaction deep in his blood, it was because he had become aware of a slight diminution, a lack of zest. It might be true that the women of Venice were a little too willing to be debauched, but it was also true that the most fastidious women had always proved Venetian in the end. And if they did not, and his blood was up, he asked no permission and never looked back. No, what he needed wasn't a different life, but a more intense version of this one—a life of sensual pleasure uncorrupted by vague dissatisfactions and elusive ennuis. What he longed for was more desire, a madness of desire, a journey into feeling so intense that he would ride through himself like a conqueror of unknown inner countries. He had perhaps become a little stale. And as he lay in the darkness of his curtained bed, with his arms crossed over his chest and his eyes closed, like the stone effigy of a king, Don Juan tried to see the new life that he knew awaited him, if only he could learn to see in his own dark.

One night an idea came to him, at first vaguely, then with

startling precision. He would leave the south, the lush, soft Mediterranean world where women ripened in the sun like oranges hanging over a whitewashed wall, and he would travel north. Don Juan was a child of Seville, who had always loved the cities of southern Spain and France and Italy; he had never been farther north than Paris. He would go farther than that—he would go all the way to England. England!—that legendary land composed entirely of fog, through which glimmered the crowns of stern kings. It was a land of blond-haired seamen in their high-prowed ships—or was he confusing it with Norway? But precisely what he liked about England was that he didn't know how to imagine the place; it was an insubstantial land, a cloudland in which he seemed to see pale-haired queens walking in dim gardens. In fact he had met a number of Englishmen on his travels and enjoyed several of their wives, but somehow those very substantial creatures—the broad-shouldered wine merchant traveling in Verona, the hawk-nosed viscount with disdainful eyes who had proved to have a passion for Roman ruins and thirteen-year-old boys, the buxom, lusty wife of an apothecary who had sung him an old song of which he'd understood only the word "never" but which had disturbed him with its melancholy beauty—all these flesh-and-blood emissaries of England seemed to have nothing to do with that mythical northern land of kings and castles and pale princesses gazing down from high towers.

He had forgotten the invitation, but it came back to him now: the odd, likable traveler he had met one night at the beginning of his stay in Venice. Don Juan had been gliding along in his gondola at three in the morning, when he'd seen a strange sight: a man standing in a gondola staring up at the sky through a telescope mounted on a three-legged support. Don Juan had drawn up alongside him and addressed him in Italian, which he knew perfectly, and the man had replied in an equally fluent Italian colored by a faint accent impossible to place. He had, he said, been looking at the moon. Don Juan's interest was aroused; the man proved amicable, and soon the two were drifting about in Don Juan's gondola, while the man showed him the wonders of the universe. His name was Augustus Hood. He was traveling through Italy with his wife and her sister. He was one of those round-faced, plump-cheeked Englishmen who seem boyish at thirty, with a small mouth and very wide eyes, as if life for him were a perpetual surprise. Within ten minutes he had impressed Don Juan with his flow of easy erudition, his knowledge of a hundred curious subjects such as the manufacture of cannon and the methods of irrigation under the pharaohs, his travels to China, Egypt, and Constantinople, his modesty, his energy, his unlikely mixture of man-of-the-world and earnest schoolboy. He asked Don Juan questions he had never been asked before—about the manufacture of Seville lace, the shearing of merino sheep, the arrangement of rooms in his childhood home. He was leaving Venice the next day, on his way to Rome and perhaps Sicily. He would return to England in a month or so; he invited Don Juan to visit him at Swan Park in Somerset. His most recent passion was landscape gardening, and he would like to show his new friend a few little things he had accomplished in that line. The Englishman had stayed with him in the gondola until dawn, betraying no sign of tiredness, and though Don Juan had quickly forgotten Augustus Hood and his telescope, he remembered everything now in immense detail. He would go to England. He would visit Swan Park, in the mist-filled shadowy North. He might stay a week or a century. He would keep his rented palazzo on the Grand Canal, leaving behind all his servants but one. It was crucial that he take with him as little as possible of his former life.

That night Don Juan dreamed that he and Augustus Hood were walking in his father's orchard on the bank of the Guadalquivir. Hood was pointing up at an orange tree with his walking stick, which he handed to Juan, who raised it to his eye like a telescope and looked at an orange that suddenly leered at him and stuck out its tongue, and when he swung the telescope at it he saw that he was holding in his hand a gondolier's oar, he was rowing through the watery spaces between trees hung with jewels, and the next day he left Venice and headed north.

I I

"Adam was the first gardener," Augustus Hood remarked, stepping from a cypress grove onto a grass path that led to a distant grotto.

"And this, then, is a second Eden," Juan gallantly replied, sweeping out an arm. They were speaking Italian; Juan held in one hand a small English grammar bound in buckram.

"In English—" Mary Hood began, in English.

"Before or after the Fall, Sir?" her sister Georgiana remarked in French, and Juan, turning to look at her, again had the irritating sense that he couldn't tell whether her remark was in earnest or whether she was being mischievous in some elusive English way.

"*In inglese,*" Mary Hood said, and then returned to English, "we say 'Eden.' 'Eeeee-den.' You see: 'tis the same word. *La stessa parola.*"

The sisters, each wearing a flat straw hat with a low crown tied round with silk ribbons, stepped onto the path rippling with sunlight and leafshade. The front and back of the wide hat-brims were turned up, and the edges of the lace undercaps showed beneath.

"That, Georgiana, depends entirely on the divine plan," Augustus Hood mysteriously remarked. "Why, here's a jolly fellow. Look! An *usignuolo*."

"Nightingale," Mary Hood said. "Night. In. Gale."

"Pouring forth its melodious song," Georgiana said.

And indeed a nightingale was pouring forth its song from a low branch at the shady border of the grove. Hood walked quietly up to the bird and, to Juan's surprise, took it gently in his hand. The squire of Swan Park was continually surprising him.

"Here," Hood said, handing the bird to Juan. The nightingale sat very still in his hand—was this a habit of English birds? "I made it myself," Hood continued. The bird was covered with real feathers; under one wing was a small pin that operated a spring.

"Your husband is a man of many surprises," Don Juan remarked to Mary Hood, who smiled pleasantly at him and lowered her hat-shaded eyes, while Georgiana Reynolds looked at him with a faint smile that might have meant "And you, Sir, are a great fool" or "What an amusing thing to say" or anything else or nothing at all. Juan examined the bird and returned it to Augustus Hood, who replaced it carefully on the branch and led them up the path.

But Swan Park was in truth a surprising place, a realm of wonders, an artful Eden, of which Augustus Hood was the presiding genius. He had designed every feature of his two hundred acres of gardens, including the grottoes, the cascades, the mounts, the serpentine streams, the sudden openings onto distant prospects, the seats under shady trees, the ruined priory, the Temple of Flora, the scenes arranged to remind the wanderer of paintings by Salvator Rosa, Nicolas Poussin, and Claude Lorrain. Beyond the gardens lay four thousand acres of parkland, which Hood had also designed and which he had promised to show his guest in the coming days. The brilliant art of English landscape gardening had swiftly replaced the dreary old rigidities of the continental style, but in Hood's view the revolution had barely begun, and in any case was not sufficiently understood even by those in the vanguard of the movement. It was all very well to turn away from artifice in the direction of the natural and wild, but those wild prospects, those tumbling cascades and rugged grottoes, were all the work of ingenious artificers. You might say that the wilder the prospect, the more cunning the hand of the maker. If the movement toward the natural were taken to its logical conclusion, there would be no distinction whatever between Nature and the English garden. No, the true way was to assert artifice even in the act of paying homage to Nature.

"Ingenious, certainly," Georgiana was saying. "But is the real nightingale any less wonderful? Can anyone possibly believe that Nature herself is without design? For my part—"

"You must forgive us," Mary Hood said. "We English are rather fond of argument."

"I am not *arguing*, Mary, I am merely saying that in this age of mechanical ingenuity—"

Don Juan listened with delight to the voices of the Englishwomen, one speaking Italian, the other French, a language he understood nearly as well—the one with a gentle, musical voice, the other more energetic and abrupt, reaching higher and lower in the scale—while greenish shadows rippled down onto the cream-colored and sky-blue silk of their hooped

gowns. It was a brilliant summer afternoon. Everything inter-
ested him: the wide, forearm-length cuffs of Hood's coat, the
tight horizontal side-curls of his wig, the figure of Moses striking water from a rock at the top of a cascade, the silk ribbons
around the sisters' necks, the Rotunda with its telescope and
its view of the river Ymber, the Garden of Shakespeare with its
sixty-four statues of comical and tragical characters in dramatic
attitudes, Hood's explanation of the construction of a rill. At
the top of the path they entered the cool grotto, passed out the
other side into a picturesque meadow bordered by a wood, and
walked along a winding path that somehow led back to the
great house.

Dinner was served at four o'clock on the broad lawn that
sloped down to the Ymber. Osiers trailed their branches in the
slow brown water; a few swans swam flickering through sun
and shade. On the grass by the riverbank was a stone bench on
which lay a yellow silk pillow, a fan with ivory sticks, and a
book bound in red morocco. A footman stood before Don
Juan, holding out a silver bowl containing bunches of grapes
so purple and glistening that they looked like a painting of a
bowl of grapes, each with its careful highlight. Juan dropped a
grape into his mouth, hesitating a moment, as if it might be
an object of wax, before biting down and feeling the juice burst
against his tongue—and while Mary Hood smiled at her husband under the shade of her hat, and Georgiana brushed an
ant from her blue silk shoulder, and the pleasant voice of
Augustus Hood was saying that a universe was not precisely
like a pocket watch, and beyond the river a field of hayricks
lay burning in the sun, Don Juan felt a rich sense of peace, of
relaxation, as if for a long time he had been clenching unknown
muscles. He felt ten years old again, listening to his father

explaining how the flower ripens into the fruit, in the orchard that went down to the Guadalquivir. Venice seemed a dark dream, a fever-vision from which he had wakened to a new morning. Don Juan had no intention of sparing the women— idly he wondered whether Mary or Georgiana would lead the way—but for the first time in his life he was in no hurry.

Over the next few days a loose, easy-flowing routine was established at Swan Park. Don Juan, who was accustomed to rising late in the morning, would come down to find that Squire Hood had risen six hours earlier and was out supervising one of his many projects in the gardens or parkland. Mary and Georgiana had eaten at nine but sat with Juan in the breakfast room as he was served the third breakfast of the day: hot brown bread, honey, hot chocolate, buttered toast, and a pot of steaming tea. The three would then walk along the river, or on one of the many garden paths, as they awaited the return of Squire Hood. He would come galloping along the riding path, swing from his horse, cry "Hah!" or "Gad, what a day!" and burst into enthusiastic talk about his projects as he took a short turn with them in the gardens before riding off with Juan to the farthest reaches of Swan Park. The gentle squire, Juan thought, was like a fire—or a Spanish rake: he was always burning. They returned for dinner at four, in the high dining room or on the lawn above the Ymber. Hood, dressed carelessly in riding boots and an old broadcloth coat, consumed platefuls of roast veal and pigeon pie washed down with cider and red port as he discussed everything under the sun: the operation of a silk loom, the superiority of timber props to pillars of coal for supporting the roofs of mines, the idea—shocking to Juan—that modern battle heroes depicted in paintings ought to be shown in contemporary garb instead of in Greek or

Roman armor. The elaborate dinner, lasting two hours, ended with bowls of gooseberries, thick wedges of currant pie, orange pudding, and pots of green and black tea.

After dinner they played charades or piquet in the drawing room, walked by the river, and sometimes drove in a calash along the graveled riding path that wound among the gardens. Then Hood retired to the library, to read a treatise on the cultivation of laburnum or the operation of a Newcomen engine, or to examine a bit of leaf or the wing of an insect through the microscope that stood on a corner table. A light supper of cold meats was served at nine-thirty or ten; afterward first Hood and then the women retired to their rooms. Juan, unused to going to bed before dawn, would climb the stairs to his apartment— a bedroom and sitting room in a separate wing—where his new valet had prepared his bed for the night. On the third day Juan had sent his servant back to Venice, unable to bear the thought of having about him the all-too-faithful partner of his Venetian revels; Hood had immediately supplied an English valet, the self-effacing cousin of a Swan Park chambermaid. In the long night Juan would play dozens of games of patience at an inlaid mahogany table in his sitting room. He would drink Madeira, look at the sky through the telescope that Hood had mounted for him on a stand by one of his sitting-room windows, and glance through the leather volumes of English poets that Mary had chosen for him from the library. Then he would sit for a long time in his bedroom armchair in the embrasure of the casement window, savoring his solitude and staring out at a distant turn of the Ymber before climbing into his canopied bed at three in the morning.

In the vast house, he was the only guest. Hood, for all his exuberance, enjoyed his solitude—or at any rate he was happy to shut himself up in the library whenever he liked. One afternoon his landscape architect, a quietly amiable man named William Gravenor, came to dinner, during which he unrolled a large sheet of paper that knocked over a glass of port; after dinner the two of them retired immediately to the library, while Don Juan walked with the women by the river. He knew that Hood liked him, but it struck him that he was also useful to the squire, who could disappear at a moment's notice.

"I *walk*," Mary Hood was saying, as she and Juan walked along the path of osiers behind Georgiana and Augustus, "every day. I *am walking*—now—at this moment. 'Tis the difference between what is customary and what is singular. I am walking beside the river."

"I am walking," Juan said, "beside the river."

"You are walking beside the river," Mary said. "You are talking beside the river. We are walking and talking beside the river."

"I am talking beside the river," Juan said. "We are walking beside the river."

"They are walking beside the river," Mary said, pointing at Georgiana and Augustus. "The birds are singing in the trees. The sun is setting in the west."

"Night is coming," Juan said. "We are walking in the north beside the river. Day is dying."

"I am going mad," Georgiana said, glancing back over her left shoulder, "beside the river."

He was making rapid progress in English. Mary had taken it upon herself to be his teacher, and he spoke to her easily, though an odd shyness prevented him from practicing his sentences with Georgiana. He was never alone with either woman; he wondered whether it was by design. Of the two, Mary seemed to enjoy his company frankly, while Georgiana held him at a playful distance, as if he were a very amusing piece of foreign furniture—just how amusing, he would show her in time. Georgiana liked to engage in serious discussions with her brother-in-law, about such matters as whether natural beauty might ever be excelled by artistic beauty, or how the impression made by a word differed from the impression made by the object represented by a word; Juan admired her brilliant gray-green eyes with their long, curved lashes, the green feathers she liked to wear in her thick auburn hair, and the green silk ribbons around her neck. Her movements were quick, even impatient; there was a tension in her hands and at the edges of her mouth that suggested secret energies. Mary Hood was gentler and more flowing in her motions. She liked to assume the role of teacher, repeating sentences patiently and giving examples, as if Juan were a child of seven and she a stern governess with excellent references; at dinner she preferred to listen. Her hair seemed to Juan a contradiction: light brown, like a paler, duller version of her sister's, combed softly back from the forehead and temples, but at the back thickly ringleted and hanging to the nape; when she moved, her curls shook continually, as if her passions were in her hair. Her eyes were hazel. She was given to sudden, unexpected fits of laughter.

Don Juan understood that his genius in the art of seduction lay not in his gift of beauty, not in his power to charm, not in his fearlessness, not even in his ferocious will, but rather in a subtle evolution in the domain of feeling: his uncanny ability to burrow his way deep into a woman's nature, to detect with precision the slight, subterranean ripples of inclination and repulsion that constituted the hidden life of women. He knew that Mary Hood enjoyed his company, and he knew something more: her interest in him quickened whenever he turned his attention toward Georgiana. Then he would sense in her body a slight stiffening, in her bottom lip a slight drawing in; and lowering her eyes, she would wait for his attention to fall on her again. Juan understood that this was not yet jealousy, but some elusive foreshadowing of it, akin to an instinct of ownership. It was as if Mary Hood had taken charge of him and didn't like him to stray. Juan understood one other thing: it was the beginning of a particular interest in him that might, in time, take a more lively turn. It was his way in.

Meanwhile, he savored his long outings with the tireless squire of Swan Park, who proved to be a passionate horseman with a fondness for dangerous descents along craggy paths and wild gallops across open downs. The outer reaches of Swan Park were in a continual state of development and reinvention, and Hood was in the thick of things, assisting laborers as they cut a glade or opened a serpentine path through a wood, directing the construction of a pond or the draining of a swamp, and discussing with tenants on outlying farms the breeding of cattle or the cultivation of turnips. He had strong opinions about a host of subjects that Juan had never given a thought to. Lakes, Hood declared, should always be wooded to the shore, their ends lost to view among trees, and he argued that the most picturesque coppice was one composed of beeches and Scots firs. He was currently overseeing a number of exciting ventures, including an interconnected series of subterranean tunnels, a hollow hill containing a library, and several curious projects that he called "living representations"—small tracts of parkland turned into legendary or historical places that blended perfectly into the forests of oak, beech, and ash, the undulating meadows and fields, the hills and valleys of Swan Park. Passing through a thick wood, they came to a region of gently rising hills and shady dales, watered by many streams. A shepherd sat on a rock under a tree, playing a reed pipe, while eight or nine shorn sheep grazed nearby. This, Hood explained, was the land of Arcadia, where real shepherds and shepherdesses dressed in authentic Greek costumes tended flocks of sheep, whose wool was sheared by tenant farmers and sold to merchants in Flanders, while skilled musicians wearing the costumes of shepherds and shepherdesses played pipes made from reeds imported from the Peloponnesus, and actors dressed like Elizabethan lords and ladies enacted scenes of love-longing, such as sighing aloud, weeping by the sides of brooks, pining away in shady groves, and writing love sonnets to hang on the branches of trees. As they rode, Juan saw one young lord in doublet and hose leaning cross-legged against an oak, staring sorrowfully at the ground; the lord looked up at the intruders on horseback, and turned his face away with an expression of angry despair.

Scarcely had they passed through Arcadia when Hood began to speak eagerly about a more recent representation—a venture into the Saxon past. After a time they came to a realm of thick forest and swampland; dark islands rose from the marsh. Here, Hood explained proudly, stood the Isle of Athelney; here during the Danish wars, when all of Wessex was on the verge of a humiliating defeat, King Alfred had retreated for seven long weeks, brooding over the fate of England, waiting for the chance to strike back at his enemies, and emerging at last to defeat Guthrum at the battle of Edington. Hood showed Juan the dense thickets of alder, the fort of the brooding king, the wild deer, a rough wooden bridge; and here and there Juan could see, deep in the alder woods, an ancient Saxon disappearing into the gloom.

But Hood could scarcely suppress his impatience to show Don Juan his latest representation, still under way in a remote corner of southwest parkland. "This way!" he cried, as he broke into a gallop across a field of yellow wildflowers. "Faster!

Zounds! I'll take you to the end o' the living world!" Juan, spurring his horse, felt the excitement of it—the irrepressible squire had a way of making you feel like a twelve-year-old boy following an adventurous fourteen-year-old brother. They dashed over meadows, slowed to a walk through narrow forest paths darkened by overhanging branches, splashed through rushing streams, startled hares and deer, burst into secret glades trembling with sunlight, until at last they came to a dark lake bordered by gloomy hills. Here Hood dismounted and motioned for Juan to tie his horse to a thick branch. Eagerly he led the way on foot along the edge of the dreary lake, which emitted a stench of sulfur. " 'Twas said that birds flying over this noxious lake would sicken and die. Hah! What have we here?"

They had come to a high cave partially concealed by dense bushes. Above the entrance hung a stone plaque in which were carved the words FACILIS DESCENSUS AVERNO. Underneath, in smaller letters, stood four lines of verse:

> Smooth the descent and easy is the way
> (The Gates of Hell stand open night and day);
> But to return and view the cheerful skies,
> In this the task and mighty labour lies.

Dryden, Hood remarked—was Juan familiar with the English poet?—had taken a strong liberty by translating "Dis" as "Hell," although the more interesting question concerned whether Avernus referred to the lake proper or, by extension, to the Underworld itself. The opinion of the learned was divided, some saying that *Averno* must mean *to* Avernus, others that it could only mean *by way of* Avernus. However that may be, he remarked as he led Juan into the cave, he had cho-

sen to call this representation Avernus, for the simple reason—
"Hah! Well! I see you enjoy my little effects." Juan had drawn
his sword as a hissing form half emerged from the shadows.
" 'Tis the Lernean Hydra," Hood explained, nodding toward
the retiring monster. "She o' the many heads. In this art, Sir,"
he added, "shadow is all." In a trembling blackness lit by small
fires, he pointed to shadowy creatures that half showed themselves and half withdrew. There lay a Gorgon, there a flame-
breathing Chimaera, there Briareus of the hundred arms—but
surely Juan knew his *Aeneid*? Beyond the tree of false dreams
lay the shore of the river Acheron: there the souls of the dead
fluttered moaning near the bank.

Hood led Juan into a broad flat boat. At one end Charon
with his burning eyes and wild tangle of white beard stood in
his filthy cloak knotted at one shoulder, gripping his pole like
a grim gondolier. " 'Tis only the buried dead may cross," Hood
said, sitting down on a wooden thwart. "The unburied must
wait on shore for an hundred years." "Are you and I the buried
dead, then?" Juan asked with a smile. "We are all buried, in
comparison with what *may* be," Hood riddlingly replied.

On the far shore of Acheron he led Juan into the flickering
dark. Here there was still much work to be done. The three
heads of Cerberus lay in a heap, and Dido, dressed in black
and looking rather bored, sat at a small table playing patience
by the light of a lantern. A fork in the path led to Tartarus on
the left and Elysium on the right, both under construction.
Hood led him to the left, through a passageway that opened
into a torchlit place where laborers struck at the walls with
picks, pushed carts laden with rocks, or sat wearily on barrels,
eating bread and cheese.

"And yet," Georgiana said a few hours later, "you cannot
deny that all of Nature is the work of a great Designer."

"Come now, I do not deny the existence of a great Designer," Hood replied, as he cut into his roast goose. "I deny only that that existence may be proved from the evidence of Nature."

"But—Augustus—what more evidence can there be, than the regularity and order of Nature? Night following day, the succession of seasons, the regular progress of the stars, the orderly development of the oak tree from the acorn and the rose from the rose seed, the marvelous mechanism of the human eye, so perfectly adapted for the sensation of vision—surely the sense of a Designer must present itself forcibly to a mind unbiased by ideas repugnant to reason."

"Indeed, 'tis well argued," Hood said. "I do not—upon my word, I do not deny the appearance of order in Nature. I deny only—"

"Appearance, you say!"

"Aye, just so: for what *appears,* may not *be.* Yet the appearance of order once being granted, I deny 'tis evidence of purposeful design. It may, with equal reason, be explained as the result of an accidental collocation of atoms, as in the system of Democritus and Epicurus."

"What! My dear Augustus, you—why, 'tis the rankest atheism!"

"Nay, my dear Georgiana. 'Tis the rankest Reason. Come, have some more port, Mary. The white is better than the red. Is it my fancy, or does our friend Don Juan look as if he has just returned from the dead? Why, I'm only joking, dear. Pray, Don Juan, do explain my little riddle, else she'll cook me and carve me and serve me up on a platter."

After dinner, Hood retired to the library to read a paper in the *Philosophical Transactions of the Royal Society,* while Juan took a turn with Mary and Georgiana along the path of osiers on the bank of the Ymber. In the early evening light, a swan and five cygnets passed near the shore. Georgiana stopped to watch for a moment, while Mary, who had been agreeing that the spelling of English was much in need of reform, and who hadn't noticed her sister's interest in the swan, walked on several steps ahead. Juan, seeing that Georgiana had been left behind, inclined his head and said in a low voice, "I fear your sister has taken a dislike to me."

"Why—why—but surely you are mistaken."

"You see how she avoids us."

"But I cannot understand—"

"Come, come," called Georgiana, "what are you two plotting?"

"We were speaking," Mary replied, coloring slightly, "about the irregularity of English orthography."

The flush in her cheeks, the reflection of the osiers in the dark water, the shimmer of the lace frill on her square décolletage, the evening light falling on distant fields, the sense of sudden intimacy caused by his words and by Mary's little falsehood, all this filled Juan with a sense of well-being, and that night, lying in his curtained bed, he recalled the pleasing scene as if it were a painting: the man standing with slightly inclined head, the woman close beside him, the second woman standing at a distance, her face turned toward them, in the soft light of dusk.

Now in the late mornings, whenever he walked with Mary and Georgiana along winding garden paths, or in the evenings when all four played together until supper, Juan seized any chance he had to exchange a word in private with Mary about Georgiana, or to speak with Georgiana while Mary watched across a distance. And Juan could feel, in the young wife, a quickening of interest, a ripple of feeling that was deeply familiar to him—for he was never mistaken, in such matters.

One afternoon after his late breakfast Juan accompanied Hood to the stable yard, where one of the grooms replaced a worn bridle and examined a shoe. Juan then rode out with Hood to Avernus, watched his friend disappear into the cave, and rode back to the house. There he sat with Mary and Georgiana in the drawing room before retiring to his apartment, where he threw himself down on the walnut armchair beside his bedroom window. It was an unusually comfortable chair, upholstered in claret-colored wool velvet. He drummed his fingers on the arm, stood up and walked into the sitting room, flung himself across the sofa, rose at once and returned to the bedroom, where he strode to the window. He opened the casement wide and stood with his hands on both sashes as he looked down at a strip of lawn, a plum orchard, a beech grove, and a distant turn of river. A moment later he climbed up onto the window ledge. Directly below was a narrow stretch of lawn, on which lay a rake and a watering can.

Juan leaped, wondering dimly if he would break a leg. On the brilliant jewel-green grass his dark green shadow appeared; as he fell he had the odd sensation that his shadow had been stolen from him and was now being returned. He broke his fall, rolled over twice, and stood up, joined to his shadow. His whole body tingled with exhilaration. And suddenly he recalled his leap into the canal, the lights on the water, the orange peel, the eyes of the merchant's wife widening in fear, the waiting gondola.

He passed through the orchard and made his way through the coppice of beech trees, past a small lake with an island, and through a pine grove to a melancholy retreat, where paths wound among yew trees, weathered statues, and a dark pool rimmed with crumbling stone. At the far end of the retreat rose an immense oak. Its half-bared roots, thick as saplings, had been artfully shaped to form two seat backs. At the base of each seat was a dark red pillow bearing Hood's crest: a swan wearing a crown. On one of the pillows lay Juan's grammar. Juan threw himself onto the other pillow, opened his grammar, closed it immediately, and studied an iridescent insect that was walking on the back of his hand.

Ten minutes later he was studying the same insect as it walked along a blade of grass that Juan slowly tipped from side to side. He looked up to see Mary approaching on a path beside the crumbling pool. The pink silk of her hooped gown rippled with light and shade, the lace ruffles at the ends of her elbow-length sleeves shook on her gloved forearms, and as she drew closer he saw that she was wearing around her shoulders a covering of translucent white fabric, the ends of which were tucked into her low-cut bodice and held in place by a blue silk breastknot.

" 'Twas impossible to come directly," she said in a quiet, urgent tone, and the trouble in her face gave her an energy that reminded Juan of her tight, trembling ringlets. "Your note—"

"Georgiana doesn't"—he groped for the correct word as he rose to his feet—"suspect?" He motioned for her to sit down.

"I told her that I had a terrible headache. I wasn't to be disturbed—not for any reason. I dislike sneaking. You had something of importance to tell me?"

"There is nothing to be alarmed about. Please sit." He considered the phrase. "Down."

"I can stay no more than a moment," she said, sitting on one of the pillows and resting the backs of her white-gloved hands in her lap, like shells.

"A moment will be more than enough. There is something I must speak to you about"—and as he sat down beside her, looking into her anxious face, examining the shadowy pale skin beneath the translucent gauze handkerchief that revealed her elegant collarbone and swelled over the tops of her breasts before plunging out of sight beneath the big silk bow, he knew that Mary Hood had already succumbed, although she herself did not yet know it, and imagined only that she was having an interesting conversation with a Spanish nobleman under an ancient oak.

"I really must go. Georgiana—"

"Hang Georgiana. I have felt—for some time—that you have been avoiding me."

"But no—why do you—"

"If I have offended you in any—"

"*You*—offend *me*—"

Juan was excited by her wide nervous eyes, by the flush in her neck, by the tense curves of her tight-gloved fingers and the short copper-colored hairs on her cheek near her ear. He could feel a hoop of whalebone bending against his thigh. He had taken her hand, he was leaning toward her—so close that he could see the individual hairs in her lustrous eyebrows, which were darker than her ringlets. Her clear hazel eyes had become cloudy and languorous. The day had grown very still. As he was about to seize her and throw her down on the grass, Don Juan hesitated for a moment, and noticed his hesitation. In that moment he became aware of a faint sound, as of a scratching or scraping. The sound grew louder. There was a thumping or rumbling behind his head—Mary looked over her shoulder in alarm—Juan leaped up with his sword in hand and whirled to stare defiantly at the great oak. A crack appeared in the bark—it was as if the whole tree were breaking before his eyes—and suddenly a door swung open and Augustus Hood stepped out.

"Mary, my dear," he said, "you look as if you've seen a ghost. You look ferocious, Sir! Faith! Do you mean to cut off my head?"

And laughing, trembling with excitement, his cheeks burning with glee, Squire Hood motioned Juan and Mary to look inside the hollow oak, where a stairway led down to an underground passage. It was, he explained as he walked with them back to the house, the most recent extension of a splendid system of subterranean tunnels that he had been working on for some time.

I I I

That night as he sat in the walnut armchair in the embrasure of his bedroom window, Don Juan brooded over his moment of hesitation under the oak tree. He had hesitated in part because he hadn't wished to conquer so easily—he had longed for more resistance, more difficulty, and had been disappointed in the cloudy look of yielding in Mary Hood's eyes. He had hesitated because Mary was pleasing to him just as she was— an earnest schoolteacher, an ally, a charming companion of his evening rambles, a shy and gentle woman trembling on the verge of destructive ecstasy—and he knew that she would become less pleasing the moment he had enjoyed her favors. He had hesitated because Augustus Hood was one of the few men he had ever liked. He had hesitated because he had hoped to find, in the mysterious North, a new life, unimagined before, a life of desire so deep that it would pierce him like a sword, and the seduction of pretty Mary Hood was a return to the old life. And he had hesitated for some other reason that he couldn't quite grasp, as if there were something about himself that eluded him, something he was on the verge of knowing but did not know. Then he thought of himself brooding there in his window like a pale philosopher, and he gave a scornful laugh, aloud to the night sky—for nothing was more repellent to Don Juan than a man of uncertainty, a hesitating, careful-stepping man, a man without a woman.

He returned to the routine of Swan Park, but with a feeling of restlessness. For a day Mary seemed awkward in his company and made a point of remaining at Georgiana's side, but she soon thawed into her old easiness, as if nothing had happened under the old oak tree; perhaps nothing had. Georgiana, who now spoke English in his presence, remained a little aloof, a little mocking. It seemed to Juan that she was rather amused by him, this fantastical don with his plumed hat. As for Squire Hood, his work on Avernus was progressing nicely, though he'd hit a snag in Tartarus: the pasteboard boulder for Sisyphus didn't have the look of stone, and he was eagerly awaiting a new rock prepared by a stonecutter—a real boulder carefully hollowed and filled with a mixture of wool and straw to prevent a telltale echo. At dinner Hood was in high form, overflowing with anecdotes of his day and arguing with Georgiana about the riddle of the universe. He insisted that the nature of Nature wasn't at all clear, since although it was true that forests, for example, suggested to the mind ideas of wildness and irregularity, it was equally true that the individual trees in the wildest forest had leaves or cones so regular in appearance that it was difficult not to imagine the hand of an artist; at which Georgiana said Hah!—by his own admission there was design in Nature, whereby one could argue the existence of an ultimate Designer. No no, Hood insisted, that wasn't at all the case, since the appearance of design was by no means proof of a designer, it being with equal reason arguable that matter had inherent within it a cause of order; and Juan felt that this conversation would never come to an end, that it was arranged expressly never to come to an end, and that the tip of Georgiana's nose irritated him, and that Mary's little glances, to make certain he was following the discussion, were even more irritating than the tip of Georgiana's infuriating nose, and that if he didn't do something soon—now—this very instant—his head would break loose from his neck and go rolling across the floor—and still he sat there, while the voices spun out delicate threads that bound him, and it seemed to him that he had always sat just that way, like a man caught in a spell.

Sometimes in the evenings he joined Hood in the library, where he bent over the microscope on the table by the fireplace and examined the little creatures teeming in a drop of vinegar or pond water or an infusion of peppercorns. Nature was so prodigious, Hood declared, that it produced universes in both directions, the minuscule and the gigantic, a vast concord of animalcula and suns; and as Juan tried to share Hood's awe at the plenitude of Nature, he felt only a discontent, a vague revulsion, as if the universe stretching away in both directions existed solely to reveal to him the fecundity of its indifference.

One morning when Juan came down to breakfast he found Georgiana standing in the drawing room with a letter in her hand, while Mary sat watching her.

"Well, Sir," Georgiana said in English, glancing up at him, "you shall soon be well rid of me."

"Madam," Juan replied, choosing his words carefully, "I would sooner be rid of my honor."

"Oh," Georgiana replied, with her eyes on the letter, "that is no very great thing to be rid of."

Juan, biting down in anger, was uncertain whether she meant to taunt him into a witty reply, or whether she intended a more malicious meaning; and once again he was aware of the odd, physical sense of imbalance he always felt in the presence of this woman, as if he were walking across an unsteady log thrown across a rushing stream.

"Georgiana has had a letter from Father," Mary said. In a letter filled with news of a quarrel among servants, farm rents, land improvement, a lame horse, and a pious memory of his late wife, he let it be known that he sorely missed his dear Georgiana. She would be leaving Swan Park for Sussex the next morning. Juan looked at Georgiana standing there with her haughty head bent over her letter, her hair in back turned up in a flat plait bound tightly in place. The sheer sight of her irritated every nerve in his body. She had received a letter from her father, the sort of letter that thousands of daughters received every day, and because of it the entire world must be turned upside down. A pleasing routine had been established at Swan Park, a daily harmony, and merely because of this prattling epistle from a fretful father it must now be interrupted, broken up, destroyed forever. Georgiana had no feeling for such things; there was a thoughtlessness about her, even a selfishness, that fit in perfectly with her distant manner and her mocking tone. And whatever she might think of *him*, a foreign guest toward whom the rules of hospitality required at most a modicum of civility, what of Mary, who without her sister would be left alone for long stretches of the day?—to say nothing of poor Augustus, who liked nothing better than to engage Georgiana in lively discussion at dinner and to walk with her along the river. And although the sight of her standing there with her insufferable letter irritated him so deeply that the mere thought of her absence filled him with delight, it was also true that the pleasure he took in her future absence was diminished by his exasperation at the knowledge of her imminent departure.

That evening Augustus Hood did not return to the library but joined the company in a walk along the Ymber. He and Georgiana strolled ahead of Juan and Mary. The precise reflections of branches in the dark water, the meadow across the river, the sound of cattle lowing, Hood's riding boots squeaking softly on the path, Georgiana's hat brim trembling slightly as she walked—all this sank into Juan as if he were seeing it for the last time. "Oh, look!" said Georgiana, pointing to the swan and its five cygnets. She stepped off the path, bending her head, pushing away osier branches for a closer look. Her hat struck a branch and fell to the grass. Juan sprang forward. "Sir," Georgiana said, laughing, "you startled me." Juan, wondering irritably whether he was supposed to apologize, handed her the hat in silence, and as she raised it with both hands to her hair, lifting her elbows like wings, he saw her looking away across the water with a cool smile.

And when he came down to breakfast the next morning she was gone, just like that: a conjuror's trick. Mary would be the next to vanish, and then Hood, and then Swan Park— and the Great Magician, with a fiendish laugh, would open his hand—nothing!—while the blue silk handkerchief fluttered to the floor. Meanwhile, it was as if nothing had changed. Mary sat with him in the breakfast room. He was still sitting at table, staring at the shortened shadow of a cup on sunlit white linen, when Hood arrived in his riding boots and spurs. In the afternoon Juan rode off with Hood to the site of Avernus and then continued alone into the countryside, where he tried to ride himself into exhaustion. At dinner the conversation turned to methods of education. Juan told stories of tutors and governesses in the house in Seville, the lessons in fencing and riding, in mathematics and Latin—oh yes, he had made his way through all twelve books of the *Aeneid* at the age of thirteen—and as he spoke he kept expecting Georgiana to leap into the conversation in some irritating exasperating way.

Two nights later he woke and saw through his partly open bed curtains a brilliant glow of moonlight in the room. He had fallen asleep fully clothed, with his sword belt still in place. Through the open casement window he saw the deep-blue night sky. He had been restless and distracted; a walk would do him good. At the casement he sprang lightly onto the sill, then lowered himself from the window by climbing partway down along two stone projections on the wall. He dropped to the grass and, keeping away from the kennels, made his way around the guest wing and down to the river. For a while he walked on the path beside the osiers, before stepping into the trees. He sat down against a trunk. Frogs croaked along the riverbank; a bird called sharply and was still. Through the hanging branches he looked out at the dark river shining with moonlight.

He was restless and irritable and melancholy—he could feel disappointment seeping into his skin. His northern journey had been a failure. He had hoped for something—something that was no longer clear to him—and he hadn't found it here. It was true that he had been happy at Swan Park—happy riding out with Augustus Hood, happy half-seducing Mary and sparing her the descent into triteness, happy even in the exasperating company of irritating Georgiana. But now there was a flatness to things, a dullness in his spirit. He had never been so long without a woman. He was probably doing himself great harm by not ravishing Mary Hood, or her maid-servant, or one of the chambermaids he saw now and then about the house. But he had wanted—he had wanted—and Don Juan, who was a man of action, unused to thinking, tried to seize it, under the tree by the river—he had wanted something else, something more, an adventure so extraordinary that all of Venice by comparison would melt away. He had been a fool. It was time for him to leave Swan Park, to return to his real life—the life of Don Juan Tenorio, conquistador. And at the thought of leaving Swan Park, of never returning to the northern Eden where it was always summer, where women looked at you from under the shade of ribboned hats or stared across rivers with cool little smiles, he felt such a burst of protest, such an inner riot of grief, that he was shaken and almost frightened—he who had faced death a score of times with a mocking laugh.

So Don Juan sat under the osier all that night and tried to seize himself, but he kept slipping away.

When he woke in his bed the next morning, his bones ached and his eyes felt heavy-lidded. At breakfast a terrible weariness possessed him; he could barely keep his head erect. Far, far away he saw Mary looking at him through quivering air, she seemed to be saying something, and when he tried to stand up he heard a great roar, as of a nearby cascade.

He stayed in bed for the rest of the day, and the next morning he was examined by Dr. Centlivre, a plump man with a very small nose, large melancholy eyes, and streaks of wig powder on the shoulders of his frock, who kept reaching into a pocket in the waistband of his breeches and removing a silver-cased watch that he held up to his ear. Dr. Centlivre announced that the patient was suffering from a fever, gave him a teaspoonful of foul-tasting green liquid that Juan spat onto the floor, let out a cupful of his blood into a basin, and recommended a regimen of rest supplemented by boiled duck and small beer. Then he examined his watch once more, returned it to his fob pocket, and proceeded to tell a long story about a fox that had killed two of his bantams. Juan, weakened by the bloodletting, was led by his servant to the sofa in his sitting room before an open window. There Mary read to him, while his mind wandered down to the river.

A weariness coursed through Don Juan. So that was it! He was not well—he who had never been ill a day in his life—and his sensation of dullness and melancholy was the sign of his illness. The news cheered him a little, for it meant that the trouble lay not in Swan Park but in his debilitating fever. It was true that the doctor had struck him as a fool, with his insufferable watch and his dead bantams. Juan had heard it said that when a physician knew nothing he always said "fever," a vague word covering a multitude of symptoms, including those of health. In fact, far from feeling warm, he felt like a lump of damp earth; and anyway, he would sooner stick his sword into the doltish doctor's plump belly than permit him to steal any more of his blood. Still, something *was* wrong with him. The word "fever" was in one sense soothing—it removed the necessity for further thought. For he was tired, there could be no doubt about that; and a languor had come over him. It was as if the act of lifting his arm were more than he could bear. Sometimes, looking up, he would see Mary staring at him anxiously with her hazel eyes. Then an irritation would seize him, for his languor was not unpleasant; and he wished he were alone, so that he might sink into himself, and drift away into a heavy-lidded half-waking drowsiness.

One afternoon Mary entered his sitting room with four or five books that she had brought up from the library. She sat down in the armchair facing his sofa, opened a book, and removed a letter. "Georgiana has written to say that she is coming back to us on Thursday. Father is *such* a dear. He says he can't keep her there for his own selfish pleasure. He feels there is really nothing for her to do in Belford, which of course is entirely untrue. She says—" Juan felt an odd rippling in his stomach. Blood beat in his temples, he had the sensation that somewhere many windows had been flung open—and he felt a surge of dark excitement, a tide of dangerous joy, so that he placed a hand on his chest as if to keep himself from bursting. And because, even now, Don Juan did not know what was happening to him, as he lay on his sofa trying to calm the rush of his blood, he said to himself, with a touch of sulkiness, "What the devil's wrong with me? That doctor is a blockhead. I'm not well, not well at all."

IV

"What I most like about this place," Georgiana was saying, as she stopped for a moment on the path by the Ymber to lift both hands in a gesture of welcome, "is that nothing ever changes."

"Why, I cannot agree with you entirely," Augustus Hood said. "For say you overlook my little improvements—the new laburnum planting beside the hermitage, which you really must make it a point to see tomorrow, the felling of pines in the grove by the northwest cascade—yet one notices small changes in Nature every day—every hour. The rye has grown measurably taller. The sun sets a little earlier, at a point farther south. The hawthorn hedge—"

"But—good heavens!—you take my meaning too literally, Augustus. Let the corn grow as high as the house, let the sun be extinguished by a sneeze. I was speaking of all that underlies such changes. Do you not feel, that underneath Nature, and all that decays, there is another Nature, supporting and upholding all? That is what I meant, when I said—"

"You, at least, my dear Georgiana, never change," Hood remarked.

The four were walking after dinner along the path of osiers, and Juan felt the calm, reassuring return of the familiar rhythm of days, under the always blue sky, in the green world of his deepest desire. But even as he took in the familiar details—the osier branches trailing in the dark water, the swan and its cygnets gliding over their clear reflections, the meadows across the river glowing in the yellow light of evening—he knew that everything had changed. Georgiana herself was so different from what she had been that he wondered whether he had ever looked at her before. The other Georgiana had been composed of three or four hasty strokes—a hat, a ribbon, a cool smile— like a woman glimpsed in a passing diligence, whereas this Georgiana was a torrent of details, which were almost impossible to seize because of a disturbing radiance that made it difficult for him to look at her. Her mouth, for example—how had he failed to notice, in the old days, the way her top lip would press tightly against her teeth when she smiled, while her nostrils, faintly reddish at the sides, seemed to quiver with energy?

He had begun to rise earlier, filled with impatience to see Georgiana, as if to assure himself that she hadn't disappeared again into Sussex or Flussex or wherever it was she had gone to. At the same time he experienced a wariness, almost a reluctance, for not to see her was at least to remain in a known condition, however undesirable, whereas to see her always unsettled him and made him feel unfamiliar to himself. At breakfast he would catch himself gazing at her naked hands, or at a thin strand of hair lying on her cheek, and he would turn violently away—or he would notice himself staring stupidly at his plate, while around him he became aware of an alarming silence. During the morning walk he was eager to have Georgiana's attention, while at the same time he wished himself invisible, so that he might observe her in peace. If he rode off with Hood he was relieved to be away from the house, with its awkwardness and strangeness, yet he was fiercely impatient to return, since he suddenly could no longer remember what she looked like, exactly. At dinner he followed her conversation closely. He liked to watch her mouth and eyes, and the way the tip of her nose, tugged by her upper lip, would move very slightly when she spoke. In the evening, if he walked beside her, he had the sense of an imperfect, blurred view, or of sharply glimpsed pieces of face and lace and flounces flashing out at him before dropping away into nothingness. Then he longed to walk behind her, where he would be able to watch, slowly and thoughtfully, the complicated movements of her gown, the late light on her hair, the green shade and pale sunlight rippling across her hat and shoulders. But when he actually did find himself walking behind her, he felt cut off, cast out, abandoned, like an outsider among a group of close friends who have agreed to endure him patiently while secretly wishing he would go away. At night he lay restlessly awake for a long time before plunging into deep, dreamless sleep, from which he suddenly woke feeling heavy-headed and weary, with throbbing temples, as if sleep had been an exhausting labor.

He seized every chance of being alone with Mary, in order to discuss Georgiana. Falling behind with Mary on the path by the river, he would say, "I think your sister is looking a little pale today. Don't you think she is looking a little pale?" or "I admire that black silk bracelet, the color suits her perfectly." When he accompanied Hood on his rounds, he would pursue a conversation of the night before, in order to feel, in the air around him, the presence of Georgiana. Once, when he complimented a pleached bower by saying that it was difficult to tell where Nature left off and Art began, Hood said, "Georgiana believes that"—and at the sound of her name, which startled him as if Hood had suddenly drawn aside a curtain, revealing Georgiana in her traveling cloak hurrying toward him, Juan banished all expression from his face, as his breath came short and blood beat in the veins of his neck.

He knew that Georgiana was aware of the change in him, for by dozens of small signs she revealed an uneasiness in his presence, a new alertness, that in another woman might have been the first sign of awakened interest. In Georgiana he detected only a desire to conceal herself more completely, to evade scrutiny. Don Juan was accustomed to the ambiguous smiles, the modest withdrawals that were secret advances, of women who agreed to the rules of the game. Georgiana simply eluded him. He understood that if she eluded him, it was because she was aware of him—but her awareness went only far enough to enable her to mark out her distance. She wasn't unfriendly. What troubled him was that she wasn't anything in particular. She was a little playful, a little watchful, a little distrustful, a little indifferent. She hadn't missed him; she did not need him; and as the days continued, it seemed to him that he had failed utterly to capture her innermost attention.

One morning after an exhausting night, when he had lain awake until dawn and then fallen into a restless half sleep, Juan hurried down from his room and found Mary seated in the drawing room. She was alone. Looking around wildly at the empty room, the desolate symbol of still another departure—this time she had left secretly and cruelly, without a word to anyone—Juan strode forward as Mary drew back and cried,

"What is it? What is it?" as if he had struck her in the face like a madman. Juan stopped, looking with surprise at his hand gripping his sword hilt and at the frightened face of Mary Hood.

"Pray pardon me, but you—surprised me," he said.

"Good heavens! One would think you had seen—I don't know what. Georgiana asked me to tell you that she is writing letters in her room and will be down in five minutes."

A feeling of tenderness seized Juan at the thought of Mary waiting for him so that she might deliver Georgiana's message. It was a message that itself showed unusual consideration, since anyone who wished such a message to reach him must have imagined his feelings of confusion and concern, and with deep sincerity he said, "Forgive me if I frightened you." Instantly a thought seized him and he added, "But you're certain she asked you to tell me? She might have said, 'I'll be down in five minutes.' And you changed her words into 'She told me to tell you.' Can you remember whether she said, 'Please tell him that I will be down in five minutes'? Do you recall her exact words?" And although an instinct warned him that he ought to stop talking immediately, that he was acting like a man who no longer respected himself, at the same time it seemed to him that if only he had the answer to this question, then his mind would be at peace and he could return to the calm, soothing routine of Swan Park.

In his effort to gain Georgiana's attention—her deepest, most inward attention—Juan found himself turning to Mary. She was always there, waiting for him to look at her, watching his face, alert to his slightest ripple of feeling. She would exchange conspiratorial glances with him when Georgiana's head was turned, fall back with him on the path, leave an empty place beside her whenever the three of them rested on the elaborately carved seats and benches disposed along the walks, watch for the moment when he wished to say something to her in a few whispered words, such as "If we can get her to take that turn, over there," draw him into the conversation or take up the slack when he chose to be silent. Juan was grateful to Mary, though he understood that her devotion to his cause was not disinterested: what she craved wasn't his success with Georgiana but her own intimacy with him. Juan was used to the adoring looks of women, and if he accepted Mary gratefully, it was also without surprise.

She had taken to slipping him notes from time to time. He would open a morocco-bound copy of Warner's *Horticultural Meditations*, brought to him by Mary from the library to improve his command of English, and in it he would discover a folded piece of letter paper on which she had written:

> *Tomorrow morning we should take the west path, past the plum orchard, in the direction of the grotto. After the wych elm, let us bear left, through the pine grove, which will take us to the cascade—a lovely walk, with many enchanting prospects, and one about which Georgiana spoke with enthusiasm last summer.*

His slight irritation at the note, with its air of whispered melodrama, dissolved at the thought of the next day's walk, with its new turn through the pine grove, shot through with dim green sunlight, which would ripple across her hands and throat as if she were composed of iridescent silk—and as he reread the note, which promised him an intimacy so necessary to his well-being that he tried not to desire it, in order not to suffer disappointment, suddenly he came to the words "last summer," that time when she walked in Swan Park without him, and it seemed to Juan that she had always walked through rippling sun and shade in a green world beyond his world, maddening and ungraspable.

Or, walking along the path of osiers, Juan would feel something brush against his hand. Glancing down he would see Mary's hand passing him a piece of paper, which he would thrust out of sight and read later, in his sitting room: *She says you are too silent.*

Once, when he was walking with Mary behind Augustus and Georgiana on the path by the Ymber, he was startled to see Georgiana's hand, in its yellow kid glove, reach behind and lightly lift up the back of her hooped overskirt, in order to prevent the hem from catching on a small branch that had fallen onto the path. The suddenly appearing hand, the agile jerk of the wrist, the exposed ankle with its tense tendon pressing against the white silk stocking, the sense of a secret and exact body inhabiting the shaking mass of her clothes, all this created in Juan a roaring behind his eyes, as if he had accidentally stepped off the path into the thick mist of a cascade, so that he was almost relieved when, a few moments later, he caught his foot on the small branch, which he kicked violently aside. Georgiana, glancing over her shoulder from under the turned-up brim of her bergère hat, looked down at the branch, raised her eyes to Don Juan's face, and seemed about to say something, before she turned away with a faint smile.

From Mary he learned that Georgiana had had several suitors, whom she had discouraged swiftly. She passed her time between her father's house and Swan Park, and seemed disinclined to pant after a husband. When Mary and Augustus traveled, Georgiana accompanied them. Augustus, Mary observed, was good to her sister, though she added without complaint that Georgiana in her own way was helpful to *him,* for Augustus worried about leaving Mary too much alone and the presence of Georgiana permitted him to do as he liked. Mary, Juan saw, was cleverer than he had thought. He tried to imagine her life, and the life of Georgiana, but quickly grew tired—he wasn't in the habit of imagining the invisible lives of women. If Georgiana puzzled him, it wasn't because of the way she conducted her life, which seemed to him no more absurd than the lives of other women—it was because she drifted before him, just out of reach, glancing over her shoulder with a little smile, like a faery creature from another world who was leading him deeper and deeper into a dark forest.

Sometimes he rebelled against his new life—a life of continual agitation and anxious brooding modified by moments of uncertain hope. Hadn't he always despised men of feeling?— the soft, delicate, sighing race of men who go trembling after a woman. After all, he was no dreamer. He was Don Juan Tenorio, scorner of gods, slayer of men, conqueror of women—a new Alexander, obeying no law except the law of his relentless will. What was wrong with him? He was no longer himself—he was no longer anything. He was a sick man—a dying man—a man who had been poisoned by a woman. Enough! It was time to act. She was nothing—nothing but a woman—and she would bend to his will—or break. He had known plenty of Georgianas— proud women, arrogant women, enclosed in the insufferable circle of their self-esteem. He had had one of them against an orchard wall in Algeciras, another on a drawing-room sofa in Seville, with his hand over her mouth. She had bitten him like a rat. He would have her—she would *pay attention* to him— he would smash his way in. Then an image would come to him, of sunlight and green shade, of a cool smile and a glance thrown across a river, and Don Juan would suddenly place a hand on his chest, as if to feel his adoration spreading in him like a disease.

He received a note describing a plan. Mary would contrive an excuse to return to the house during their morning walk; he would be with Georgiana, alone. It seemed to him unlikely, an impossible scheme doomed to failure, but the next day it happened: he found himself alone with Georgiana on a winding path not far from the first grotto. Sunlight fell on the oak and beech trees. In the warm air the rich green odors burned his nostrils like firesmoke. Nearby he heard the rush of a cascade, punctuated by the repeated cry of some animal that might have been a fox. The warm air, thick with dusky light, the heavy scents of green, the edges of Georgiana's gown brushing against bushes, the two of them moving slowly through green shade and green sun, all this made Juan feel drowsy and heavy-headed, as if he could barely push his way through the rich, cloth-like air. He spoke very little. When he did speak, the sound of his voice struck him as grotesque. After a short time, or perhaps it was a long time, they returned in silence to the house.

"How was your little walk?" Mary called from a window.

"Most extraordinarily remarkable," Georgiana replied. "And how goes your headache?"

"Oh, much—*very* much better, thank you, I—"

In his sitting room, Juan stretched out on his sofa and recalled the time in Seville when he was fifteen years old and the chambermaid had looked at him strangely. She had suddenly reached for his hand and placed it on her stiff black dress, over her breast. Juan had removed his hand, considered a moment, and then plunged it deep inside her dress. As he lay on his sofa, bitterly reviewing his wasted walk, he compared the boldness of the boy with the ludicrous confusion of the thirty-year-old man. And with a little burst of anger he thought, "Those doctors don't know anything. There's definitely something wrong with me."

It was about this time that Hood one afternoon invited Juan and Mary and Georgiana to visit Avernus. Work had been progressing splendidly; it was complete, except for a few minor details. In the early afternoon the party set out along the broad riding path, in the calash drawn by a bay. The graveled path wound through the gardens, passing a tea pavilion, a small lake with an island, and a statue of Morpheus sleeping on a shady rock. Soon they entered the parkland, where they rolled through dense forests and sunny meadows, along the banks of rushing streams, between cliffs where hawks rose from their nests. Once a deer came bursting out of the woods and startled the horse—Mary cried out as the carriage rocked and threw her against Juan, who had been staring at Georgiana's throat rippling with light and shade. The woods grew darker and thicker; the carriage came to a halt at the shore of a gloomy lake. Hood, walking with Georgiana, led Juan and Mary along a path to the great cave mouth, where all four paused while Mary read the inscription aloud.

"Careful—steady—hah!—look sharp, now," Hood said, as he led Georgiana into the cave.

"Oh! This is terribly exciting!" Mary exclaimed as, drawing close to Juan, she followed them in. A moment later she gave a little shriek at the hissing Hydra, which abruptly withdrew, while Georgiana, drawing her shawl tightly around her shoulders, remarked that with so many heads it must be difficult to make up one's mind. They passed the Gorgon, the flame-breathing Chimaera, hundred-armed Briareus, the tree of false dreams. On the shore of the river Acheron, Georgiana said that Charon reminded her of their old governess, Mistress Grindley. Mary whispered, "You are incorrigible!" and burst into nervous laughter that she instantly stifled.

All four entered the flat boat and were rowed across to the far shore, where Juan pointed out three-headed Cerberus with his neck of wriggling snakes. That dark woman over there, who looked savagely at them before turning away—that was the shade of Dido. And Juan, startled by her passionate, ravaged face, glanced suddenly at Georgiana, who was adjusting her hat. Hood meanwhile had seized a lantern that hung from a hook in the wall and was leading the party along a dark path; at a fork he turned left, toward Tartarus.

They came to a torchlit region where Juan saw a great wall looming beyond a river of fire. From the other side of the wall rose a clamor of groans, the clanking of iron, the crack of lashes. "Stay close!" cried Hood, as they approached a stone bridge that led over the fiery water; halfway across he tossed over the rail a piece of paper, which turned orange and then black as it drifted down.

On the other shore they came to a dark-gleaming gate that rose high above their heads. Hood shouted into the air, over the rush of flaming water and the noise of clanking chains, and Juan saw at the top of the wall a high tower, where a dark figure stood. Hood explained that she was Tisiphone, one of the Furies, who guarded the entrance to Tartarus. Even as he spoke, the great doors began to open on shrieking hinges.

They entered Tartarus and soon came to the iron-railed rim of an enormous pit, where Juan looked down into blackness, lit here and there by small fires. From the pit rose cries and groans, the bang of iron, piercing shrieks, the rumble of stone. A railed flight of stone steps led downward. Hood, holding up his lantern, began the descent. When he turned to look back, motioning them to follow, Juan saw his cheeks glowing in the lantern light like red iron.

At the bottom he led them through the fire-crackling, smoky dark, past groaning men and women who lay on the ground, toward an alcove where the shadows of flames moved on the walls. Juan stepped up to the opening and saw a figure bound to a wheel of fire that turned slowly on an axle. The man, barely visible in the flames, screamed as he turned; his eyes glowed with a kind of weary horror. Mary put her hands over her eyes, while Georgiana turned disdainfully away, but Juan stared in melancholy fascination at the fiery man turning in torment on his hellish wheel.

The wheel began to turn more slowly; gradually it came to a stop. Almost upright, though still bound to the wheel, and wearing only a blouse and breeches, the man looked at the visitors and said: "I am Ixion." With awkward dignity he bowed his head. "You see!" Hood cried above the groans and the clashes of iron. " 'Tis false fire!" Juan, stricken with disappointment, asked Hood if Ixion might return to his torment, while Mary moved away and Georgiana said, "Sir, I see you have a taste for horrors." And as the actor on the wheel began to turn and howl in agony, Juan watched for many minutes, until Mary tugged at his arm.

"But who is that?" Juan asked, as they came to a low wall of stone that enclosed an immense man who lay groaning on his back. A vulture sat on the giant's open chest and tore at his liver. "Why, 'tis Tityus, the Euboean giant," Hood cried, "who offended the gods by attempting the honor of Leto. Here he lies forever, while a vulture eats his liver, which grows again with each circle of the moon. I can explain the mechanism." But Juan, not wanting to hear, moved a little away and watched as the vulture tore at the bloody liver, while the giant's hands clenched and unclenched and his great lips stretched over his teeth.

"Let us leave this horrible place, Augustus!" Mary cried, as Juan strolled to a quieter region where, on a steep path, Sisyphus bent his fierce body against the great boulder pressing against him. Nearby, a bearded man with burning eyes stood up to his chin in a pool of black water. "Here's a jolly fellow," Hood was saying. "Behold Tantalus—a precious rogue, whom Virgil omits from his masked ball. 'Tis from Homer I fetched him hence." Tantalus, licking his dry lips, bent to drink from the water, which sank away from him; and raising his weary head, he reached for the fruit that hung just beyond his grasp, his eyes dark with remorse and longing.

" 'Tis well represented, Augustus," Georgiana said. "But I do not much care to spend the whole of a summer afternoon walking in the bowels of the earth listening to ceaseless shrieks of torment." And Juan, who would have liked nothing better, looked with regret at the cruel fruit, the vulture's beak, the twisted mouths and hopeless eyes, as they made their way out of the pit and up the flight of steps.

"This way lies Elysium," Hood said, leading them along the right-hand path. "I think you will prefer it, Georgiana." Suddenly, around a bend, the path opened into a brilliantly lit realm of meadows and streams, of shady groves and riverbanks. The ceiling was painted bright blue, with here and there a white cloud, blue-shadowed. A large lake held a scattering of islands.

"What a perfect place for tea!" exclaimed Mary. Hood, his cheeks flushed with pleasure, led them to the shore of the lake, where a smiling ferryman ushered them onto his boat and poled them to an island. Tea was served by a footman in livery under a spreading oak.

"Now tell me, by my soul!" Hood cried, lifting an arm. "What think you of my Paradise?"

"Oh, Augustus!" Mary cried. "I could stay here—oh, my!" Covering her mouth with a hand, she gave a little laugh. "Why, I almost said: forever."

"Sir," said Georgiana, "you look displeased, here in Elysium."

"Madam," Juan answered, "upon my word, 'tis all a wonder. And yet, I hope it may not strike you as fantastic, but some prefer Tartarus."

At this Georgiana burst into laughter; Mary started to smile, forced herself to be serious, and suddenly began laughing uncontrollably; Hood laughed until tears poured from his eyes; and Juan, sitting on a cushioned chair in Elysium, surrounded by the good-natured laughter of friends, smiled tensely as he bent to sip his tea.

Two nights later he found himself pacing back and forth in his moonlit bedroom. As if idly he stepped to the open casement window. There he stood looking out at the sharp tree-shadows on the grass below and a distant glimmer of river. A moment later he sprang onto the ledge, climbed partway down the wall along the two projecting stones, and leaped lightly to the ground. Quietly he made his way around the guest wing to the sloping front lawn, which he followed down to the river. He walked among the osiers, pushing aside branches that made lines in the surface of the water. After a while he stopped, resting one hand on a broad osier branch at the height of his shoulder. With a sudden motion he pulled himself up onto the tree, and as he did so his arm remembered something from long ago, when as a boy he swung himself into an orange tree in his father's orchard. Juan climbed several branches and settled halfway up, resting each leg along a separate branch. He sat looking out at the clear dark water on one side of his tree and, on the other side, the moon-bright house, sharply outlined against the blue-black sky. Up there, near the top of the slope, he became aware of two dim forms. They were drifting down toward the river. The long, full gowns glowed in the moonlight, and in the stillness he could hear the lap of river water against the bank, the cry of insects, a sharp bark from the kennels, the sound of silk rustling on grass.

"... mysterious message that you ..."

"... do not wish to be overheard by ..."

They began to walk along the osier path.

"... strangely, Mary. This urgent matter you speak of—does it really require nocturnal flight, hushed whispers, and perambulation beneath a canopy of stars?"

" 'Tis not entirely for my sake that I—"

"Do you mean—"

"Rather, for mine," Juan said, dropping lightly from the tree and sweeping his plumed hat to the ground. "If you would allow me but a single—"

"Is it the fashion in Seville, Sir, for men to jump out of trees?"

"In Seville, Madam, 'tis the fashion for men to jump out of clouds."

"And in your cloudy Seville, Sir, has it never happened, that two women accosted at night have cried out for help? What say you to that, Sir?"

"Madam, 'tis I who am desperately in need of help, which you alone—"

"But where on earth is Mary?"

"Not far," she called, invisible among the osiers.

"I fear I have deeply offended you."

"My sister has offended me. Come, Sir, we can walk a little way, if you like."

Juan, walking beside her along the osier path, was aware of nothing but the moonlight rippling over her silk gown and lace cap, as if she were dissolving into the summer night. A melancholy exhilaration seized him: he was walking at night, alone, along the river, with a Georgiana who was nothing but the dream of a summer night—for how could it be otherwise? He had waited for this moment too feverishly, and now that it was here he could only walk, rippling beside her, a dream beside a dream. And that was good; that was as it should be. For when you are flesh and blood, Georgiana, then you keep me at a distance, with your cool smile and your eyes glancing away, but when you are a dream we can walk forever in the flesh-dissolving night. And because everything is permitted in a dream, Don Juan walked close beside her, so that along with the smell of the river and the trees he could inhale the subtle scent of her face and hair; and bending his face to hers, he whispered the words, the dream-words, the foolish words that he had uttered ten thousand times without giving them a thought but that now, in his dream-walk by the river, seemed to be charged with a new, mysterious meaning: "I love you"— whispered them with such fervent quietness that he wondered whether he had only imagined them, there at the edge of the world. But at once Georgiana stiffened and drew back, saying, "I *must* go back now. Mary!"—and Juan, stung with the sharp sense of coming up from the bottom of the sea, heard the crushed-paper sound of her gown hurrying up the lawn and saw, as he turned to look after her, his hand suspended in the air, as though he had forgotten it.

The next day Georgiana kept to her room. She wasn't feeling well, Mary reported, a little breathlessly, throwing him a look. In the unforgiving sunlight Juan rehearsed the events of the night with fascinated revulsion: the childish plan, the idiotic leap from the tree, the wordless walk, the breathed-out words that had affected Georgiana like a lash across the cheek—and again he saw himself leaning close to her, his eyes red with exhaustion and longing, an unhealthy flush in his cheek, a repulsive vein beating in his neck, and Georgiana stiffening, drawing back, and a look in her eyes—or had he imagined it?—of rage and sorrow.

The sight of Mary, eager to console him, her eyes heavy with sympathy, filled him with anger. In the morning he rode hard, in the open countryside. When he returned to the house he went up to his sitting room and flung himself across the sofa. He came down to dinner at four, saw that Georgiana was still absent, and returned to his rooms. All night Don Juan lay brooding in his bed, and the next day, when he tried to rise, it seemed to him that he was being held down by a great weight resting on his chest. As he lay there, in the curtained light of morning or afternoon, breathing with difficulty, his heart beating rapidly against the bones of his chest, his cheeks warm and his eyes burning, Don Juan saw that he was not alone.

Rising over him, pressing into him but soaring through the canopy to the height of the ceiling, stood a dark angel with wings of fire and an upraised flaming sword. The angel pressed into him heavily, so that Juan thought his chest would crack, but at the same time the creature seemed to be composed of trembling light or fire. Its gaze was directed straight ahead, in an attitude not so much of pride as of absolute authority. And Juan knew that this triumphant angel, the angel of his inner fever, was the terrible angel of Love, who crushed his victims, destroyed the power of their wills, humiliated them in every fiber of their being. But it did not stop there. For like a conqueror who can never be content with mere destruction, the harsh angel demanded of its victims that they lift their voices in praise. And Don Juan seemed to hear himself say, as he lay there broken in spirit: Praise be to you, O fiery one, O angel of my devastation, for without you I would have known only a terrible calm.

When he opened his eyes the angel had gone. Mary was seated in an armchair beside the bed. Her maid stood somewhere in the background, looking away.

"You cried out in your sleep," Mary said.

"I need—" Juan said. "I need—"

"I will bring you what you need, Don Juan," Mary said, lowering her eyes.

When he woke it was dark. A candle burned on the small table where four volumes of English poets—Spenser, Milton, Waller, and Pope—lay one on top of the other, turned in different directions. In the chair beside the bed sat Georgiana, looking at him with an expression of interest.

"Good evening to you, Don Juan. I hope you are feeling a little better."

When he said nothing, she continued.

"I am told you are suffering, Don Juan. Suffering because of—me. Nay, Sir—pray don't speak. 'Tis highly irregular for me to be here—in this room—at this hour. My maid is posted at the door, but I must hurry. Your attentions—flatter me, Sir. When you first came among us, I confess I did not like you very much. It seemed to me you were a proud, self-loving man, who looked upon the world as a feast prepared expressly for his own pleasure. I have come to think better of you, Sir. I will say that to you now. But I will also say, Don Juan, that I can never return your feelings in the way you might wish. I tell you this not to cause you unhappiness, but to spare you needless . . . sorrow. I will tell you one other thing. You should leave this place, Don Juan. You should leave this place at once."

She stood up. The kindness in her voice had soothed him, had masked, to a certain extent, a harshness that he preferred not to contemplate at the moment, and it seemed to him that it was absolutely necessary to keep her standing there beside his bed, looking down at him, for when she left there would be nothing to prevent the harshness from rushing in.

She looked at him kindly, with her faint smile. Suddenly she bent over and placed on his forehead a cool, chaste kiss.

She straightened quickly and drew back a little, but continued to look down on him.

"Good night, Don Juan. May you have a good night's rest."

She turned to go. Perhaps it was the kindness of the kiss, perhaps it was the aloofness in that kindness, perhaps it was the sight of her body turning to go, but something seemed to give way deep in Juan's chest, and he heard himself groan—an unpleasant sound that might have come from an old man—and tears began to fall along his cheeks. He had last cried at the age of six, when his father had struck him in the face for cringing before a rearing horse. "Never show fear," his father had said with outraged eyes. "Fear is for women and animals." Georgiana had half turned at the sound of the unpleasant groan and stood looking at him with a frown. Juan felt the deep shame of his tears, and he scorned himself, for wasn't he weeping like a child? But at the thought that he, Don Juan Tenorio, was weeping like a child, a pity came over him, for the grown man stricken in his bed, and the tears came hot and fast, in great heaving desperate convulsions—which almost comforted him a little, as if, by abandoning himself to his unhappiness, he were protecting himself from some deeper harm.

V

If Georgiana's kiss had been cool and chaste, if her night visit had had about it all the signs of a farewell, it was also true that she had been kind to him—kinder than ever before—that she had placed her mouth against the burning skin of his forehead, and that she had remained in the room until he fell into uneasy sleep. Encouraged faintly by these signs, as well as by the fact that she hadn't expressly forbidden him to see her, Don Juan rose the next day and returned wearily to the life of Swan Park. He had the sense that he had entered a new era of feeling—an era of hope no longer believed in, of hopeless hope and joyless longing relieved at times by dim and unpersuasive illusions of distant happiness. Georgiana no longer avoided him. She was friendly and even attentive; but there was a propriety in her friendliness, a discipline in her attentiveness, that stung worse than dismissal. She no longer mocked him, or openly disdained him, but instead watched carefully over his feelings. It was as if she would do anything to prevent another outburst. The new watchfulness troubled Juan, for it was the opposite of intimacy: she paid close attention to him in order to hold him at the precise distance that allowed her to bear his presence at all.

Exhausted with longing, oppressed by obsession, Juan found that he was soothed a little in the company of Mary. He knew that Mary was drawn to him, even in love with him—in the old days he would have considered her easy prey. He'd had scores of women like her, the pretty, not unhappy, faintly discontented wives of busy husbands. Now she seemed to him a fellow sufferer. She doted on him, longed for his company, hungered for a sign of tenderness; in her pretty hazel eyes he sometimes saw a look of terrible yearning. He felt for her a delicate, wounded sympathy. She was his sad sister—they were members of the fellowship of the forlorn. It comforted him to speak to her of Georgiana, who sometimes left them to themselves, but it also comforted him to feel her own formidable despair. He studied the plum-colored pouches under her eyes, knowing that she lay awake at night thinking of him. He tried to recall whether her face had always been so pale and cheerless and drawn. And a tenderness came over him for poor Mary Hood, who had fallen so foolishly in love with Don Juan. He understood that his tenderness was itself painful to her, because it was the tenderness of a brother toward a sister; and sometimes he felt a little angry at her, for failing to inspire passion in him, for failing to be Georgiana.

One morning at breakfast Mary began to rise from her seat, stopped suddenly, and stood with her hands on the table, her head bowed, her eyes closed, before falling very slowly to one side. A footman caught her as she fell; Georgiana rose dramatically. Mary was carried into the drawing room and placed on a sofa, where Georgiana soon revived her with hartshorn and water fetched by a maid. "You don't eat properly, Mary," Georgiana said, but Juan, looking at the pale woman lying wearily on the sofa, felt in his blood the restless nights, the devouring fantasies, the ferocious longing destined to disappointment.

Later that day, as he climbed the stairs to his apartment, Don Juan stumbled for a moment and had to seize the broad handrail to steady himself. Blood drained from his face, he felt a touch of dizziness; it was over in a moment; and when, later in the day, he reported the incident to Mary, he saw on her lips a small, melancholy smile.

Don Juan had never given much thought to the sexual relations of husbands and wives, which had always struck him as tedious, ludicrous, and utterly superfluous, but sometimes he wondered a little about Hood and Mary. They had separate bedrooms, which might mean anything; Hood seemed fond of her in a dim way, sometimes patting her on the arm and sometimes commenting on the color of her gown, but more often appearing rather surprised that she was there at all. It was as if he misplaced her each night and found her again the next morning. He had once said to Juan that he was pleased, for Mary's sake, that Juan had come to stay at Swan Park, for he himself was devilish busy with his projects, and Mary— an angelic wife, who never complained—was often without employment.

Sometimes it seemed to Don Juan that there were two lives: a public, proper, entirely uninteresting life witnessed by everyone, and a secret life of bliss and torment that had nothing to do with that other life. In one life he sat sipping a cup of green tea, among friends, in the pavilion of an English garden, while in the other he was lying rapturously beside Georgiana on the floor of a hut in the middle of an impenetrable forest at the bottom of a hidden valley surrounded by impassable mountains. Mary Hood smiled over a cup of tea, but in her eyes was a night-world where she and Don Juan wandered hand in hand forever through the rooms of an abandoned country house filled with beds and sofas. And what of Georgiana, pointing at a bird singing on a branch—is it one of *yours*, Augustus?—or urging Mary to eat a biscuit?—she too must be the mistress and goddess of a secret world where, unknown to Juan, she led her other life, the one she concealed from him behind her cool smile and quiet gaze. Hood was no less difficult to unriddle, since he lived in a world of contrivance and artifice, of secret mechanisms and skillful illusions, as if, desperately dissatisfied with the actual world, he must continually replace it with another. In Hood's case, then, it might be said that the secret world was repeatedly erupting into the first world. But Hood, for all his frank friendliness, was also elusive, like a child or an elf, so that perhaps he too concealed, behind his restless activity, another life that he inhabited more deeply than this one. Juan, who was unaccustomed to working things out in his mind, felt suddenly exhausted, and studied the rim of his cup without interest.

Because Georgiana did not love him, because he could not compel her deepest attention, Don Juan had grown to dislike himself, and above all to dislike his face. Staring into the mirror in his sitting room, at a face so famous for its beauty that women had been known to swoon when he entered a room, he saw only a repellent mask: the sharp beard that looked like a dagger pointed at his chest, the teeth too white and too sharp, like instruments for inflicting pain, the nose a blade, the forehead harsh, the whole face tense with will—and the dark eyes, fierce with sorrow, staring up out of deep pits like drowning rodents.

One afternoon when he was sitting in an armchair by a window in the library, trying to concentrate his attention on a book about the harrowing of ninth-century Wessex by Danish Vikings, while imagining that he was alone with Georgiana on a green island in a blue lake in Elysium, he was irritated by a sudden knock at the door. Georgiana entered and closed the door quietly behind her. Juan stood up. Georgiana walked to an armchair on the other side of the high window. She sat down and said, "Pray be seated. Forgive me for—disturbing you."

Juan, who could scarcely look at her because the sight of her hair against her cheek made him want to cry out in pain, opened his mouth to make a witty reply, closed it, and sank wearily into his chair.

"You are looking tired, Don Juan. But I've not come to speak to you about that. I've come to speak to you about Mary. She worries me, Sir. She does not eat; she is growing thin; yesterday she grew dizzy again on the path. She refuses a doctor, insists she is well. She is behaving strangely. 'Tis plain she is fond of you; she watches you. Be kind to her, Don Juan. I fear some terrible disaster."

Juan looked at her sadly. "Am I unkind to Mary?"

"Pray forgive me. I did not mean that you have been unkind to her. I meant that I wished you to be particularly kind to her, since she is unhappy. Hush!"

Georgiana held up a hand to command silence and tilted her head to listen. Rising quickly, she strode across the rug and pulled open the door.

Mary, standing with her arm out as if to turn the handle, gave a little jump.

"You frightened me, Georgiana."

"He is in the library," she replied, striding out with a loud rustle of silk.

Mary closed the door and walked across the room to the empty chair beside the window, where she sat down.

"I was looking for you, Don Juan. I didn't know you were with Georgiana. I thought you *might* be, but I didn't *know*. May I sit here? I shall be very quiet while you read. I don't know how it is, but I wanted to sit with you, for a while. There is no reason. Don't you find that very strange? That there should be no reason for things, I mean."

Juan, who was so tired that the bones of his face ached, did not know whether she was speaking nonsense or uttering profound truths in riddles. Meanwhile, he tried to understand what Georgiana had said to him. He was already spending a good deal of time with Mary—was she asking him to spend more? Was it possible that she meant something else, that she was asking him—but surely she could not have been asking him to become the lover of her married sister. Perhaps she was being kind to him again: since you cannot have *me*, Sir, I offer you *her*. He felt that he was not thinking clearly, or perhaps too clearly. Mary sat in the chair. Suddenly he stood up. Mary looked at him with wide, nervous eyes. He placed a finger severely over his lips, then walked swiftly across the room and pulled open the door. No one was there.

"I thought I heard something," he said, as he returned to his armchair and picked up his book, which he immediately closed.

"I hear things," Mary said. "In the dark."

Juan leaned back his head and closed his eyes. Through the high window, sunlight struck his face. He was lying back in a warm gondola with the sun on his face, listening to the lapping of water and the distant song of a gondolier.

"Oh, look," Mary said, and when Juan opened his eyes he saw her studying a spider on the back of her hand.

"I used to be afraid of spiders," Mary said. "But not any more. Hello, little spider. Do you want to play with me? Oh!" She shook her hand violently. "He startled me. Poor little spider." She began to look for it in the folds of her overskirt, but the spider had disappeared.

Don Juan had always known exactly what he wanted from

life, and it exhausted him to recognize that he no longer knew. At night, lying restlessly awake, he posed questions to himself that seemed crucial and unanswerable, as if he were a stern priest administering the catechism to a bewildered pupil who knew nothing but feared eternal damnation. If you were allowed one night of bliss in the arms of Georgiana, followed immediately by banishment, or a lifetime of chaste friendship, which would you choose? If you were permitted to ravish Georgiana night after night for the next ten years with the knowledge that she despised you, or to leave tomorrow with the knowledge that she loved you passionately, which would you choose? Would you love Georgiana if she were a leper? A dwarf? An idiot? If you were given the choice of leaving Swan Park for thirty years with the knowledge that when you returned she would love you, or of remaining forever with the knowledge that nothing would ever change, which would you choose?

Sometimes he had the weary sense that Georgiana had been a little more kind to him than on some other occasion. Then he would find an excuse to be alone, in his sitting room or the library, where he savored the moment, turning it over in his mind, before it had a chance to be damaged by the little knife-points of indifference that glittered through her friendliness. At other times he tried to lose himself in the routine of Swan Park, as if the familiar motions of strolling along the river-bank or riding out with Hood would stimulate in his mind an earlier exuberance. But the familiar motions had suffered a change: Georgiana walked with a more measured and attentive tread, Hood watched Mary carefully, and Mary, tense and pale, her eyes large and restless and burning-dark, a hand fluttering now and then to her hair or to her gown, talked in sudden breathless bursts or not at all.

Dr. Centlivre, with his powdery frock, his watch in its polished silver case, and his melancholy eyes, had visited Mary in her sitting room, and had left behind a small brown bottle and strict orders for plenty of bed rest and no mental agitation. Juan wondered which would agitate her less: his absence, his presence, his speech, his silence, his coolness, his kindness—but he was so sunk in apathy, a restless, feverish sort of apathy, a nervous languor, a drowsy sluggish fire of leaping and falling feeling, that it was all he could do to put one foot in front of the other, after which you were supposed to put the first foot in front of that—an absurd succession of slow deliberate footsteps, leading with maniacal precision to inevitable death.

Late one night when Juan was sitting before his casement window, staring out at the glimmer of distant river under the moon, he became aware of a figure moving on the lawn below. It was white, with whiteness shimmering around its head, and Juan's first impression was that a ghost such as he had often read about in his childhood had come floating out of a book in the library and was drifting across the grass. A moment later he recognized Mary's walk and her cap of Brussels lace. He hesitated long enough to see her turn into the plum orchard; then he stepped up onto the windowsill, climbed partway down the wall, and leaped softly onto the grass.

He followed her at twenty paces through the orchard and the coppice of beech trees and entered a darker place, where paths wound among yew trees and weathered statues with broken forearms and decaying shoulders. Juan passed a headless woman with two broken arms who stood in the heavy marble folds of a moss-covered mantle, baring to the moon a single broken breast. Beside her in the grass lay her upturned head. At a dark pool rimmed with crumbling stone he stopped. Mary, white and black in the moonlight, like a drawing in a book, stood on one of the cushioned seats carved into the roots of the great oak. She was touching the tree with both hands, caressing the bark as if she had come out for a midnight tryst with a lover who had been turned into a tree. Suddenly something stirred and Juan saw the door in the tree begin to open. Mary stepped up and disappeared into the oak. Juan strode along the length of the pond, stumbling on something white that might have been a marble arm, stepped onto the cushion in the carved root-seat, and climbed up into the hollow tree.

Dim moonlight falling through the leaves of the oak revealed a stone stairway going down. Juan made his way down the turning stairs, which wound around a column of stone. As the moonlight rose above his head the darkness became blacker, until he felt that he was pushing his way through a thickening mass of blackness as palpable as feathers. He pressed one hand against the central column and one against the concave wall. Below he heard a steady soft silken sound, like a distant rustle of high grass stirred by a wind; he imagined Mary's wide gown brushing against the column and the wall, dragging behind her on the turning steps. His hand dislodged a bit of stone, which fell clicking on the stairs and suddenly stopped. As he descended he had the sense that he was dissolving in a solution of blackness, that soon there would be nothing left: one day on a stone stair in a hollow tree forgotten by generations of squires a young woman with gray-green eyes who happened to be walking in the woods would discover a ring, a skull, a rusty sword.

Now the darkness seemed to become thinner, as if it had been penetrated by an alien substance, a faint light glimmered, and when he came to the bottom he could see a passageway stretching off to the left and right.

Here and there dim lanterns in wall niches gave off a

gloomy half-light. He saw Mary turning out of sight along the winding path, from which other passageways branched off on both sides. Hood had spoken of his *system* of passageways, and Juan imagined a vast underpark of crisscrossing paths, connected to the upper park by circular stairways emerging in grottoes, rotundas, ruins, summerhouses, tea pavilions, hollow statues and trees. Mary turned into another passageway. The path became broader; Juan noticed a narrow rivulet running along one side. The streambed sank lower, the water widened, and when he turned a bend Juan saw Mary stepping into a boat. The oarsman stood high on one end, holding his oar; the boat was long and narrow and curved upward at bow and stern. As the oarsman began to push off, Juan stepped into the boat and sank into the dark cushions of the seat across from Mary.

"Why, Sir Juan! You must be a dream—or a ghost. You're pale as a ghost—so wan, Sir Juan!—oh, I shall call you Sir Wan. I really do think you must be a ghost, after all. So am I, too: the ghost of Mary Hood. You remember Mary Hood. First she was glad, then she was bad, and then she was very, very sad. And now she has disappeared! Indeed, I cannot find her anywhere. Nothing left but us ghosts, Sir Juan. That is what happens to us, once we disappear. And we can never never rest because—because—oh, I forget *why* we can never rest. 'Tis our punishment, I think. For our wicked thoughts. Do dons ever have wicked thoughts, Sir Don? Oh, my."

The boat had rounded a sharp bend and was entering a broad waterway. There were the great palazzi, looming in the torchlit dark; there were the arched bridges, the stone steps leading into the water, the passing gondolas, the masked revelers. Hood had even fashioned a night sky of twinkling lights, a round moon, and blue-black clouds. " 'Tis but recently begun," Mary Hood said. "Augustus was hoping to surprise you. I heard him speaking of it to Georgiana. Georgiana thinks I am too much alone. And yet I do not lack society. My thoughts are my daily companions, and at night—why, at night I lie down with Despair. Oh, Johnny had a wife, and a right fine wife, and yet she was a maid, Sir. And how that may be, I cannot cannot tell, and fol de rol de rol, Sir. Georgiana says—oh, look."

Mary was pointing to a gondola in which a young lord wearing a plumed hat sat leaning back against the cushions. Hood had captured everything: the cut of the sleeve, the insolent grace of the man, a certain tilt of the face as he said something to his gondolier, who wore a straw hat set back on his head. The face was perhaps too youthful, too lovely in a languorous way, but the line of the nose, the slope of the forehead, the small sharp beard, all composed a remarkable likeness. A masked woman in a passing gondola called out to the young lord, who turned his head in her direction and spoke a few words. In every gesture of his face and hands he revealed the supreme confidence of a man accustomed to the attentions of women. He laughed lightly as he turned away—and Juan, startled by the sound, and pressing himself down on the cushions so as not to be seen, tried to remember when it was that he had last felt laughter rush through his throat.

"Do you suppose she is happy?" Mary was saying, as a band of revelers burst into shouts of laughter on a nearby bridge; and when Juan turned to look at her, he saw that she was gazing after the masked woman with sorrowing eyes.

"Pray, that way," Mary said to her gondolier. They were approaching a building where an arched doorway with an iron portcullis came down to the water. The portcullis rose as they drew near, and the gondola entered a watery courtyard bounded by stony ground strewn with trestles, buckets, and barrels.

Long wooden beams slanted up from the ground and rested high against the back of the palazzo facade. The inner surface was unfinished; in the light of lanterns Juan could see the unpainted boards, which on the outside had been painted to resemble ancient stone. At a small pier an old man with a boat hook pulled them in. Juan followed Mary out of the gondola and up a flight of rickety wooden steps that led to a winding passageway. Under a dim lantern an arch revealed a stone stair. He climbed behind her, round and round, and now he had the sense that the darkness was unraveling and trailing behind him, fold after fold, until it lay at the bottom in a heavy black pile. He smelled leaves; a moment later he emerged behind Mary through a door in a tree on the bank of the Ymber, far upstream.

"Oh look, Sir Juan! A spy." Juan placed his hand on his sword hilt, but Mary was pointing to the brilliant summer moon.

"Come, Mary," Juan said wearily, and as he walked with her along the winding river in the direction of the house, it struck him that they must have emerged on the distant bend of river that he liked to watch at night from his casement window.

Mary was not at breakfast the next morning; Georgiana said she was headachy and dull. "She said she dreamed about you all night," Georgiana remarked, glancing at Juan and looking away. Juan, opening his mouth to reply, was seized suddenly by a shuddering yawn, which he violently repressed. His eyelids felt hot. Somewhere a fly buzzed. Georgiana fidgeted with her tea.

Sometimes he tried to imagine that Georgiana was playing an elaborate game, that she was trying to provoke his interest by an apparent indifference that concealed a secret passion.

Because he did not believe what he imagined, which was contradicted by every visible sign, he was able to sustain the illusion only by avoiding Georgiana—an act that enabled him to imagine that she was aware of his avoidance and was moved by it to tumults of feeling she could scarcely suppress. When, helplessly, he found himself in her company, he would force himself not to look at her face. Instead he concentrated his attention on Mary, whose wide eyes looked at him with sorrow, or on his own hand, which lay before him like a hand broken from a statue and set down for his inspection—and sometimes, suddenly, he raised his eyes to Georgiana, whose head would be turned the other way.

He was always tired. At night he lay exhausted and awake, with burning eyes, and in bright sunlight he narrowed his eyes tightly, as if someone were flinging sand in his face. He tried to remember when it was that he had last slept well. As a boy in Seville he had slept in a big bed with gilt hawks on the posts. In the mornings his mother would come in and touch his face with her hand. Remembering, he touched his face with his own hand. He immediately withdrew it, as if something unpleasant had been pressed against his cheek, like the forepaw of a dead animal.

One night as Juan lay in his bed, staring through the parted curtains at the night sky framed by the casement window, he heard the sound of an opening door. He sat up in bed, bent to peer around a curtain, and saw Mary coming toward him in a hoopless white negligee. "Did I wake you, Sir Juan? Pray forgive me. I cannot sleep and have been wandering through the house these many hours. 'Tis strange, Sir Juan. Though I am always tired, yet I can never sleep. Is it not strange? Sometimes I fear my mind is not right. Georgiana says I never eat. But that is not true. I eat sorrow. I am very tired, Sir Juan. I will lie down here now." Mary pulled aside the curtain and climbed into the bed. She lay down on her back beside him and did not move.

Juan, in his long nightshirt, crossed his legs irritably and wondered what the devil he ought to do. It occurred to him that never before in his life had he been in bed with a woman and wondered what the devil to do. And after all—after all!— why not? She had come to him in the night. She was a pretty wife—he liked pretty wives—and she was lying next to him on her back in his bed. It was not an impossibly difficult problem requiring the help of a mathematical tutor from the University of Seville. But say a second woman was present in the bed. Say she was a phantom woman with glowing eyes, who lay between you and the living woman beside you. Don Juan had slept with two women in a bed before. But what if the phantom woman was an enchantress who tied you in chains of fire while she lay against you, untouchable, twisting her body into every shape of desire? The living woman lay beside him, in her gown the color of moonlight. But when Don Juan tried to see her, she vanished in the glow of the other woman, who was a fire that burned out his eyes. For the phantom Georgiana was an un-woman, a more-than-woman, an absent presence who harmed him and mocked him and fevered him too. He thought of the monks, his laughable enemies, sickly haters of pleasure who tormented their bodies for the sake of heavenly visions. Now he too had become a monk, pious Brother Juan, a repellent abortion of a man. Nightly he was visited by his succubus. She lay on him like smoke, like the fur on an animal. She breathed in his ear and sucked out his breath through his mouth.

He looked over at Mary, white and still in his bed. And he felt an irritable, exasperated tenderness for poor Mary Hood, his pale sister in sorrow. There she lay, bound in her sad enchantment. He didn't, after all, *not* desire her. For wasn't it true that all women were the same woman, in the difference-dissolving night? Daylight was the element in which forms became distinct, the realm of analysis and discrimination, whereas in the night all things flowed and mingled. And wasn't it true that he was not finicky in his choice of women, no fussy bourgeois who chose a woman the way you might choose a piece of furniture for the drawing room? No, he was Don Juan Tenorio, conqueror of thousands, who had ravished not only women so disturbingly beautiful that other men, seeing them once, had been changed forever, but also squint-eyed hags, blind beggar women with stinking breath, witch women, hump-backed women, diseased women with suppurating sores. Once he had bedded a bitter woman with one leg, who cursed him and wept. No, he didn't *not* desire pretty Mary Hood. Rather, his desire had been consumed by the blast from a fiercer fire—diverted from the bodies of living women by the spell of a demoness.

His eyes burning with weariness, Juan slid down on his back and lay beside his sad sister. Her face was in shadow; a patch of gown shone white-luminous in a streak of moonlight. She might have been Georgiana—didn't she look a little like Georgiana, if he turned his head a certain way? Three times he moved toward her, tricked into desire, for what did he care whether she was Mary or Georgiana or anyone on earth or in hell or heaven? Three times he fell back with an angry burst of breath. Toward dawn he woke her and led her from the room, for Augustus was sure to be up at any moment. No point in killing his friend over a woman untouched in the night.

He ate breakfast alone, in a shady corner of the breakfast room with a view of the sunny Ymber. His valet, appearing suddenly beside him as if he'd been conjured into existence by the mumbling of a spell, informed him quietly that the mistress of the house was not well and that her sister was tending her. Juan nodded dully, feeling a gloomy pleasure in his solitude and abandonment, and scarcely noticing as his valet dissolved into the bright morning air. After breakfast he went to the library and sat down in an armchair with a copy of *The Philosophical Magazine.* Immediately he sprang up and began pacing. He strode to the double doors, pulled them open, and nearly collided with a startled chambermaid in a long black calico dress and a white apron, hurrying past with a chamber pot in both hands and a dust brush tucked under one arm.

Outside he went round to the stable yard, where he stood inhaling a sweetly acrid smell of straw and dung before he swung onto his horse. He nodded at the groom and rode out along the graveled path through the gardens and into the parkland. For a while he kept to the riding path, then branched off onto a narrow woodland trail, coming out near the Isle of Athelney and riding until he found himself on the outskirts of Arcadia. A shepherd was sitting on a rock in the shade of a tree, playing his reed pipe. Half a dozen black-faced sheep grazed nearby. Juan sat on his horse. Idly he wondered whether the sheep were ingenious systems of turning gears covered with wool dyed to look dusty brown. It struck him that all of Swan Park was nothing but a gigantic mechanism, wound up and kept in good working order by that master watchmaker, Augustus Hood. And yet the squire of Swan Park would never allow the evidence of design in Nature to argue for the existence of an unseen Designer, because the universe, my dear Georgiana, is not Dr. Centlivre's watch, but a riddle without an answer, a mystery that eludes your questioning. So by reason we climb by slow degrees to unreason: in the silence of the mystery, wonder is born. For love, my dear Georgiana, is not a watch in a pretty case, but a merciless angel bearing a sword of fire.

Don Juan rode on into the green Arcadian countryside. Plump sheep with delicate dark legs grazed here and there—somehow the legs reminded him of knitting needles sticking out of lumps of yarn—a forlorn shepherd sat sighing under a tree, and the warm air trembled with a dim sound composed of stream water, bees, the distant notes of a reed pipe, and the faint tinkle of sheep bells. Juan came to a solitary place, where he dismounted. He tethered his horse to a low branch and walked on a little way. A broad shady tree, with round-lobed leaves he did not recognize, grew on a slope not far from a narrow stream.

He sat down and leaned back against the tree. One wrist rested lightly on his raised knee; the other hand lay on the ground beside his outstretched leg. His eyelids began to close, the brown stream flickered with spots of yellow sun and tea-colored leaf shade, and it seemed to him that he was about to fall into a deep sleep, though at the same time he was painfully alert. Across the stream a dense, cool-looking thicket of gnarled trees retreated to form a sunny opening, a small, secret glade at the edge of the stream. As he half watched, shifting his heavy gaze from dark to bright, he saw a movement in the thicket, and a shepherd boy stepped out of the trees into the bright place.

He was thirteen or fourteen years old and wore the white Arcadian tunic, which came down to his knees and was fastened loosely over his left shoulder; his right shoulder was bare. Looking toward the thicket from which he had emerged, he beckoned with his fingers. A moment later a shepherd girl stepped out of the trees, smiling and reaching out her hand. Her straw-colored hair was pulled back lightly on both sides and gathered in back with a comb. She wore a loose white tunic bound at the waist with a belt of straw; whenever she moved, the cloth tightened for an instant against her small breasts, which seemed to appear and disappear. They stood holding hands, smiling at each other as if they were about to burst into laughter. Suddenly the boy dropped her hand and ran to the stream, where he crouched down to scoop water into his hands. He rose carefully, carrying the water to the girl, who bent over his hands to drink.

From under the tree Juan watched, not hidden from view though protected by the shade; and as he watched, keeping very still so as not to startle them, he had the sense that the boy had caught sight of him on the slope across the stream—indeed, he was certain of it, for the boy began glancing deliberately in his direction—and soon the girl began casting quick looks at him, the dark stranger watching in the shade. But instead of growing shy, instead of moving back or escaping into the trees, they seemed to become bolder in his presence. Now they began flicking drops of water at each other and leaping away, as if for the amusement of the watcher across the water. Then the boy closed his eyes, reached out both hands, and began searching for the girl, who kept laughing and stepping aside. Once his hand seized her hip before she twisted away. Suddenly they bound up their tunics under their legs and waded into the stream. They held hands as they bent over to search for things in the water, glancing up now and then to catch sight of the stranger watching them. After a while they climbed out of the stream and sat on the grass, where they stretched out their brown legs glistening with water, leaned back on their arms, and flung their heads back, eyes closed against the sun. For a time they stayed that way, as if to invite a secret inspection by whoever happened to be looking at them: here we are, two young bodies, male and female—study us well.

The boy grew restless first. He glanced at the girl, whose eyes remained closed, her face upturned and glowing in the light of the sun. He looked about, then picked a blue wild-flower that grew near his shoulder. Bending toward her, he placed it carefully in her hair. In the brilliant sun her pale hair, straw-colored but shot through with whitish yellow and milky brown, gave off little glimmers, as if it contained flecks of metal. The boy tipped back his head to study the effect of his wildflower, leaned closer to make an adjustment. She gave a slow, drowsy smile, raised one hand lazily to her hair, and touched the flower. Smiling at each other, they seemed to come to an agreement. The boy stood up, reached out his hand, and lifted her to her feet; and throwing a bold, unmistakable look at Juan across the stream, they walked hand in hand out of the sunny glade and disappeared into the trees.

And Juan was shaken: they hadn't mocked him, but they had displayed themselves proudly before him. They had drawn him into the circle of their not-quite-innocent love play, in the spirit of those who must proclaim their happiness, must reveal their superiority to all mere mortals who are born, grow old, and die—and especially to all solitary watchers in the shade, whose task it is to witness the unbearable joy of laughers in the sun. And after all, hadn't there been a touch of mockery in it? For how could they fail to be amused by the sight of a shadow-man banished from sunlight, a no-man who had crept out of the rush of things into the secret, bitter shade?

Juan stood up. He had become a pathetic creature. Children laughed at him—at him, Don Juan Tenorio—the grim man brooding under a tree. No doubt others were laughing at him too. It was very quiet, and as he listened he seemed to hear sounds of laughter rising all about him: the laughter of shepherds and shepherdesses in Arcadia, the laughter of actors playing Charon and Dido, Tantalus and Ixion, the laughter of farmers plowing their fields and laborers swinging their picks, the laughter of chambermaids and footmen and gardeners and grooms—a low, rippling hum of laughter like a sound of cicadas in high grass. It was the sound of all those who walked in the midst of life, who didn't sit off to one side, dreaming in the shade. What was he? Who? He was no longer Don Juan. He had wandered away from himself, he couldn't find his way back. Who are you? I am the one I no longer am. *Basta!* He would *have his life.* He would go to her room that night. He would beg her—or kill her. He would take her by force. He would kill anyone who got in his way. He would *do* something. For love, my dear Georgiana, is not a sad man sitting under a tree, but a raging sword flashing with blood and fire.

Don Juan walked over to his horse, untethered it, swung up into the saddle, and rode out of Arcadia.

When he returned to the house he found Georgiana in the drawing room, looking tired as she leaned back on a sofa and held flat in her lap, in one limp hand, an open fan that pictured a landscape. "Oh, there you are," she said, glancing up at him as if she had something more to say, but saying nothing. Juan went up to his sitting room and stretched himself across the sofa, where he lay yawning repeatedly, as if something were wrong with his jaw. At dinner there was still no sign of Mary. Georgiana seemed distracted, and Hood told a long, rambling anecdote about a laborer in his under-realm who had been trapped with his pick in a collapsed tunnel. The poor fellow had hacked his way in another direction, advancing slowly with diminishing strength and gradually losing all sense of time; on the point of death, he felt his pick break through the wall and found himself in China. The solution to the mystery was that he had broken into a Chinese temple constructed under Hood's supervision years ago, abandoned, and soon forgotten. The laborers who rescued the poor man said he seemed confused and kept insisting that he had reached China. "Which of course he had," Hood added, as they walked along the Ymber at dusk. "For say a man reads of China, dreams of China, and does not go to China. And say another man hacks his way through a wall and enters a Chinese temple. Now riddle me this: which China is more real?"

"They are each of them false in different ways, surely," remarked Georgiana.

"A third man," Hood said, "sails to China. Upon his arrival he is stricken with a peculiar madness, which makes him believe he is in London."

"And is the world composed only of dreamers and madmen, Augustus?"

"Aye, and landskip gardeners, too. Now say a fourth man, an English merchant, travels to China. 'Tis the very opposite of your dreamer. He cares for naught under the sun but trading good English wool for Chinese silk. Thirty years go by and your good merchant can recollect but two things: the storm that nearly destroyed his ship, and a green river with yellow boats, which might have been in Japan. Now, by Heavens, tell me: has this man traveled to China?"

"A fifth man," Don Juan said, "travels to China. He likes the country, travels for many years, and never returns home. *Poco a poco*—mmm, little by little—his early life becomes vague, dreamlike. He too has never traveled to China. He has always been there."

"Oh, Gemini! You sound like Augustus," Georgiana remarked, and Don Juan gave a sharp, nervous laugh—a single syllable that ended abruptly.

That night Juan sat in the walnut armchair before the casement window, looking out through burning eyes at the bend in the river as he waited for the great house to fall asleep. For some reason he thought of a dragon circling round and round its cave, settling in a corner, lowering its head onto its dangerous, peaceful claws. Deep in his chest he felt the beginning of a yawn. It rose slowly to his jaw, shuddered along the bones of his face, and floated to the top of his head, where it clung to his skull like a bat. His tiredness was so ferocious that it had become almost interesting, almost a thing of beauty. All this idiotic early rising was bad for a man. It was an unnatural form of exercise, harmful to health, disastrous to mental vigor, even—yes—morally questionable. For why should a man wrench himself from his bed in the miserable middle of the morning, after a useless night, solely in order to breathe the dangerous air surrounding a woman crackling in her clothes like fire? Better to go back to bed, close your ruined eyes, and die into the naked body of a devouring succubus. A dog barked three times, stopped, and barked once more. Juan looked about. Where was he? He was sitting in a room—in a house—in a garden—in a park—in England, a wholly imaginary country called up from depths of dream by a lustful friar hunched over a book of spells, a country inhabited by demon-women so desirable that to look at one of them for a single second was to go mad. Juan stood up. A sudden yawn shuddered through him, as if he were being lashed by an inner whip. He walked across the room, pulled open the door, and set forth in search of Georgiana.

He stepped into a corridor so black that he had to feel along the wall with one hand as he made his way slowly forward. Georgiana's bedroom was somewhere at the far end of the house. He knew that to reach it he had to descend a staircase and make his way across the main drawing room, the dining room, the library, and a second drawing room to a stairway that led up to the apartments in the family wing. But he had never mastered the plan of the meandering mansion, with its long and sometimes turning corridors, its various wings, each with so many rooms that it was impossible for him to make his way by day across any wing without becoming lost, its many stairways going up or down, its galleries, its hidden chambers reached only by secret passages known to servants long since deceased, its wine cellars and storage rooms, its coin room and medal room, its chambers half built and suddenly abandoned, its forgotten rooms into which a chambermaid sometimes strayed with a gasp. In the corridor his fingers found the top of a flight of stairs. As he made his way down into the darkness of the drawing room, he understood that the heavy curtains had been drawn; no glimmer of moonlight on glass or polished wood indicated the way.

He advanced with his left hand outstretched, his right hand grasping his sword hilt. Suddenly he felt something cool and hard and smooth that might have been the side of a vase or the cheek of a bust. He tried to picture the drawing room carefully in his mind, but the imagined furniture kept shifting and sliding about—and in the slippery blackness he wondered whether he might have entered some other room, after descending a stairway he had never used before.

He continued forward, through the room that ought to have been the drawing room, holding out his hand in empty space. It was an odd immensity of space, as if he had accidentally stepped through a door into a black meadow—and who was to say he had *not* stepped into a meadow, or into the orchard that went down to the Guadalquivir? Slowly he advanced across the meadowy room. Then he began to wonder whether he was moving in a straight line, perhaps he was veering a little with every step, so that he was doomed to turn forever in this desolate black place, a Sisyphus without a rock—and as he set down one foot after the other, in the deliberate and thoughtful manner of a man who had every reason to suppose that he would arrive at his destination, even though he no longer remembered it, the outstretched fingertips of his left hand seemed to quiver, like the antennae of an insect.

Something struck his knee. It was neither soft nor hard, a soft hardness that might have been part of a piece of furniture, but when he bent to feel it he could feel only empty air, as though an animal had come up against him and wandered away. Then his shoulder knocked into a hard object that wobbled, began to fall, and did not fall. He took another step. His fingers struck something flat and smooth—it appeared to be a wall—and following the smoothness, Juan came to a closed door that opened into another darkness.

It should have been the dining room, if the meadow had been the drawing room, but as he advanced along the wall he came to what seemed to be a carved cabinet. He tried to remember a carved cabinet in the dining room, though wasn't there one in the drawing room?—in which case he was already hopelessly lost. For that matter, the cabinet had begun to seem less like a cabinet than like a large beast carved in wood. On the other side of the chest-beast he felt the wall again, then the edge of something that might have been the frame of a mirror or the high back of a chair, and again the wall. Soon his fingers came to an opening that seemed to be a doorway without a door. He passed through into another blackness—perhaps a new room, perhaps only a recess or alcove—and as he stood wondering whether it might be possible to return through the no longer visible opening, he became aware of a small light glimmering in the dark.

He saw the shape of a far doorway, through which a figure with a candlestick was advancing slowly. The white gown was unhooped and flowing, a ghost in a wind. On her head was a pale hat with a wide brim.

As Mary came closer, she raised the candle toward his face and said teasingly, without surprise, "Why, Sir Juan! You really are a ghost. I'm feeling much better, thank you."

Her face, radiant in the candlelight, seemed to glow from some inner light. When she stopped before him she dropped her voice to a conspiratorial whisper. "Shhh. You mustn't tell anyone, Sir Juan. 'Tis a secret, you see. But I can tell *you*." She hesitated. "I'm going down to the river. I mustn't be late. Don't tell Georgiana." She laughed lightly, then became grave. "You look tired, Monsieur Jean. Why are you not asleep? Oh, but I know. Night after night they roam the earth from dark to dawn, never resting. That is what ghosts do. 'Tis our job, Sir John. I'faith we cannot do otherwise. Shhh. Soon everything will be all right." By the light of her candle he saw with surprise that he was in the supping room, an informal room off the main dining room where, as Hood had once explained, supper used to be served, although now he was converting it into a second library. She lowered her voice again. "You mustn't follow me tonight. No-no-no-no." Slowly she wagged a warning finger back and forth. In her wide, childish eyes he saw trembling candle flames. "Sleep well, Don Juan," she said, moving past him toward another doorway. He watched her light until the darkness devoured it.

By continuing carefully in the direction from which Mary

had come, he managed to enter the far doorway with only a slight bump on the shoulder. But now, instead of the familiar dining room he had imagined, he found himself in a soft, sagging chamber, a chamber of velvety wall hangings and a rug so thick that he seemed to be sinking up to his ankles, and he tried to remember when he might have been in such a place, which felt like a big, furry animal—he was walking on the back of a sleeping bear, at any moment it might wake up and fling him off. Something fell to the floor with a soft thud. Juan crouched down and patted about, feeling suddenly a glass globe the size of his fist.

When he rose, holding the globe, he sensed that he was moving in a different direction; perhaps he had passed through a doorway into still another room.

Now wearily, without hope, he made his way through the fertile and prolific dark, striking against unknown objects that sometimes fell over, pausing once to place the glass globe on what seemed to be a small silk cushion. As he passed from room to room in Hood's inexhaustible house, which kept growing new corridors, chambers within chambers, additional stories, entire wings, he had the sensation that he was leaving bits and pieces of himself in every room, an arm here, an elbow there, the bones of his chest over there, so that if he ever arrived at Georgiana's room there would be nothing left of him—nothing but a faint agitation of air. But he no longer believed in Georgiana's bedchamber. It was so far away that it was in a distant land, where the inhabitants were said to have one eye in the center of their foreheads and long blue hair. He thought of knights who had to cross mountains and rivers and oceans and slay giants the size of entire towns in order to gain admittance to the bedchamber of a lady at the top of a tower so high that gradually it grew vague, as if it were turning into mist or dream. He thought of the multitudes of animalcula in a single drop of water, of infinite suns. He came to another stairway, another room. Wearily he opened the door.

Moonlight shone on a canopy bed with rose-colored curtains. On a small glass table he recognized a large fan with ivory sticks, which Georgiana had once asked her maid to fetch from her room.

As Juan advanced toward the foot of the rosy bed he felt a desire to postpone his arrival, in part because he wanted to make certain that his mind wasn't suffering from an illusion brought on by his weariness, and in part because, if it proved to be an illusion after all, he wished to let it continue for as long as possible before the bed began to tremble, waver, and melt away. At the foot of the dream-bed he paused before the closed curtains, the lower half glowing a cool silver-rose in the moonlight from the open window. He reached out his hand, which glowed suddenly as if it had burst into flame, and drew a curtain back.

In the shadowy depths of the bed Georgiana and Augustus lay side by side, their shoulders and heads raised by pillows. He could barely make them out, there in the shadows, as if they were reluctant spirits summoned out of the invisible world. He was not surprised to see them lying there, waiting for him to speak, for hadn't he always known they liked to be together? They seemed to gaze at him as he stood holding the curtain aside. Georgiana had pulled the sheet up to her neck, but carelessly, so as to expose one shadowy shoulder and part of a dim breast. Her scarcely visible hair fell over one shoulder and vanished onto the coverlet. He thought he was able to make out a gaze that was frank, slightly amused, slightly irritated, as if to say: "So you have found me at last, Don Juan." And indeed he had found her at last, though now there was nothing left of him, after his long journey. Hood's eyes in his boyish face, he was sure of it, were large and melancholy. Raising one arm as if in a gesture of welcome, Hood said with deep feeling, "My dear Juan." Then he allowed his hand to fall back heavily on the bed, where it bounced once and lay still. Juan wondered whether the words he had heard were part of a sentence abruptly terminated, or whether they represented the complete and exact expression of an elusive thought.

Juan stood holding the curtain aside, feeling their ghost-gaze upon him. Then he opened his fingers and watched as the curtain plunged back into place. He stood staring at it, as if trying to remember how it had come to be there, then yanked it open with a violent rattle of rings. He drew his sword and felt a tremor pass along his arm. In the air beside his face he saw with surprise a naked sword.

He thrust it back into the scabbard and said, "I will be leaving in the morning." He took one step back, removed his hat, and bowed low, sweeping the plumes to the floor. Then he turned and walked out of the room.

A change seemed to have come over the night. Perhaps dawn had begun to break, perhaps his eyes had grown used to the dark, in any case Juan made his way through rooms filled with dim masses and murky forms that sometimes took on the shapes of cabinets and couches. He heard movement; the servants were up; and here and there the heavy curtains had been drawn back from the windows, admitting moonlight in some rooms and faint dawnlight in others.

He descended a staircase. At the bottom stood a cluster of chambermaids and scullery maids and footmen, talking at the same time. He heard "Mary" and "the river." Over the front lawn he saw that the sky had begun to turn pearly gray.

Don Juan made his way through the vestibule and down

the steps onto the sloping lawn, where servants were moving in many directions; it occurred to him that he had never seen more than two or three at a time. He followed a groom and a chambermaid down toward the river. Three footmen came through the osiers, carrying Mary. She lay with her head flung back and water dripping from her hair. "She's alive, Sir. No need for alarm. She'll pull through, she will." Someone thrust a wet piece of paper into Juan's hand. "We found this, Sir. Pinned to her gown." The note read, in neat, stiff letters: HERE LIES MARY HOOD, WHO DIED FOR LOVE.

The sun was coming up. A high window opened and a chambermaid leaned out, holding her arms wide as if to greet the new day.

In the coach headed south for Dover, Don Juan leaned back and closed his eyes. Late-summer sunlight warmed his cheek and the back of one hand. A leathery creak of springs mingled with a clatter of wheels and the dark, soothing thud of hooves. Don Juan saw light playing on the bridges of Venice, trembling on the sides of gondolas. Through the coach window he heard the single sharp call of an unknown bird.

The King
in the Tree

The Queen is a whore—cut off her nose. The Queen is lecherous—burn her. Such are the interesting remarks one hears at court, from those who dislike the King's new bride. Others, it is true, speak of the Queen's exceeding beauty. By this they mean the Queen is guilty and should be hanged. For my part, I believe the young Queen is beautiful and must be watched closely.

I, Thomas of Cornwall, faithful counselor of a once happy King.

The King is a vigorous man, well favored in countenance, deep-chested and hard-muscled, youthful in appearance despite his forty-four years. His forehead is smooth, his eyes large and dark. His broad hands, well tested in the managing of horse and sword, are remarkable for their long fingers, which lend a suggestion of grace and even delicacy, though I have seen him crush a man's collarbone with a single blow of his fist. When, in his crimson mantle trimmed in ermine, he walks beside the Queen, the eye is pleased with its vision of power joined with beauty.

There is nothing in the King that can incite ridicule.

I have noticed one change. Before his marriage to Queen

Ysolt, the King was master of his countenance: no one studying the King's face could see anything behind the smooth brow,
the broad planes of his cheeks, the still mouth, the clear, intel-
ligent eyes. Now, in that well-loved face, one can see adoration,
suspicion, jealousy, yearning, sudden doubt.

The ladies of the court speak continually of love.

Love, they say, ennobles the heart and exalts the soul. Love
is a divine gift that permits us to enter the Earthly Paradise, from which we have been banished because of our base
natures and which is a type and reflection of the Heavenly
Kingdom. I have heard the wife of a baron maintain in
the middle of a summer afternoon that love is a purifying
flame which burns only in a lofty heart, and I have seen that
same baroness in the dark of night standing against the wall of
the granary with her robes raised above her waist while her gal-
lant lover, grunting like a bull, charms her with his delicate
attentions. Love, I have heard the court ladies say, is not a con-
tractual obligation upheld by the brute authority of law, but a
form of spiritual consent, freely given. By this they mean that
love is possible only outside of marriage. It is these same ladies
who whisper about the Queen, glance at her with malicious
disapproval, gossip about the King's nephew, and smile kindly
at their husbands while devoting every instant of their waking
hours to the arrangement of clandestine meetings with their
virile young lovers.

The ladies of the court are very beautiful.

The immediate source of the court rumors is Oswin, the chief
steward. It is he who first reported to the King the glances

exchanged by the Queen and his nephew. The steward is a loyal servant of the crown, skilled in all that relates to household management, scrupulous in his accounts, exact of speech, proud, censorious, secretive, disinclined to laughter. He is fond of rich cloaks trimmed in miniver, jeweled rings, cups of gold. He has two weaknesses. Because he is the son of a burgher and has made his way at court through talent, tireless work, and steadfast purpose, he nurses a grievance against the rich and well-born. This failing leads him to overestimate his own considerable accomplishments and to imagine slights in the eye-blink of a baron. His second weakness lies in his displeasing looks. Although Oswin is not an ugly man, his features make a disagreeable impression: his eyes are small and cold, his nose thrusts forward, one upper tooth grows at an angle. The lady Fortuna, he believes, has treated him unjustly, while lavishing upon fools her gifts of landed estates, hereditary titles, and pretty teeth. His lust for highborn ladies, which appears inexhaustible, is not pleasant to contemplate. His successes never satisfy him.

Oswin follows the Queen ruthlessly with his eyes. His lust shows on his face like a knife-gash.

It is easy to imagine that Oswin's report to the King was caused by injured pride and thwarted desire. When the Queen smiles at the steward, her gray, faintly melancholy eyes do not see him; more often she passes him by without a look. His invisibility, his terrible transparency, must exasperate him beyond measure. But such an explanation, however reasonable, is true only up to a certain point. In judging the motives of a man like the steward, one must bear in mind his loyalty to the crown; Oswin's obedience has never been in doubt. It is his duty to report to the King any sign of disorder in the household, any form of behavior unbefitting a vassal or a wife. In this sense his spiteful report is the laudable act of a servant devoted to his master. It is also true that Oswin has always been jealous of the King's nephew, whom the King loves immoderately.

No one can deny that the young Queen and Tristan take pleasure in one another's company.

The Queen's beauty is remarkable but difficult to account for. Each of her features, considered separately, is exceeded in perfection by the exquisite eyelid, the flawless cheek, the incomparable lip of a court lady, and yet, united, they compose a pattern of beauty that surpasses any other at court. Is it the harmony of her parts that is so beguiling? I believe the secret lies elsewhere. The Queen, like all beautiful women, has about her a remoteness, a coolness of perfection, such as one feels in a jewel or a silver goblet. Such beauty holds us at a distance, chills us, in truth repels us a little. In this sense it may be argued that the highest expression of beauty is nothing but a rare and enigmatic form of ugliness. But working against the chill of the Queen's beauty is some other force—a force of imperfection, of unruliness. Her plaited yellow hair, a hint of which is visible at her temples, where the wimple is joined to her head covering, is so richly golden and perfectly arranged that it appears to have been fashioned by a master goldsmith with repeated blows of his small hammer, yet here and there a strand escapes and glitters in the sun. These are the strands that break the heart. Her lips are perfectly formed, but when she smiles, one side of her mouth begins to turn upward before the other. Her left eyelid dips at the outer corner. Her elegant nostrils, shaped by the delicate chisel of a carver of Old Testament scenes on the panels of a cathedral door, do not match precisely. When she laughs, however mildly, something leaps into her cheeks and eyes that was not there before—something that bursts out of her like a force of disruption.

The secret of the Queen's beauty lies in what shatters it.

Is it surprising that gossip and slander have joined the young Queen and Tristan? They are radiant with youth, disarming in beauty. When the King, the Queen, and Tristan are seen walking together, the eye helplessly binds the young Queen and Tristan, separating them cruelly from the King. It is also true that the King has formally requested Tristan to love and protect the Queen; when the King is meeting with his counselors in the great hall, or following his hounds in the royal forest, she is always with Tristan. They walk in the Queen's garden, stroll among the trees of the orchard, ride in the forest, talk in the women's quarters above the royal bedchamber. Such behavior can lead only to malicious gossip. The Queen is very busy, say the court ladies: she has one husband by night, and one husband by day. They fail to understand that it is precisely the King's love for Tristan that makes him place his beloved Ysolt under his protection. Would they leave her open to the attentions of the steward?

Tristan is honorable. He would lay down his life for his King. The Queen walks beside him with downcast eyes. Strands of her yellow hair catch the sun.

They are too much together. I do not like these rumors.

This morning I was summoned to the King's private chamber in the northwest tower. I found the King seated alone at a small table before his chessboard. He motioned for me to sit down across from him and, after taking thought, moved the white king's pawn two squares forward. His long fingers lingered caressingly on the artful folds of the sleeves of the stern-faced pawn, before releasing it; of his nine sets of chesspieces, these are his favorite, carved from walrus tusks. In reply I moved the pawn of my black king two squares forward. He immediately moved the queen's pawn two squares forward, inviting a capture. At this point an odd look came into his eyes, and he raised his hand to stop me from moving. "Now, Thomas," he said, "if you were King of Cornwall, which move would you anticipate?"

"If I were King of Cornwall, my lord, I would anticipate one of three moves: a direct capture, the move of my king's knight to the square before the bishop, or the advance of my queen's pawn."

The King, who plays chess well, listened closely to this uninteresting reply. He stared down at the three pawns and looked at me again. "I have never forgotten what you said to me that day in the garden."

The King's fondness for this memory, which in truth I can scarcely summon, always pleases me. He was twelve years old—a Prince in his father's castle. I was a young man of twenty, knighted and well tutored in my uncle's manor, brought to instruct the Prince in fencing and dialectic. We often played chess in his mother's garden, in a bower of lime trees. It was an old story, which he liked to remember over the chessboard.

"You pointed to the three pawns and said, 'The last move of the game lies right here, if we could but see it.' "

"We could indeed see it, if two conditions were true: if we could always anticipate our enemy's moves precisely, and if our own moves were always perfect."

The King pushed back his chair and stood up. I rose immediately. The chess game was over. He walked to the chamber window, which looked out upon the orchard and the forest, glanced down without interest, and moved before a wall hanging that showed a bleeding stag surrounded by silver greyhounds.

"Do you think the Queen is happy?" he said.

"She appears well content, my lord."

"Ah," he said, in a tone of impatience. "But you know, Thomas, I sometimes think—a young woman brought to a foreign court, a place of strangers. How difficult it must be for her! I should like you to keep an eye out for her. Let me know if she is ever—unhappy."

"Very well, my lord."

"I know I can rely on you, Thomas." He swept his arm toward the window. "Look! A fine day for hawking."

It is night now, and I haven't been able to dispel a sense of oppression. The meaning of our interview is all too clear: the King wishes me to spy on his wife. He has not been himself since the steward whispered in his ear.

I would think nothing of the Queen's keeping company with Tristan, whom the King has set over her as a protector, were it not for certain looks that sometimes pass between them. Even those looks might easily be explained as entirely familial, since each has been instructed by the King to love the other well. Might they not love each other as brother and sister—she in a strange land, he without father and mother? The reverence she owes her husband requires her to cherish his nephew. Oswin says the Queen gives herself to Tristan in every bed, upon every stairway, behind every tree.

I fear that something is going to happen.

. . .

There are those at court who would not be unhappy to witness Tristan's disgrace. Tristan has always attracted an ardent following, especially among the younger knights, but the extreme love of the King for his nephew has bred secret jealousies. Among the barons, some fear his prowess in battle, some are jealous of the King's favor, some resent the King's long refusal to marry for the sake of making his nephew heir to the throne. Others, to be sure, remain bound to him in passionate friendship. Yet even they may sometimes feel, at the center of their loyalty, a secret tiredness, such as one feels at the back of the neck after gazing up too long at a splendid tower.

I do not mean that Tristan is disliked. Even those who are jealous and resentful acknowledge his daring, his fearlessness, his high sense of honor, his love of comradeship. The story is told how Tristan, hunting one day with companions in the royal forest, came to a spring. As the company kneeled to drink, Tristan's servant presented to the young lord a single bottle of wine, which he had brought along to slake his master's thirst. Tristan, seizing the bottle and holding it high, cried, "*Thus* do I drink!" and poured the bottle of wine into the spring, inviting all to partake of it.

The King's love for Tristan runs so deep that it is like the love of a man for his own life.

Oswin the Proud, Oswin the Lascivious, is not the only source of disorder at court. Often he is seen in the despicable company of Modor. Of the three dwarves at court, Modor is the only one of consequence. Modor!—a strutting little ugly man, tyrannical, boastful, obsequious, vengeful, a puffed-up little piece of malevolence. He bullies the other dwarves cruelly, sends them on trivial errands, humiliates them before laughing barons. His harsh face puts me in mind of a clenched fist. His sole passion is intrigue. The barons laugh at him but are uneasy in his presence; he is believed to be skilled in the art of poison. He professes to revere Tristan, while letting it be known that the King favors him unduly; he ingratiates himself with the Queen, while whispering against her; his loyal service to the King does not prevent him from hinting to Tristan's followers that the King's marriage to Ysolt of Ireland will deprive his nephew of the promised kingship. He betrays everyone and is universally detested. Why then is his presence tolerated? It is more than tolerated: Modor is sought after eagerly. Is it that an idle court, weary of familiar pleasures, seeks the diversion of the grotesque? Or is there a deeper reason? Modor is the concentrated essence of everything base and ugly in the soul of a courtier. To see him is to experience a thrill of recognition, as when anything hidden is brought to light, followed at once by a pleasing sense of moral superiority.

When I see Oswin and Modor standing together in the angle of a shady wall, or walking side by side on a path at the edge of the forest, then I confess that I am overcome by a feeling of gratitude to the Creator for the wisdom and goodness of His divine plan, whereby the end of life is the beginning of punishment, and death is inevitable.

Something has happened—something disturbing and unexpected—something I cannot understand. I am seated at my writing table late at night, gripping my quill tightly, with trembling fingers. I must make an effort to calm myself. Calm yourself, Thomas! Writing will calm me.

It is my custom, before I retire for the night, to leave the castle by the postern and take a walk in the orchard. The rows of fruit trees—quince and pear, cherry and plum, apple and peach—stretch for acres beyond the castle wall. Here and there cleared paths, broad enough for wagons to pass at harvest-time, run all the way to the palisade of pointed stakes that encloses the orchard and makes of it another garden. Beyond the palisade flows the river, which at this point is no wider than a brook, and on the other side of the brook rises a second palisade, which marks the boundary of the royal forest. It is pleasing, on a warm summer night when the moon is nearly full, to leave the orchard paths and walk among the fruit trees themselves. Here, away from the voices of the castle, in a world of black leaves and white moonlight, a world of silence broken only by the cry of an owl, the rustle of a mouse among the grass, and the distant bark of a greyhound in the courtyard, one can possess one's soul in peace.

Tonight I walked a little farther than usual, making my way along the wagon paths, striking suddenly into the trees, crossing a stream, entering open places not yet under cultivation, plunging again under the branches—for I was restless and wished to tire myself for sleep. Overhead, like a piece of glass stained deep blue in a cathedral window through which the sun is shining, the night sky was blue and radiant. I had come to a stretch of orchard not far from the palisade when I saw a movement in the shadows and heard a footfall. I halted, placed my hand on my sword hilt, and was about to call out when I saw two figures walking among the trees.

I knew at once it was Tristan and the Queen. They were walking so slowly that they were scarcely moving, and they seemed to lean against each other lightly. Their hands were clasped at their sides and their faces were turned toward each other, his more sharply than hers. Shadows of branches rippled across their faces and backs. The Queen's mantle, which trailed on the ground, was decorated with small crescent moons made of silver. Over her hair she wore a simple head covering, fastened around her temples by a fillet of gold. Now and then they stepped from the rippling shadow-branches into the sudden light of the moon, before the shadows reclaimed them. As I watched their slow, dreamlike walk, under the silence of the moon, I seemed to forget that I was witnessing an act of treason punishable by death, and I felt—but it is difficult to say precisely what I felt. But I felt I was witnessing something that was of the night—an emanation of the night, as surely as the moonlight dropping softly on the leaves and branches. It was something old, older than marriage, older than kingship, something that belonged to night itself. Then I seemed to feel, rising from those scarcely breathing shadows, an exalted tenderness, a night ecstasy, an expansion of their very being, as if at any moment the night sky would crack open and reveal a dazzling light; and I turned my face away, there in my spying place, as if I had been rebuked.

When the lovers had advanced beyond earshot, I turned quietly and made my way back to the castle.

One detail I neglected to mention. Upon first seeing the pair, I had gripped my sword hilt, with the instinct of an old warrior. When I finally turned to go, I discovered that my hand was still on my sword, the fingers tense, the tendons thrust up, the muscles of my arm sore, as though I had just returned my sword to the scabbard after a battle.

Up at cockcrow, after little sleep. It is good, when the mind is troubled, to walk in the courtyard in the early morning. In the half-light of dawn, the grooms were sweeping out the stables. Peacocks and peahens strutted about. A servant was emptying a chamber pot into the cesspit. A second servant, carrying an arm-ful of rushes for the floor of the great hall, climbed the outer stairway at the base of the keep and disappeared into the arch above. At a great wooden trough, the big-armed laundress was soaking tablecloths and sheets, which she would later pound and hang up to dry in the morning sun. Through the door of the forge I saw the smith examining a broken cart-axle. I stopped for a moment before the mews, to look through the small win-dow at the falcons on their perches, the long-winged peregrines and gyrfalcons, the short-winged goshawks and sparrow hawks. I continued past the well, with its windlass and bucket; a hen fluttered up to the stone rim. The greyhounds were feeding in the kennels, barrels of live chickens stood piled by the kitchen gate, bales of sweet-smelling hay stood before the door of the granary, and on the high walls, against the graying sky, men-at-arms with crossbows were replacing the night watch.

In the afternoon I was alone with the King and did not speak. He waited for me to speak, but I spoke of other things. My silence I condemn as an act of treason against the crown. What bound my tongue was not doubt about whether I ought to speak, but the knowledge that, if I spoke, I would be guilty of an act of disloyalty to the Queen, whom I dislike, and to Tristan, whom I do not love as I love the King.

My duty is clear. Is my duty clear? I have no proof of adultery. Tristan is the Queen's protector and is often alone with her. The King from the beginning has encouraged their intimacy, has repeatedly praised Tristan for attending to the Queen. What is it that I know? I know that the Queen and Tristan were walking together in the orchard late at night. Is this a fact to be lightly reported to a jealous and suspicious King, in an atmosphere of gossip and slander? A word from me, the King's trusted counselor and companion, carries more weight than the malice of fools. It is also possible, however unlikely, that there are reasons for their nocturnal walk which, once understood, will set everything in a new light. I did not witness a kiss or a single embrace—merely the holding of hands, as if they were children. Perhaps the unusual hour, my mental agitation, the enchantment of moonlight, an overzealous imagination, a pardonable but highly questionable sense of foreboding, united to produce in my mind the troubling sensations of that night. I must observe them carefully, and accumulate more telling evidence before reporting to the King.

A madness of preparation has seized the court, diverting its attention from the Queen. The Count of Toulouse and some two hundred attendants will be arriving on these shores within the week and will lodge with us for some days before making their way to London. Oswin complains bitterly that there is no room in the stables, that the visitors will devour our pigs and sheep and capons, kill our deer, seduce our women, steal our treasure; he speaks as if he were anticipating a plague of locusts. The King laughs and orders him to spare no expense. Already, in the southwest field outside the castle walls, new stables are being erected. Bedchambers are being cleaned, tents set up, horses curried, walls hung with silks. Wagonloads of hay and grain roll in from the outlying farms. There is talk of feasting, games, entertainments of all kinds. The King hunts all day; Tristan visits in the women's quarters, or is seen passing with the Queen and her handmaid into the Queen's garden.

From high windows, ladies look out expectantly, searching for the first sign of movement on the horizon.

Is it possible I was mistaken? They walk together like the best of friends. No one speaks of them, in the tumult of preparation. Only now and again, as I step round a corner of the stables, or emerge from the shady arch of a doorway, I see the steward staring after them as they pass into the tower that opens into the Queen's garden.

These men of Toulouse do nothing but sing, dance, and play from daybreak to midnight. Laughter rings out from every tent and stairway. Are they a race of children, these knights and nobles of Toulouse? No, in truth they care nothing for childhood: they are of a race who celebrate the joys of full-blooded youth. One can see it in their fashions, in their games and amusements. Their minstrels sing of love—only of love. Never do they sing of battles, of fallen heroes, of ruin and misery. Their songs know nothing of our stern world, with its bitter burdens and sorrows; for them all is youth, zephyrs, the green buds of a perpetual May. The Count is a man of fifty, who wears his unnaturally blond hair to his shoulders. He is said to be a musician and a scholar, a poet, a skilled chess player, a bold swordsman, a lover of the chase who never travels without his hawks. He presented to the King a silver ewer in the shape of a knight on a horse; when the ewer is filled with water and tipped, the water pours from the horse's mouth. The Count and the King spend hours bent over the chessboard or walking in the King's garden. Today they hunted in the forest, with a large company. The Count is good for the King, he distracts him from jealousy.

Last night the Count's minstrel sang for us in the great hall, seated on a low stool and accompanying himself on a harp. The songs were all love songs, written by the Count himself. Afterward the King's minstrel, seated on a cushion and accompanying himself on the vielle, sang an adventure of Reynard the Fox and Ysengrim the Wolf, which was well applauded. It was after this, as the singer rose to give way to a juggler of knives, that a curious incident took place. A stranger entered the hall, dressed like a pilgrim in a broad-brimmed hat and a hooded cloak, bearing in one hand an ashwood staff and carrying a harp on his back. Seashells were sewn onto his cloak, as a sign that he had traveled in distant lands; his feet were bare. He approached the Count and asked if he might play a song before the court. To the consternation of the King, the Count laughed and urged the pilgrim to entertain the company if he could. Thereupon the stranger took the harp from his back and played his melancholy song with such surpassing skill that the company listened in hushed wonder. When he had finished playing, there was great applause; the Count, visibly moved, said he had never before heard playing of that kind, and asked where he learned to play so well. "In Lyonesse," replied the pilgrim, who at once tossed off his humble cloak, beneath which was a purple surcoat with silver sleeve-borders decorated with gold lions, and removed his pilgrim's hat, revealing himself to be—Tristan. Then there was great laughter and rejoicing in the hall, for these men of Toulouse like nothing better than a bold and playful spirit.

. . .

It is only two days since my last entry, but everything has changed. Disaster has struck. The Count and his followers departed at daybreak. The spirit of revelry has been broken, the fraternal warmth between the Count and the King has suffered a chill. The Queen refuses to leave her chamber, the King paces alone in his garden, Modor sits in the tower prison. I am partly to blame, for I sensed trouble but was unable to foresee the direction from which it erupted.

The idea for a mime appears to have come from the Count, although I cannot believe that Modor did not guide him from the very beginning. It is unimportant. The Count's love of pleasure, his need for diversion, his childlike delight in surprise, his openness to suggestion of every kind—all this was bound to present itself as a temptation to Modor's sharp sense of opportunity, his habit of machination, his single-minded devotion to furthering his own ends. The Count's two dwarves proved to be his way in. These are the clownish dwarves one often sees in the entourage of a great nobleman, dwarves without pride or dignity—dwarves who accept without protest their repellent destiny as the playthings of the strong. Their grotesque names were Roland and Bathsheba. They were man and wife, both skilled in small entertainments such as juggling, tumbling, and mime. A small harp had been specially constructed for him, a little set of bells for her. Modor has always detested dwarves of this kind; he quickly befriended them. The mime was to take place in the evening, after supper, when the King and the Count had returned from the hunt.

A stage was erected on the dais, surrounded by seats for the King, the Queen, the Count, and the highest nobles of both courts; all others sat on benches in the lower part of the hall. Tallow candles in iron candelabra lit the stage, bare except for a single stool on which sat an emerald-green silk cushion. When Modor appeared, gasps and murmurs sounded. His brash impudence astonished me. He wore a brilliant crimson mantle, edged with ermine—the unmistakable robe of the King. On his head sat a gilt paper crown. With ridiculous majesty he strode to the cushioned stool and sat down on that throne with his arms folded across his chest. Enter Roland and Bathsheba. He wore the jeweled mantle of Tristan; from Bathsheba's shoulders hung the crescent-covered mantle of the Queen. Her hair, only partly concealed by a head covering, had been dyed a gaudy, brilliant yellow—the yellow of bitter laughter. Tristan le Petit led his little Ysolt to King Modor, who took her hand and gawked at her with oafish adoration. As Tristan walked away, she turned to watch him and stretched out one arm in a gesture of yearning. Now Dwarf King and Dwarf Queen leave the stage and Dwarf Tristan is seen groping his way among invisible trees. He stops, cups his ear. Ysolt appears. They embrace passionately. Beside me, the King drew in a sharp breath. On stage, King Modor appears, wearing his crown. He sees the lovers and throws off his mantle; he is wearing a white-and-gold surcoat over a shirt of ring mail. He draws his sword. Two dwarf attendants appear and swiftly arm him: they pull on the mail gauntlets, fasten his leg mail, lace his helmet, present him with a shield. Ysolt-Bathsheba gives a silent cry, presses both hands to her cheeks, and flees. Dwarf Tristan throws off his mantle: he wears an azure surcoat over a glittering hauberk. In the flamelight one can see the small interlocking rings of iron on his arms. The dwarf attendants complete his armor.

The sword fight between Modor and Roland was a brilliant piece of stagecraft. Their short but dangerous blades flashed in the light of candles, rang out in high-pitched tones, flung showers of sparks. Both dwarves were expert swordsmen—Roland more graceful, more resourceful, more constrained, as if he disdained to make a single motion more than was absolutely necessary; Modor fierce, nimble, relentless, at times awkward, a lover of the wild and unexpected motion. His eyes in the flamelight glittered like magic stones. Suddenly the edge of Modor's sword strikes Tristan's upper arm, cutting through the mail. Blood runs through the iron rings. Dwarf Tristan falls to one knee and drops his sword. As if maddened by the sight, Modor strikes wildly with his blade—rings of iron go spinning into the air. Suddenly he plunges his sword into Tristan's side. Dwarf Tristan falls forward and lies face down on the stage.

Now Modor bends to unlace the helmet, swiftly removes it. He flings his own shield over his back, where it hangs by the shield strap, raises his sword in both hands, and in a single blow cuts off Roland's head. Ladies cry out, the Count rises from his chair. Modor, his face crazed with triumph, seizes the dripping head by the hair, strides to the King, and holds it up to him. The Queen cries out, raises one arm across her eyes, and falls sideways in a swoon. The King, roused from his trance, holds the Queen awkwardly and attempts to rise. On the stage, Bathsheba utters a piercing scream.

The Count, inconsolable over the loss of his favorite dwarf, agreed to accept thirty thousand pieces of gold, three greyhound bitches, and an annual gift of grain. Modor sits chained in the tower prison. It is difficult to know which is worse: the murder of the Count's dwarf or the humiliation of the King. The King speaks to no one. What I find interesting in these troubling events is the moment when Modor held the head up to the King. I had the distinct sensation that the King was about to stretch forth his hand, before coming to his senses and calling for his guards.

This morning the King summoned me to his tower chamber. His face was drawn, his eyes melancholy and streaked with very fine lines of blood. He came directly to the point. There was no proof against the Queen, no evidence of wrongdoing, but the atmosphere of suspicion and gossip had put him in an intolerable position. Although Modor's murderous rage was inexcusable, he did not entirely blame the dwarf, who in his brutal and bloody way had delivered a timely warning. The King was able to see three possibilities of action. First, banish Tristan from the court. Second, allow Tristan to remain at court, but forbid him to be alone with the Queen. Third, set a trap and take them unawares. The first possibility was repugnant to him, for two reasons: first, he did not wish to punish Tristan without evidence, of which there was none, and second, he loved Tristan as a son and the mere imagination of his absence made his heart hurt. The second possibility—allowing Tristan to remain at court, but forbidding all intimacy with the Queen—was likewise unacceptable, for three reasons: first, he did not wish to deprive Tristan unjustly of the Queen's company; second, he did not like to publish his suspicions by a decree resulting in a conspicuous show of change; and third, he did not wish to deprive Queen Ysolt of the company and protection of Tristan, for not only did she feel warm friendship for him, as was only proper, but she was protected by him from the unwanted attentions of other members of the court, some of whom he knew to be far less honorable and trustworthy than his loyal nephew. The third possibility—the trap—though distasteful to him, was therefore the one he favored, for if the two were indeed guilty of treason against the crown, it was important to have evidence before bringing charges against them for a crime punishable by death.

As the King spoke, he became animated, as if the act of utterance were filling him with decisive energy, but his eyes remained melancholy, withdrawn, and—an impression that struck me—as if indifferent to the strategy he was urging.

He knew, he said, that I disliked Oswin, who nevertheless was trustworthy in most ways. Oswin had reported to him that the Queen had been meeting secretly with Tristan, at night, in the orchard. The steward had followed them twice to their trysting place, where a broad apple tree grew beside a brook. There, although Oswin had not witnessed it himself, he believed they consummated their treasonable love. The King proposed to have Oswin lead him to the spot, whereupon he would dismiss the steward—on pain of death—and conceal himself in the tree. He would arm himself with a bow and two arrows.

It is my duty to lead Oswin back to the castle, after which I am to return and join the King in the tree.

I loathe this plan, which seems to me to carry with it something alien to the King, something that belongs to Oswin, like a borrowed sword.

For my part, I think of the Count of Flanders, who, when a vassal sighed in the presence of the Countess, ordered that the man be beaten and suspended head first in a cesspit.

The King is pleased by his decisiveness, which is nothing but the cunning form assumed by his indecisiveness.

It is very late, but I cannot sleep before setting down the surprising events of this memorable night.

Not long after the King took his leave of the company to

return to his bedchamber, I made my way alone to the orchard, where I lay in wait for the King and Oswin not far from the gate in the orchard palisade. I soon saw the gate open and the King and Oswin pass through. I followed, keeping well behind. The moon, a brilliant crescent, was low in the sky—a clear night, dark, with many stars. Oswin did not speak. He led the King silently along wagon paths, through clusters of fruit trees and arbors of grapes, over streams and ditches; in the starlight I saw an abandoned wagon, a pile of empty baskets, a broken wheel with tall grass growing between the spokes. In time we came to an older part of the orchard, where thick-branched apple trees rose high overhead. A narrow brook ran nearby. At the base of an immense apple tree that grew beside the stream, Oswin stopped. One low branch, thick with leaves and small unripe apples, grew out over the stream. Handing his bow and quiver to Oswin, the King with a sudden leap seized a branch and climbed into the tree. Swiftly he concealed himself in the middle branches. Then he reached down for his bow and quiver, which Oswin handed up to him.

"Why are there three arrows, Sire?" Oswin asked.

"The third arrow is for you," the King replied, "if you fail to return to the castle. Thomas will see you safely to the gate."

At this I stepped forth. Oswin, outraged, banished all expression from his face and accompanied me in silence back to the orchard gate, where he took his leave coldly. Only when the gate closed did I make my way back through the orchard to the apple tree beside the stream. There I stood looking up at the thick-leaved branches, until the King ordered me to climb up and keep watch with him.

When I was settled not far from him on a neighboring branch, the King said in a whisper, "Tell me, Thomas. When did you last climb a tree?"

At once I saw myself in the orchard of my uncle's manor, plucking a handful of cherries.

"Forty years ago," I whispered.

At this the King gave a sudden, disarming grin, a mischievous grin, as it seemed to me, and my heart was moved, for despite the solemnity of the occasion, he was still boyish, in some things.

His mind darkened as we waited. He seemed restless, sorrowful, gloomy with anticipation, half inclined to abandon the grotesque enterprise—for how could he desire to discover what he could not bear to know? And beneath his burst of boyish high spirits, I sensed that he was ashamed to be hiding in a tree, spying on the Queen and Tristan; for he was no comic cuckold in a minstrel's tale, but King of all Cornwall.

Suddenly Tristan was there, under the tree. I had not heard a sound. Shadow branches showed sharp and black on the moonlit grass. He seemed uneasy and kept pacing, keeping a careful watch in the dark.

At the sound of the Queen's footsteps I felt the King grow violently still, as if his body were a hand that had closed over a struggling bird.

Tristan did not step forward to meet the Queen. Instead he drew back, almost as if he wished to avoid the meeting. As Queen Ysolt came near I could see her face in the moonlight, anxious and uncertain. She stopped some ten feet from Tristan, who stood directly below us.

"Why have you asked me to come here?" she said, in a cold, majestic voice I had never heard before. I had the odd sensation that I was watching a court play.

"To ask for your help, my lady. Enemies have turned the King against me; God knows the love I bear him. If, in your kindness . . ."

So they declaimed, two actors under the moon. For I understood—suddenly and absolutely—that they knew they were being watched, up there in the branches. I felt like leaping down and crying, "Well done, Tristan! A fine speech!" On the ground, among the leaf shadows, I saw the shadow of the King's face. Tristan must have seen it there and passed a signal to the Queen. So the two played out their little drama under the apple branches: the Blameless Lady and the Injured Knight. It was well acted, though a little long; the speeches, though rather florid, were delivered with strong feeling. And I marveled at the sheer daring of it, the air of impassioned conviction with which they assumed their parts. Of course they were in a trap, fighting to get out. But wasn't there more to it than that? Tristan truly did love the King, who had taken him into the Cornish court at the age of fifteen and brought him up like a father; the Queen surely considered herself blameless, for she had been married against her will—and in any case, what can one do against the power of Love? And what of the King? Can he really have been deceived? I believe he grasped at the little drama gratefully, eager to be deluded—for the one thing he could not permit himself to find was the truth he sought.

When the two had left—first the blameless Queen, and later, after a proper interval, the melancholy and misunderstood knight—the King said nothing for a long while. Then he turned to look at me from his branch. With passion, with a kind of crazed delight, he whispered, "You see, Thomas! You see!"

"I see our shadows, my lord," I replied sharply, but the King, with a burst of energy, swung down from the tree and looking up at me cried out, "Come down, Thomas! What the devil are you doing up there? A grown man like you! Come down, Thomas, come down!"

. . .

Oswin is in disgrace. The King dotes on the Queen, sings Tristan's praises, hunts the red deer and the fallow deer and the roe deer, drinks deep from his gold flagon, throws back his head in laughter: all is splendid, all is well. Only I am uneasy. Is it because I detect in the King's heartiness a note of excess, as if by sheer effort of will he hopes to banish the doubt that devours him? His eyes glitter with a mad merriment. He embraces Tristan, looks admiringly at the Queen. "Thomas!" he cries. "Is she not beautiful?" "Yes, my lord." The Queen lowers her eyes.

Because the King cannot bear the thought that his wife and Tristan are lovers, he has again placed her under Tristan's protection. In this way he demonstrates to himself that they are innocent and he is wise—for if they were guilty, he would be a fool to leave them alone together. All morning and afternoon he hunts in the forest, while Tristan attends the Queen everywhere. He walks with her in the garden, climbs the winding stairs that lead to her tower chamber. Oswin is forbidden to be in her presence, on pain of imprisonment. In the early evening, Tristan returns Ysolt to the King. The King and Queen retire early. At night, in the royal bedchamber, I hear cries of lovemaking.

Anyone who reports ill of Tristan or the Queen is threatened with banishment.

It is precisely now, when the Queen and Tristan ought to exercise exceptional caution, that they behave as if the King's trust, his air of cheerful unconcern, has deceived them. They exchange glances full of longing, flush and grow pale, emerge from hidden chambers drowsy and languorous. When Tristan hands the Queen to the King, his face is full of tender sadness. The Queen, walking beside the King, looks about for Tristan, catches his eye. Are they mad? One might almost think they are trying to provoke the King into punishing them. Is it possible that his inflexible good cheer, his stubborn insistence on being deceived, exasperates them into public shows of affection? Do they feel he is tempting them to see how much he can bear? Or is it that, swept up as they are by an irresistible power, they do not think about the King at all?

Really, they go too far. Have they no sense? No shame? The King has been absent for two days. He announced that he would spend two nights in one of his hunting lodges and not return until the third day; in the presence of his Council he placed the Queen in Tristan's care. All day they walk like lovers, seeking out secluded places. A servant saw the Queen and Tristan emerge at dawn from the door at the base of her tower that leads into the garden. At dinner they sit side by side at the royal board; he permits his hand to graze her hand while her throat flushes above the gold brooch clasping the lappets of her brilliant green mantle. Fearing the King's wrath, everyone turns away, remains unwatchful and ill at ease. Oswin stares at them coldly. One can almost hear, from the high prison of the southeast tower, the rattle of Modor's chains.

A trap! Was it a trap? In the middle of the night I was wakened by the King's hand on my shoulder and the light of a candle glaring on his cheek. He had returned alone, secretly, in the night. My door remains always unbarred, so that the King may find me when sleep eludes him. In his hunting lodge he had dreamed that Ysolt had been gored in the side by a wild boar. I rose quickly from my bed, groped for my tunic and sword belt in the flickering dark, and followed the King to the royal bed-chamber. Slowly he pulled aside the curtain, which rattled on its rings. He thrust in the candle. The bed was empty.

The King motioned me to follow him. We climbed the winding stairs to the women's quarters; the guard admitted us into a large hall with curtained bench-beds along the walls, where the Queen's companions sleep. Here and there on the rush-strewn floor, servant women lay on quilts beneath bed-covers. A small adjoining chamber served as the Queen's pri-vate quarters. The room with its bed and clothes chest was empty.

We descended to the courtyard, crossed to the northwest tower, and climbed the winding stairs to the Queen's high chamber. With a large iron key the King unlocked the door. Dark bedposts topped by gilt wooden swans glowed in the moonlight; the bed curtains were open. On the coverlet lay a silk girdle brocaded with gold. We descended the dark stairs to the ground floor—a storage chamber with locked chests— where a narrow door admitted us into the Queen's garden. Under the summer moon we walked along the sanded paths of the garden; a shimmering peacock moved before us and dis-appeared. The King stepped behind a tree, peered into wall recesses supplied with turf seats, turned suddenly at the sound of a rat. At an arched opening in a hedge he drew his sword and led me into a maze of hedgerows, which brought us to a grove of fruit trees. Nothing stirred in the moonlight.

We returned through the garden and made our way across the courtyard to the castle keep. On the broad steps leading up to the great hall we passed a sleeping black hen. Through an arch I followed the King up the winding stairs. I had thought we were returning to my chamber, but the King stopped before Tristan's door. With another iron key he entered.

The curtains of Tristan's bed were closed. At the top of the bedposts sat carved falcons with gilt beaks and wings. The King, holding his candle and beckoning me to follow, approached the bed and slowly drew aside the curtain.

The Queen lay in the bed, alone and fast asleep. The covers were partly thrown back; she was fully dressed, and wore a head covering, held in place by a gold fillet set with emeralds and jacinths. In the light of the candle I saw the King's uncertain, sorrowing eyes.

"My lord," said Tristan, standing behind us. The King, turning quickly, splashed candle-wax on his hand.

"I hope your hunt was successful," Tristan said, sheathing his sword. He was fully dressed, in green tunic and crimson surcoat; in the flamelight a network of tiny pearls glittered on his mantle, one end of which was thrown over his right shoulder. He nodded at the bed. "The Queen was frightened—a rat in the dark. I have guarded her with my life."

"Indeed you have," the King replied. "But as for me, the wild boar escaped. A long day—I'm tired now. Come, Thomas."

"Shall I wake the Queen?" Tristan asked.

"By no means," replied the King. "But when she wakes, please tell her that her husband bids her good morning."

I made my way with the King to his chamber, where I wished him good night before returning to my bed.

A new feeling is in the air. The lovers, no doubt alarmed by the King's nocturnal visit, have become uncommonly circumspect, while the King, abandoning the strategy of frivolous jollity, watches them with visible suspicion. He continually sends for the Queen on trivial pretexts: asks her if she is satisfied with her attendants and servants, inquires after her health, requests her to play the rote or harp for him. The Queen is resolutely obliging, but it is clear that she finds his attentions wearisome. Tristan spends long hours following his hawks. Once, when the Queen was playing a melancholy song on her harp, the King suddenly ordered her to stop and began pacing restlessly. "Continue to play for Thomas," he said irritably, and strode from the chamber. For a moment the Queen raised her eyes and glanced at me, before taking up the harp again. We both understood that the King had suspected her of dreaming of Tristan, as she played her mournful song.

It is not good to pity one's King.

When I try to imagine Queen Ysolt, I see only an enigma, a contradiction. In all her dealings at court, she is honorable, forthright, and entirely trustworthy; and yet, whenever it is a question of Tristan, she does not hesitate to lie. Although she is frank by nature, she conceals a treacherous secret; although she is obedient by habit, her obedience surrounds and conceals a fierce, unwavering disobedience. One is tempted to think that she is loyal in all things pertaining to Tristan, and disloyal in all things pertaining to the King, but such a formulation provides I think far too easy and shallow a way of grasping her: for although she is loyal to Tristan, she is also loyal to the King, and although she is disloyal to the King, she is also disloyal to Tristan. She is loyal to the King because night after night she lies naked with him in the royal bed, night after night the sounds of lusty lovemaking come from the King's bedchamber. It is possible, of course, that at such moments she is thinking of Tristan. But who can imagine that, even as she longs for Tristan, she is entirely forgetful of the King?

I have said that although she is disloyal to the King, she is also disloyal to Tristan. For if, when she is with the King, she is haunted by Tristan, is it not also true that when she is with Tristan, she is haunted by the King? To be Tristan's lover is to betray the King; the act of love is an act of disobedience. But disobedience, by its very nature, includes an awareness of the one who is disobeyed. The Queen can never be alone with Tristan; even as she lies in Tristan's arms she will see, rising before her, the King's troubled face, she will feel, falling across her, the shadow of the King.

Sometimes, when I watch the Queen unobserved, the calmness of her pale, smooth face and heavy-lidded eyes takes me by surprise. Then I notice a slight tensing between the eyebrows; the beautiful dawn-gray eyes stare unseeing; and, like someone for whom the outside world has fallen away, she raises a slender hand to her forehead, as if to wipe away a loose hair.

Is it possible? Even now I scarcely believe the news. Just when an uneasy harmony has been restored, just when caution and propriety have become the order of the day, the King has taken the very step that many felt he should have taken during his period of false heartiness. He has banished Tristan. More precisely: he has forbidden Tristan to pass the bounds of the castle wall, or to enter the orchard or the forest.

He informed the Council that the action was made necessary by charges of misconduct injurious to the reputation of the Queen, the King, and Tristan, and touching upon the honor of his court and kingdom.

With Tristan he was gentle, even tender. Rumors had come

to his attention. The Queen's reputation was at stake. He gazed at Tristan fondly. For a moment I thought his eyes would fill with tears.

The barons friendly to Tristan say the King's decree is arbitrary and unjust, but they fail to understand the subterrestrial workings of a jealous and fretful mind. When Tristan and the Queen were parading their love, devouring each other with their ardent gazes, the King was unable to act because to act would have been to draw attention to the inadmissible, to display his secret fear. Only now, when the lovers have become circumspect—when, in a sense, it no longer matters—does the decree of banishment become possible.

For my part, I believe it is a mistake the King will learn to regret. With many opportunities for secrecy and solitude, the lovers were able to afford the luxury of discretion. Separation breeds recklessness. Can the King have forgotten Tristan's talent for adventure, his habit of daring?

Oswin is once again in the King's good graces.

In the afternoon, the order was given to release Modor from the tower.

The King, fearing some bold stroke by Tristan, has set extra guards at the main gate and the postern and has placed the Queen under the protection of the steward. She is not permitted to be out of Oswin's sight when the King is absent, unless she is in the women's quarters. The Queen shuts herself up all day with her women and leaves only to walk in the garden with her handmaid, Brangane. She is cold to Oswin and will not speak to him. She eats little and never laughs.

The rigor of her bearing is unnatural and disturbing, as if

only a relentless vigilance over every motion of her body can prevent collapse.

The King rises before dawn and hunts all day. When he returns he consults with Oswin, walks in his garden, seems restless and preoccupied. Sometimes, after the last candle has been put out, after the knights and men-at-arms have retired to their barracks in the courtyard, after the horses are asleep in the stables, I imagine that I can hear, through the stout oak planks of my unbarred door, the King in his chamber, pacing and pacing over the rush-strewn floor.

It is almost daybreak and I am writing quickly. Two visits!— like dreams in the night. Or was I dreaming after all? The first was from the King, who shook me awake. I dressed quickly and followed him across the courtyard and up the winding stairs to his tower chamber. A single candle burned on the table beside the chessboard. He sat down and I sat across from him. For a long time he stared at the pieces, then picked up the white king's pawn, seemed to hesitate, closed his fist over it, and leaned back, out of the flamelight.

"Have you heard news of Tristan?" he asked, a shade speaking to a shade.

"Nothing, my lord. Is he still in Cornwall?"

"No one knows. The Queen is unhappy." He paused. "Speak."

"You've tried to find him?"

"No. Yes: of course. Was I unjust to Tristan?"

"There were rumors."

"There are always rumors. There was no proof."

"They were much together."

"By my orders. By predilection. You believe I was unjust."

"I believe you acted as you found it necessary to act."

"And if I had asked for your advice?"

"I would have advised you to wait—to watch."

He looked at me. "Thank you, Thomas."

The King rose in the dark. "Tristan is true. I would cut off my arm to have him back. If you hear anything—"

"Of course."

The King started for the door and abruptly returned to the table. I waited for him to speak, but in the light of the candle he silently replaced the white pawn on its starting square.

The King's visit was not in itself disturbing, for he has long had the habit, when he cannot sleep, of coming to my chamber and inviting me to walk in the garden, or play chess, or follow him through one of the secret passages in the walls of the castle to one of his hidden chambers. What troubled me, as I made my way back across the courtyard, was the knowledge that the exile of Tristan had not put an end to the King's suffering. What further troubled me, as I climbed the winding stairs to my chamber, was the knowledge that the return of Tristan was also not going to put an end to the King's suffering. As I approached my door, holding in one hand a candle on an iron stick, I became aware of a movement in the dark. I reached for my sword and heard a single whispered word: "Please."

In the light of the flame I saw a young woman staring at me with fearful but determined eyes. My surprise was so great that I did not immediately recognize the Queen's handmaid, Brangane.

I ushered her into my chamber, where she stood stiffly with her hands clasping her elbows and her arms pressed against her stomach. She refused to sit at my writing table or on my clothes chest. For a few awkward moments I stood looking at her with my candle held out before me. Her eyes were darker than the King's. Coils of hair, visible at the edges of her head covering, were black and shining as the ink in my oxhorn. With a sudden motion of one hand she closed the heavy door behind her. As if in obedience to a sign, I set down the candle on my table and turned to face her in near darkness.

"The Queen sends her greetings," she began.

"The Queen honors me."

"The Queen believes you are a just man."

"The Queen flatters me."

"The Queen"—she stepped toward me and lowered her voice—"begs for news of Tristan."

"There is no news." I stepped back. Had the Queen sent her handmaid to me in a moment of desperation? Or had she detected in me a softness that she wished to explore?

Brangane looked at me as if to take my measure. Abruptly she retreated toward the door, into deeper darkness.

Almost invisible, a black ghost, she breathed forth in a whisper, "I fear for the Queen's life." I heard the door opening and listened to her footsteps hurrying away.

Every action is composed of two parts: the outward, visible part, which reveals what the actor wishes us to see, and the inward, invisible part, which is its true meaning. Outwardly, Brangane had come for news of Tristan. But inwardly, did she not have a deeper purpose, the purpose of discovering how far the Queen might go in making use of me? The Queen, emboldened by longing, desperate for news of Tristan, sends her woman to the King's trusted companion and counselor. She is taking a chance, but not a very great one, for although my allegiance to the King is well known, so is my discretion. It ends with a master stroke: "I fear for the Queen's life." That is to say: "If you reveal this visit to the King, you will kill the Queen." And this: "You can save the Queen's life by finding Tristan."

Another thought comes, far more troubling: that my attempts at understanding are superfluous, that the Queen already knows she can rely on me.

Four days have passed since my last entry, and again I am seated at my table late at night. This evening, as usual, I took a walk in the orchard. On my return to the courtyard I stopped not far from the wall of the Queen's garden, beside the granary. The wall rises to a height of nine feet and is composed of blocks of cut stone secured by mortar and topped by three thousand tiles of many colors. High overhead, in the blue-black night sky, stands the northeast tower, at the top of which is the Queen's private chamber, where she retires whenever she craves solitude. A dim light shone at the upper window. Was the Queen sitting on her window seat, looking down at her garden? I could see no one from where I stood. I turned my gaze to the northwest tower, where the King and I play chess in the uppermost chamber, above the King's garden. A dim light shone there too. As I gazed at the two towers, imagining the Queen alone in her chamber, looking down at her garden, and the King alone in his chamber, looking out at the Queen's tower, I became aware of a nearby sound and stepped back against a wall of the granary.

At the base of the garden wall I saw a figure in the dark. Something about its stealth—its wary silence—put me in mind of Oswin. As my fingers closed over my sword hilt the figure leaped, gripped the top of the wall, and pulled himself nimbly up along the stones. For an instant he crouched like an animal at the top of the wall, before plunging to the other side. In that instant I recognized Tristan.

I released my sword and became aware of the tumultuous beating of my heart. What was it that so unsteadied me, there by the garden wall? Was it an old knight's love of youthful daring? Or was it some more dubious feeling, a secret sympathy with wayward and forbidden things? There was no question of reporting what I had seen to the King: and as I turned away, I felt in my chest—my arms—my throat—a dark, secret exultation.

One imagines that it is no longer necessary to fear for the Queen's health.

I have had a note from Brangane. She pressed it into my hand as she passed me on the winding stair leading from the great hall to the bedchambers above. In it she thanks me for my kindness in receiving her and says that the Queen's health is much restored. Does she mean for me to read through these too-innocent words to the unwritten message, that Tristan has returned? Or is it her intention to throw me off the scent, to dismiss me, now that the Queen has found her cure?

Much to the court's surprise, the Queen has begun to spend a good part of each day in the company of Oswin. Sometimes she even sends Brangane in search of him. The whisperers are busy and begin to weave lascivious designs, but the true explanation is surely less tedious. Made wretched by Tristan's absence, the Queen loathed Oswin as the cause of that absence.

Now, made happy by Tristan's presence, she need not shun Oswin. Indeed, she makes use of him: she deceives the world into believing she is obedient.

Two weeks have passed since I last sat down to record my thoughts. Events crowd thick and fast. Already great changes have taken place. How shall I begin?

The castle walls are twenty-two feet thick. They are built of blocks of ashlar, smoothed by the mason's chisel and topped by crenellated battlements; between the outer and inner layers of stone lies a core of rubble, composed of crushed rock, pebbles, and mortar. Here and there a portion of the core has been removed, leaving a hollow passage large enough for a man to walk in. The walls are in fact honeycombed with passages of this kind, located at different heights, some joined to the ones above and below, and here and there the stone has been hollowed out to form small, hidden chambers. Although only the King is permitted to know the design of these labyrinthine tunnels and the location of the many chambers—information that is passed to him, during the ceremony of coronation, in a letter sealed by the previous king—it is a tradition among the kings of Cornwall to reveal parts of the design to one or more trusted companions, who are sworn to secrecy; and so complex is the pattern of these intersecting passages, many of which lead nowhere, that it would be impossible for a single mind to hold them in memory, even if, as is certainly not the case, the passages corresponded faithfully to the information contained in the sealed letter. In the course of the twenty-four years of his reign, the King has taken me a score of times into the labyrinth; and on several of those occasions, he has invited the steward or Tristan to accompany us.

The passages are entered through concealed openings in four of the castle's twelve towers. Narrow spaces between blocks of stone are hidden behind painted wall hangings. The stones on each side of the narrow space are hollow and are pierced by an iron rod that permits them to be turned; they then form an opening wide enough for a single man to enter.

Some of the small chambers contain locked chests in which are stored royal documents, deeds, treaties, lists of vassals. Others are storerooms containing old hauberks, battered helmets, crossbows, piles of swords, fifty-pound rocks for defensive catapults. Still other chambers are empty, or house mysterious objects, such as the decayed robes of a vanished queen or a small casket containing the bones of a child; and it is said that there are passages and chambers no one has ever seen, hidden in the depths of our mighty walls.

Three days ago, as I was climbing the winding stairs of the southwest tower on my way to the wall walk, where I wished to stretch my legs and look out from the battlements at the clear sky and the dark forest stretching away, I heard above me the sound of hushed, urgent voices, coming from what I knew to be a recessed window not yet in sight, which looked down at the courtyard. I hesitated, stopped; one of the voices was that of the steward, with its clipped, overprecise syllables, and the other was the Queen's. "Tomorrow," Oswin was saying. "Very well, very well," I heard her say, with a kind of impatient weariness. I prepared to make my presence known, thought better of it, and withdrew quietly.

I disliked the hushed tones, the sound of irritable acquiescence in the Queen's voice, above all the word "tomorrow," for the King had announced that he would be hunting all day and would not return before nightfall. Once in my chamber I considered whether to keep the steward under close surveillance—

several household servants act for me as spies, when I have reason to think the King's interest might be well served in this manner—but I decided to send first for Brangane.

We met at the wicker gate of the King's garden. I opened the gate for her and led her past beds of white and red roses to a turf bench beside the fountain of leopards. I had last spoken with her in the dark, and in the sharp light of day she surprised me; she seemed timid and mistrustful, like a child accused of stealing an apple. I came to the point quickly. I swore her to secrecy, reported what I had overheard, and asked whether she knew anything she might wish me to know.

She hesitated, then turned to me with an almost angry look. "The steward follows us—everywhere. I don't like him."

"And the Queen?"

"The Queen hates him—but doesn't fear him."

"And you fear him?"

She looked at me with contempt. "I fear for my lady." She paused. "He wants to show her something—a place he speaks of. A bower."

"And she goes tomorrow?"

"After morning mass, when the King hunts."

"Thank you." I stood up. "I will have him watched."

"The Queen is in danger?"

"All will be well."

She stood up and followed me to the wicker gate. "Thank you," she said simply, looking at me with eyes that partly thanked and partly searched me.

When I returned to my chamber I sent for one of the steward's servants, whose life I had once saved and who performed for me small favors from time to time. Behind my thick oak door, double-barred, I asked him to watch his master closely and report to me any action of a suspect or unusual kind.

The steward, a rigorously correct but secretive man, was the subject of a number of rumors, one of which concerned a grotto or bower said to be located deep within the labyrinth of passages in the castle wall. There he was said to amass treasure stolen from the household, to seduce male and female servants, and to practice magical arts.

After supper I sat with the assembled company in the hall and listened distractedly to the songs of a visiting Breton minstrel in a feathered cap before climbing the stairway to my chamber. At the door I found Oswin's servant waiting for me. Once within he reported that directly after supper the steward had crossed the courtyard to the sixth tower, where in a storage chamber on the ground floor he had moved aside a painted cloth picturing a deer and disappeared.

I instructed him to keep his master under close watch and to report to me any movements or actions that concerned the Queen. I then returned to the King, who was still seated beside the Queen at the royal board, and with whom I requested a word in private. The King led me up to his bedchamber and barred the door. I was deliberately mysterious, for I knew his immoderate love of hunting. I implored him not to join the hunt tomorrow but to let it go forward without him and to meet me secretly in my chamber. The King, displeased by the prospect of a delayed hunt, but scenting adventure, impatiently agreed. Suddenly he leaned forward, seized me by the shoulder, and said, "You have something to tell me, Thomas."

"Tomorrow," I replied, and it was as if I were on the stair again, overhearing Oswin as he said: "Tomorrow."

I returned to my chamber, where I lay wondering what the next day would bring.

In the early morning, directly after chapel, I climbed the stairs to my chamber to await the King. His hunting party had left at dawn. When he entered I saw at once that his mood was dangerous, wavering between curiosity and irritation. He paced restlessly, went to the window, which looked down upon the courtyard, sat on my bed, continued pacing. "Well, Thomas!" he cried. "And why have you imprisoned me in my own castle?" The image pleased him, distracted him. He pretended that he was the victim of a plot: I was scheming to usurp the crown. He often assumed a playful air of this kind, attributing to me secret designs, but today the tone was a little wrong, there was an edge in his playfulness; he did not like to miss his hunt. I was about to reveal the conversation I had overheard between Oswin and the Queen when the King said from the window, "One of Oswin's lads is running this way."

The servant appeared breathless at my doorway, reporting that Oswin had just led the Queen under the deer.

I hurried with the King down the stairway and across the courtyard to the sixth tower. The painted linen hanging pictured a white hind attacked by a greyhound biting into a foreleg. A bright red gash showed in the flank. On the opposite wall a torch burned in an iron ring. Under the hanging I turned the stones. Quickly I lifted the torch from its ring and led the King into a narrow black passage.

The path was strewn with small stones. I walked ahead of the King, holding high the sputtering smoky torch. Sparks scattered in the dark like handfuls of flung sand. The walls were so close that our mantles brushed the rough rock; bits of mortar and chipped stone sifted down. On the path I stepped on something soft that scampered squeaking into the dark.

Behind me I heard a shrill scrape of iron against stone— the King had drawn his sword, and in the narrowness of the passage his blade had dragged against the wall. As I turned with my torch, I saw the gleaming blade held out before me. A rat hung from the sword-tip. Dark blood dripped onto the ground. He shook the creature off—it landed with the sound of a dropped sack.

The King sheathed his sword fiercely, looking up in angry surprise as the blade again scraped against the wall.

As we continued forward I noticed that side paths had begun to appear, some wide enough to enter and some no broader than a sword blade; all at once we came to a branching of the main path. It was impossible to know which passage to follow. "This way," I whispered, turning in to the broader way. Soon another branch appeared; and after a time I understood not only that I had forgotten the many branchings and forkings of these secret paths, but that I was leading the King deeper and deeper into a maze that might be taking us farther and farther from the steward.

The King, sensing my doubt, had begun to question me in urgent whispers, when a shout or cry sounded in the dark. I turned in the direction of the cry, which seemed to come from behind us; and following the King, who strode boldly forward with drawn sword held upright like a torch, I found myself on a broadening path covered with sweet-smelling rushes. The path led to a stout-looking oak door set in an arch. Muffled sounds came from behind the door; something appeared to have fallen. "Open!" cried the King as he rattled the iron handle. "In the name of the King!" Behind the door I heard an iron bar slide back through iron rings. The King pushed the door open and I stepped behind him into a flickering chamber hung with silks and lit by many candles resting on corbels on the walls.

Tristan stood with drawn sword over the supine body of

Oswin, who lay at his feet staring fearfully up at the sword at his throat. Beside Tristan stood the Queen, staring coldly, clinging to Tristan's arm.

"You must guard the Queen more wisely, Uncle," Tristan said, leading her to the King.

In one corner of the chamber stood a bed with gilt bedposts hung with crimson curtains. On a small table stood a gold goblet of wine and a basket of glimmering grapes. A second goblet lay on its side. Above the table the ceiling was decorated with intertwisted vines, whose gold and silver leaves glittered in the flamelight.

The King looked at Oswin lying on the ground, at Tristan standing over him, at the motionless Queen. In the candlelight the King's eyes were dark as stones.

"Tristan!" he cried, sheathing his sword violently and holding out his arms to receive Tristan in a fierce embrace. Tears cut the King's cheeks like streaks of blood.

Dawn is breaking. I cannot write another word.

I seize these few moments to finish the narrative begun in my last entry.

We returned from Oswin's Bower to the light of day, where three events took place: the Queen retired to the royal bedchamber, Oswin was led away by a guard to the tower prison, and the King and Tristan and I climbed the stairs of the northwest tower to the King's private chamber, where Tristan told his tale.

He had received a message from Brangane, warning him of Oswin's invitation to the Queen. Queen Ysolt, who disdained the steward and therefore did not sense danger, had agreed to accompany Oswin into the depths of the wall, where he proposed to show her his secret bower. Brangane had supplied her with a dagger which she concealed in her robes. Tristan, who had heard tales of Oswin's Bower, and who in any case distrusted the steward as a companion for the Queen, returned to the castle disguised as a Breton minstrel—the very minstrel in a feathered cap who had played for the assembled company on the evening when I returned to my chamber to find the steward's servant at my door. That night, Tristan made his way under the white hind and through the labyrinth of passages to the bower, where he concealed himself in Oswin's bed. In the black chamber buried in the depths of the wall he could hear nothing, not even the crowing of the cocks. The sudden jangle of keys was like the ring of a hammer in the forge. Candle flames leaped up. Oswin spoke to the Queen of his bower, which he called a garden of delights. He described the shaping of the vines and leaves in the shop of a goldsmith, and showed her several precious objects that he explained in detail, such as a silver drinking cup lined with gold, a copper figurine playing a silver trumpet, and a pen case of walrus ivory carved in relief with human-headed beasts. He offered her grapes and wine. The Queen asked to leave. "But I must show you the bed, a work of great cunning," Oswin said. When the Queen refused, he seized her arm and attempted to lead her toward the bed by force. At that instant the curtains opened and Tristan sprang out, sword in hand. Oswin started back in terror. He struck the table, knocking over the goblet of wine, and fell to the tiled floor. A moment later the King's voice cried out, "Open!"

There were many things in this narrative to disturb the King—how, for example, had Brangane discovered Tristan's place of exile, and did the Queen know of it too?—but he listened closely, asked no questions, and at the end thanked Tristan warmly.

The next morning the King met in Council with his advisers and chief barons, who were divided over the question of punishment for Oswin. Some urged death by hanging, others demanded that the steward be blinded for the crime of looking upon the Queen lasciviously, and still others pleaded for mercy because of the steward's record of long and honorable service to the crown. In the end the King took a middle course: he ordered that one of Oswin's eyes be put out, as a warning to the second eye, and that the steward be confined in the tower prison, his duties and privileges to be assumed by the understeward, John de Beaumont.

The King praised Tristan as a protector of the realm and a true and loyal knight.

After the Council, a festive dinner was held in the late morning, in celebration of Tristan's return. The feast began with a boar's head decorated with red and green banners, and there followed peacocks and plovers, cranes and suckling pigs, platters of swans roasted in their feathers. Pears spitting out juice turned slowly over the hearth fire. The Queen sat at the King's left hand, Tristan at his right. All the court could see the King turning his head from one to the other, his eyes shining, his face eloquent with affection.

In the afternoon the King gave up his hunt to walk in his garden with the Queen and Tristan. Afterward, in the King's bedchamber, Tristan played the harp and drew tears from the King's eyes.

Games, songs, and dances are planned for the evening. It is said that two acrobats from Anjou will dance on balls while juggling apples.

The King hunts rapturously from early morning to nightfall, leaving the Queen and Tristan behind. More: he has requested Tristan to keep watch over the Queen, to remain in her company whenever possible, to guard and protect her, to cheer her when she is sad, to read to her from the royal chest of ivory-bound books, to play the harp for her. Tristan and the Queen are much alone.

Sometimes I see ladies exchange knowing glances, after the Queen and Tristan pass by.

This afternoon I overheard a baron speaking in a low voice to two admiring ladies. Does the King know what he is doing? the baron wondered. Does he understand that he is inviting his own betrayal?

To be satisfied with such questions—questions that naturally present themselves, and that seem to strike boldly at the innermost workings of the King's mind—is to reveal nothing but a courtier's worldly cleverness. In order to understand the King, we must be at once more simple and more devious. The King is by no means oblivious; he has not forgotten the rumors surrounding his wife and Tristan. But the King's love for Tristan runs deeper than his jealousy, and what he loves in Tristan is above all his trustworthiness, the purity of his honor. When the King leaves Tristan alone with the Queen, he is displaying to the world the drama of his deepest conviction: my wife is beautiful, my wife is desirable, but Tristan is true. Whisper, barons, whisper, world—but Tristan is honorable. The King is not ignorant of the whispers; he may even wish to encourage them, in order to sharpen his trust against them.

To say it another way, the King arranges opportunities for betrayal precisely because it cannot take place. In the same way, he does not arm himself before Tristan, for he knows that Tristan will not suddenly draw his sword and plunge it treacherously through his side.

These thoughts, in the pauses of my day, do not bring peace.

Last night the King reported to me a marvelous dream. He was standing in the middle of a dark chamber between two windows that faced each other. The windows were brilliant with light, but the light did not enter the room. He looked now at one, now at the other, and felt a great yearning to see the view. His body began to strain in both directions. With burning pain he felt himself ripping and tearing; there were sounds like breaking sticks. One half of his body moved toward one window, and one half toward the other. Blood, black and thick, poured from the open sides.

He did not ask me to interpret his dream.

Sometimes at night I hear, in Tristan's nearby chamber, the sound of the iron bar sliding back, scraping through rings of iron. I listen for the prolonged creak of the door, like the cry an animal might make if it had been turned to wood, and the pad of Tristan's footsteps as he leaves his chamber. Sooner or later I hear the more distant cry of another door; footsteps emerge from the King's bedchamber. The two pairs of footsteps move off together and vanish in the night.

Where do they go? Upstairs, through the women's quarters, to the Queen's private chamber? Across the courtyard into the Queen's garden or tower? Through the postern that leads out into the orchard?

And if the King should wake?

It cannot continue much longer. The King, clinging fiercely to Tristan's loyalty, but troubled by doubts and suspicions, studies his nephew's face sharply while contriving new occasions for disaster. Today the Queen and Tristan went hunting with the King and his barons. I too was of the party. The King, observing that the Queen grew tired, led her to one of his well-furnished hunting lodges, where he instructed her to remain with Tristan until he returned to fetch them at nightfall. The Queen protested; the King insisted. Scarcely had we ridden off when the King came to a halt and asked me to wait while he returned to ask something of the Queen. I waited in great uneasiness, dismounting and mounting again. Not long afterward the King came riding through the trees, looking displeased.

"Is the Queen well?" I called.

"After all," he cried back at me, "I did not wish to disturb her." He spurred his horse sharply and rode off in the direction of the hunt.

In the night the King came to me. I sat up in readiness, but he urged me to lie down, for he wished only to talk. He climbed into the bed and lay down beside me in the dark.

"Like old times, Thomas," he said, and I remembered the days when the young Prince would come to my chamber at night, to lie down beside me and speak his heart.

"In the night," the King began, "one can say anything."

"I know what the court is saying," he said.

"And yet," he continued, "it is absolutely right that they should wish to be together. Who dares to say no? Speak, Thomas."

"No one, my lord."

"I want Tristan to love her."

"Then all is well."

"All is not well. Rumors—touching upon my honor—the honor of my court—"

"You invite them to be alone."

"When she is with Tristan, she is with me."

"Then she is always with you."

"Tristan—Tristan would never shame me. He would die for me. Thomas! Speak from the heart."

I hesitated for the breath of an instant. "Tristan would die for you." It was true: Tristan would defend the King to the death.

I could hear the King breathing heavily in the dark. I thought of Tristan walking with the Queen in the orchard, their hands clasped, walking so slowly that they were scarcely moving.

The King seized my arm. "Thank you, Thomas." Within moments he had fallen asleep beside me, while I lay waking in the dark.

How much longer? Two days have passed since the King's night visit, and he is more suspicious than ever. This morning he announced that he would not go hunting, then suddenly changed his mind and rode off furiously, but returned at midday. He found the Queen alone with her companions in the women's quarters. Tristan was at the mews, training a young falcon to stand on his wrist.

The day before, when the King was hunting, I sent a message to Brangane. We met at the King's garden, in the shadow of the wall. I opened the wicker gate for her and led her to the turf bench beside the fountain of leopards. Gone was her timid and mistrustful look; she was now alert, expectant, tensely still. Her hands lay not quite crossed in her lap, one hand grasping the wrist of the other. There was no need for courteous indirection. I spoke of the rumors, and of the King's suspicions, and urged her to warn her mistress to be more careful—to avoid behavior that might give rise to talk.

She took it in thoughtfully—I imagined her turning over my words as if they were pieces of fruit she was examining for bruises—then turned to me sharply. "The Queen is in danger?"

"The Queen's reputation is in danger."

"The King sends you to say this?"

"I send myself."

She sat brooding there; then—"The Queen fears nothing."

Her vehemence surprised me. It was as if she were saying that everything was lost.

"It isn't a question of the Queen's courage," I said.

I waited for her to speak, but she only looked at me, waiting.

"But rather of her—honor."

"Honor comes from within," she declared, and rapped her breastbone with her knuckles.

I hadn't summoned the Queen's maid to discuss the fine points of honor. She must have felt something flash from my face, for she then said, "And the King believes these rumors? You believe them?"

"I don't know that he believes them. He dislikes their existence."

"So does the Queen," she said, looking at me as though in triumph.

"If you would urge her to be more careful—warn her—"

"And this warning is from—a friend?"

I considered it. "From someone who isn't an enemy."

She looked at me. "I will speak to her. The Queen—does as she likes."

I rose and accompanied her to the gate.

"The Queen—thanks you," she said, pausing for a moment as if she intended to say more, but instead turning abruptly into the courtyard.

What troubles me about this conversation is the unexpected image of the Queen. The Queen fears nothing? The Queen does as she likes? Suddenly the Queen has become a bold woman, scornful of authority, impatient with duty—a woman for whom a King is an irritating encumbrance—a woman who declares to her handmaid, as a hard-won truth wrung from experience, "Honor comes from within." Consider: the Queen has been thinking about honor. "Honor comes from within." What can this mean except: honor comes not from what I do, but from what I feel?

It is the philosophy of a dissolute baron.

And the King's honor? What of that?

It is difficult to reconcile this Ysolt, the fierce Ysolt sprung from the words of her handmaid beside the fountain of leopards, with that other Ysolt, the gentle, courteous, and mild Ysolt who has been growing slowly within me, like a pear tree in a walled garden.

I know nothing of the Queen.

But the Queen is wild! Is mad! She searches for Tristan eagerly, devours him with her eyes, hurries from the King's side to greet her darling Tristan. Is she feverish? Delirious? At the royal board she looks only at Tristan, leans in front of the King to

seize Tristan's glance. It is as if she wished to defy the King—
to provoke his wrath. Can this be the fruit of my warning to
Brangane?

Tristan is ill at ease. The King pretends to see nothing and
suddenly turns his head to look at the Queen, who impatiently
adjusts her gaze, searching beyond the edges of his face for
Tristan.

This morning I saw the King inclining his head to Modor
in the shade of the garden wall.

Shortly after noon, as I walked in the courtyard, Brangane
stepped out from the narrow alley between the wall of the
Queen's garden and the granary.

"I have spoken to her," she said simply.

"Did you tell her to mock the King?"

"She feels—she doesn't like to be accused."

"No one accuses her."

"She thinks you plot with the King against her."

"Splendid! You think so too?"

"I told her I thought—I believed—you can be trusted."

I was startled by a burst of gratitude, like a rush of wind.
Why should I care what these women thought of me?—I who
loved my King and would gladly have died for him.

"The King is unhappy," I then said.

Brangane looked at me as if waking from a trance. "We're
all unhappy!" she said; it was almost a cry. "Goodbye," she said,
and was gone.

As I sit at my table, writing these words in the light of a single candle, I can hear, through my partly open door and the
closed door of the royal chamber, the noises of love, a sudden
cry from Ysolt, silence. It is the second time this night. In
Tristan's chamber, two sounds: the scrape of a table leg, the
bang of a shutter thrown open or shut.

Sometimes a strange thought comes: to murder the lovers in their sleep, to destroy this ugly plague of love that causes nothing but ruin and despair.

It is even worse than I feared.

This morning the King called a meeting of his barons in the great hall. He announced that the rumors surrounding his wife and nephew were harmful to the honor of the court and the kingdom; that although he had no evidence of dishonor, it was plain to him, and to all the court, that his wife and nephew bore one another a love beyond that which was proper and fitting; that although it was within his power to exact punishment, he would not, for the love he bore both of them, take revenge, and demanded only that they leave the court together, to seek in another place the life denied them here; that he had tried to live in a fellowship of three—the King and Ysolt, Ysolt and Tristan, Tristan and the King—but that he could do so no longer, for he saw that they were against him, in a fellowship of two; and for the love he bore them, he wished them well.

This speech—which made a deep impression—struck me as most artful. The King, while speaking continually of the love that was in his heart, was at the same time driving from his castle, and from his protection, the objects of that love. He forgave them for the wrong they had done him, while by the decree of banishment he left no doubt that he had been terribly wronged. He sent them forth to live their lives together, lawfully, without interference from him, while letting it be known that those lives were so shameful that they could not be led at the Cornish court, bright home of honor, but only elsewhere, in some other world, invisibly.

The Queen, who stood beside the King during the entire performance, never once lowered her eyes.

The King has surprised me. He is cheerful, energetic, full of schemes. The absence of Tristan and the Queen, which I feared would be harmful to him, appears to have freed him from some impediment in his nature. He inspects the wall walks and gatehouse, consults with a visiting military engineer about defense catapults to be mounted on the towers, bestows a large gift on a Cistercian monastery, speaks with the chamberlain about new curtains for his bed and new tiles for his fireplace. Above all he oversees a burst of castle repairs and construction: carpenters extend the length of the stables, masons construct a new wall for the bake house, the old wooden granary has been torn down and in its place rises a sturdy building of dressed stone. In the chapel the cracked wooden statue of the Virgin, her right arm extended and one finger raised, has been replaced by a new statue in bright colors, while a sculptor repairs the wings of a stone angel.

The King has invited to the court an artificer, Odo of Chester, a monkish man remarkable for his long face, his long nose, his long thin fingers, and his large moist mournful eyes. On one of his fingers he wears a black stone carved in the shape of a tiny hand. Odo has brought with him a curious device: a wooden box with a small window and a handle on one side. When you look through the window you see a rural scene: a windmill, a stream, a tree, a barn. But turn the handle, and behold!—the windmill turns, the stream flows, the leaves of the tree shake in a breeze, the barn door opens and a cow steps out.

This toy is well liked by the ladies of the court.

The King spends many hours closeted with Odo of Chester in his tower chamber. They are preparing something; in the King's face I can read a quiet excitement.

The King has revealed his secret. I confess I was taken entirely by surprise.

In the early afternoon, directly after dinner, the King summoned me to the royal bedchamber, where I found him seated on a clothes chest speaking with Odo, who leaned back on a window seat with one long leg resting along the stone. Together with them I descended to the courtyard and passed the stables and the mews on our way to the King's tower. I had expected to climb to the privacy of the King's high chamber, but instead the King led us to the storage room on the ground floor, where in a dim corner behind a locked chest stands one of the four entrances to the inner labyrinth. The King supplied each of us with a small horn lantern, turned the stones, and led us into the castle wall. Like the passage that leads from beneath the white hind in the sixth tower, this one began to branch and turn. The King moved slowly but without hesitation, taking now one branch and now another, until he came to a small chamber hollowed out of the rock. A wooden bench with two silk cushions faced a wall, upon which hung a linen cloth painted with a likeness of the King in his crimson robe trimmed in ermine. On each side of the cloth, a small horn lantern hung from an iron ring on the wall. The King set down his lantern and sat on the bench, where he faced the cloth and motioned for me to sit beside him.

Odo—long, gaunt Odo, with his bony nose and his chin like the knob of a chicken bone—stood at one side of the wall hanging. Reaching up with his pale fingers, he pulled what appeared to be a cord concealed behind the edge of the cloth. Slowly the cloth divided, breaking the image of the King in half. The two cloths had been placed side by side so artfully that I had not been able to detect the jointure.

Behind the curtain stood the Queen. She stood very still, in her mantle of green samite trimmed with sable and ermine, fastened at the throat by a gold brooch. She wore a head covering and a white linen wimple. Her head was turned to one side, her lips parted slightly. Her right arm was raised and extended toward us; the finger beside the thumb was lifted a little, as if in supplication or admonition. Her cheeks and eyes shone in the dim light of all five lanterns. She was very lifelike. Only the turned head, the parted lips, the raised, extended arm with its lifted finger brought to mind the old wooden Virgin in the chapel. The face, half concealed by the wimple, had been powdered and vermilioned like the Queen's. Yellow hair showed beneath the head covering, which was held in place by a gold fillet set with emeralds and jacinths.

Now Odo reached behind the Queen and withdrew his hand. Slowly the extended arm rose higher; the head began to turn. She looked directly at us, her eyes large, tender, welcoming. The arm began to lower to its original position; slowly the head turned away. The Queen stood motionless with slightly parted lips.

When I turned to the King, he was unnaturally still. His arm was raised as if frozen in the act of reaching toward the

Queen, his head erect, his eyes wide, his lips parted as if in speech.

The King has released Oswin, who at once resumes his position as chief steward with all its privileges and powers. It is very strange. Perhaps the banishment of the Queen has rendered the steward's imprisonment superfluous. Another explanation is possible: the King, tormented by longing for the Queen, feels a kinship with the disgraced steward, who also has desired the Queen. Oswin wears a patch over his blinded eye and behaves with impeccable propriety. He meets no one's gaze, sits rigidly at the royal board, avoids the company of Modor, and tyrannizes over his servants, whom he punishes mercilessly for the most trivial faults.

Odo of Chester has departed for the court of the Count of Toulouse, where I have no doubt his art will be celebrated as a wonder of the age, while deep in the castle wall the King continues to visit the Queen in his secret chapel. I do not like these visits. Sometimes the King asks me to accompany him, in order to operate the curtain and the lever. Sometimes he visits the Queen alone. The visits take place suddenly, at any moment of the day or night. Last night, summoned by the King from sleep, I followed him to the chapel, where I drew open the curtain and pressed the lever concealed in the Queen's back. When I turned to the King, I saw him staring fixedly at the slowly moving Queen, his eyes wide and unblinking. He then began to make low sounds, a mumble of speech that alarmed me. "My lord," I said. The King seemed to awaken, and giving me one of his mischievous grins, which did not sit naturally on a face marked by sorrow and longing, he said, "Now tell me, Thomas. Isn't the Queen looking well?"

The King's sorrowing face, made oddly youthful by melancholy—the face of an unhappy boy.

No! My speculations have proved to be mistaken. The King's reason for releasing Oswin lies elsewhere.

This afternoon I was summoned by a royal messenger to the prison tower. I was admitted by the guard, who thrust back the double iron bar of the door. Inside it was so dark that at first I could see nothing. A single small window, the width of an arrow loop, sat high up on the wall. A shaft of sunlight, frenzied with silent dust, lay slantwise across the dark air and struck the middle of the opposite wall. On the wooden planks of the floor I made out a crude pallet of straw and, in one corner, an iron chamber pot. Against a dark wall sat the King. He was wearing his royal robes; his hair, not bound in a net, lay loose on his face.

"Sit, Thomas," he said. I immediately sat down beside him, on the bare floor.

"Assure them," he then said, gesturing vaguely with one arm, "that all is well."

"All is not well."

"All is as it must be. Only this: they feed me too well. Water and bread: you will speak to Hainault."

"There will be talk. The barons—"

"It is by my order. Let them know. Assure them, and they will be content. Your word, Thomas."

"You have my word. They will not be content."

"They will be less discontent."

I remembered my sharp-minded pupil, fourteen years old, sitting in his father's garden, battling with me over some question of logic. If each of the three persons of the Trinity has a real existence, how can it be maintained that God is a unity? If each of the three persons of the Trinity does not have a real existence, in what sense are they three?

A sudden flutter startled me. I leaped to my feet with drawn sword. In the deep dusk of the chamber I saw the King's raven, settling on his knee. I felt uneasy—even ashamed—standing in the half-dark above my King, holding a sword.

"Let me leave my sword," I pleaded.

"Prisoners have no swords."

"And if it had been a rat?"

"Then I should have made him an archbishop, to absolve me of my sins."

"The court misses you."

"Court? There is no court. Here is my court: three spiders, a raven, and a fly. Am I not richer than the King of Cornwall, who rules nothing but an empty kingdom?"

"My lord—"

"I am tired, Thomas."

Outside the prison door I instructed the guard to observe the King closely and inform me in detail about his diet, his health, his words, his movements—his thoughts, I wished to say. I then returned to my chamber.

The King has ordered his own imprisonment. Evidently he desires to punish himself, but the reason behind his desire is less clear. Does he feel that he must punish himself because he has wronged the Queen and Tristan by banishing them without proof, with nothing to justify his judgment but suspicion and rumor? Or is there a less elementary explanation? The King is suffering because he cannot live without the Queen and Tristan. By having himself imprisoned, he isn't so much punishing himself as finding a way to display his suffering, to give it a definite and recognizable shape.

There is yet another possibility. The King, heavily burdened by the duties of kingship, longs for the purity of a suffering that eludes him. Freed by imprisonment from the distractions that prevent him from suffering enough, at liberty to enter his unhappiness as completely as he can, does the King sometimes feel, in his new kingdom, a dark consolation, a secret joy?

The royal bedchamber is empty. The King is in prison, Tristan and the Queen have been banished into the realm of faery, the castle tosses in its sleep—and I, Thomas of Cornwall, sit at my table before a sheet of smooth-scraped parchment, dipping my quill in ink blacker than night, writing words that gleam for a moment in the light of my candle like drops of black blood.

For six days the King has remained his own prisoner, sleeping on straw, eating crusts of bread, seeing no one. The knight entrusted with the King's care reports that the King moves very little, standing only to cross the small room to another wall, where he sits with his great head bowed. He has asked for his crown, which he wears like a heavy punishment. Sometimes he removes the crown to strike weakly at a rat. His eyes, when he opens them, are unusually large above his hollow cheeks. He stares emptily, looking at nothing. Mostly he sleeps.

. . .

On the ninth day of the King's self-imprisonment, a knight came striding into the great hall, while we were at supper. This was his story.

He had been hunting in the Forest de la Roche Sauvage, some three leagues from the King's forest, when, pursuing a stag, he crossed a stream and entered a thicker and wilder part of the woods, where he made his way with difficulty among the trees. In the near distance he saw a small clearing with a rude hut. As he drew closer to the clearing, the door of the hut opened and a man stepped out. He recognized Tristan. The knight, abandoning all thought of the hunt, spurred his horse toward our castle.

I informed the King, who upon hearing the news rose unsteadily to his feet. Leaning on my shoulder, he left his wretched cell and returned with me to the royal bedchamber.

Tomorrow, despite his weakened condition, he insists on leading a hunting party into the Forest de la Roche Sauvage.

I will try to record only the most important events of this memorable day.

The King, refreshed by nourishment and sleep, but still seriously weakened after his nine days in the tower, rose at dawn, attended mass at the chapel, ate a breakfast of bread and ale, and ordered our party to depart. Except for a moment of faintness immediately after he mounted his horse, he sat erect in the saddle; I marveled at the return of his strength, while at the same time I had the uneasy sense that he was animated less by physical vitality than by the unnatural glow of a devouring fervor. In the Forest de la Roche Sauvage—named for the bare crag rising at its eastern extremity—our party of two dozen broke into pairs. Each man carried an ivory hunting horn, which he was to sound at the first sign of Tristan or the Queen. I rode with the King.

It is possible to ride for days in the Forest de la Roche Sauvage without coming to a clearing. Sometimes the growth is so thick that one can ride no farther; here and there among the oaks and pines stand towering tangles of thorn, with immense black spikes the size of spear points. The King's proud face, with its still-gaunt cheeks, had begun to show signs of weariness. Urging my own tiredness, I persuaded him to dismount and sit with me on the mossy roots of a massive oak, through whose dark and prickly leaves only small pieces of blue sky were visible.

A white brachet hound, which had accompanied us on our journey, sniffed about as we sat against the broad trunk. The King, settling back, half closed his eyes. Suddenly the brachet darted off after a rabbit, disappeared into the undergrowth, and was gone.

This was one of the King's favorite hounds. He called out to it, then rose with a sigh to fetch it back. I followed him through trees growing so close that no horse could have entered. The undergrowth thickened, ferns as long as sword blades thrust up, and suddenly we came to a small opening in the trees. Before us stood a peasant's hut. It had a roof of thatch and a frame of rough timber, filled in with clay over a weave of branches that poked through here and there.

The King placed his hand on his sword, and I followed him across the sun and shade of the clearing to the single small window in the side of the hut.

On an earthen floor covered with rushes, the Queen and Tristan lay asleep on their mantles. They were fully clothed, in tunic and surcoat, and lay facing each other so that their mouths were no more than a hand's width apart. Between them on the blanket lay Tristan's naked sword. A ray of sunlight, coming through the window, lay slantwise along the dark, striking the Queen's cheek, the tip of the sword, and Tristan's shoulder.

The King watched for a long time as the two lay there breathing gently. A wisp of the Queen's hair stirred in Tristan's breath.

I looked at the King's face, with its terrible tumult of despair and joy, and turned my face away.

Raising a finger to his lips, the King drew his sword and made his way stealthily around the hut toward the door. Through the little window I watched the door open. The King stepped over to the sleeping pair and stood looking down at them with his sword held out as if in readiness. Then he bent over, carefully lifted Tristan's sword, and laid his own sword between them.

He looked down at Tristan and the Queen lying side by side, the sun on her cheeks, wisps of her hair stirring in Tristan's breath. For a moment I had the strange sensation that he was going to lie down beside them. Then he turned and made his way out of the room, into the clearing.

Not until we returned to our horses did the King speak. "Lovers lie naked," he said. At a nearby rustling he whirled, gripping Tristan's sword.

It was only the white brachet, bursting through the undergrowth, its tail wagging wildly, its coat matted with burrs.

Lovers lie naked; the Queen and Tristan are innocent. Between them the sword: the very sign and symbol of that innocence. Tristan and the Queen, wronged by jealousy and evil rumors, flee to the dark forest, where he watches over her like a brother. When she bathes in a stream, he stands guard beside the water, his sword drawn, his eyes scanning the woods for danger. At night they remove only their mantles. The sword lies between them when they sleep.

How deeply, in order to believe this, the King must have suffered.

There is great rejoicing in the castle. In the high hall the tables and benches are removed for games and dancing; minstrels sing the adventures of Arthur and Gawain. Tristan and the Queen have returned!—summoned by the King, pardoned in Council, welcomed before the entire court. The King's laughter rings out among the revelers. Tristan sits at his right hand, the Queen at his left; he looks from one to the other joyously. It is as if we were celebrating the visit of a young prince and his bride.

He has given them freedom to go and come as they like. Indeed, the King has asked the Queen to stay close to Tristan, whenever he himself is not with her. As the days pass, the King absents himself more and more, hunting with his knights and barons in the royal forest beyond the orchard. One has the impression that he is abandoning the Queen to Tristan by day, in exchange for the Queen in his bed at night.

They, for their part, do not devour each other with adoring looks but behave with modesty and discretion, as befits the King's wife and nephew. It is true that the Queen, accompanied by Tristan, occasionally visits the women's quarters, or her walled garden, but these absences are of such short duration that they cause puzzlement rather than slander. It is almost as if, since their return from the Forest de la Roche Sauvage, the Queen and Tristan had agreed to remain apart from each other, in order to demonstrate their gratitude to the King.

Is it possible that something has changed between them?

Stranger and stranger. A week has passed, and the Queen and
Tristan continue to behave with a circumspection so complete
that it becomes difficult to think of them as lovers at all. He is
gentle toward the Queen, listens with interest to all that she
says to him, smiles mildly, is perhaps a little pensive. At supper
he speaks vigorously with the King, throws back his head in
laughter. Has their ardor cooled? Did they enjoy each other so
ferociously in the Forest de la Roche Sauvage that they are now
content to be only amicable? Is it possible that they were never
what they seemed to be, that the rumors have been false from
the beginning?

Even the King is aware of the change that has come over
them. He studies their faces, unable to surprise a surreptitious
glance, a revelatory pallor. They are gentle and innocent as
children. Sometimes Tristan goes hawking with the King, while
the Queen plays the harp or embroiders among her companions in the women's quarters.

The King, who was unable to bear the ardent looks of the
lovers, is made uneasy by this new decorum.

At night the King makes love to the Queen in the royal bedchamber. No longer do I hear the sound of the creaking oak
door, or the pad of footsteps stealing from Tristan's chamber.

A great peace has come over the castle.

I have it! I have it! A small incident occurred this morning, which revealed to me, in one of those sudden bursts of
understanding—sharp as a smell—swift as a sword thrust—
precise as a scarlet oriflamme against an azure sky—but whence

these rhapsodic flourishes, highly unpleasing in an old knight scarred in battle? Calmly, Thomas.

It happened late this afternoon at supper, directly after grace. The King had returned from his hunt somewhat earlier than usual, and sat in his carved chair at the head of the table, with the Queen at his left side and Tristan at his right. Suddenly he reached out both arms and seized the Queen's hand and Tristan's hand, looking at each of them in turn with a gaze of ardent affection. He released their hands and turned his attention to the pantler, who was approaching with a platter of bread and butter. At that moment the Queen and Tristan exchanged a look so rapid that it was less a look than the failure of a look, less a look than a pause in a gaze directed elsewhere—but in that flicker of a glance, in that shadow of a pause, I understood, in a flash of feeling that made my skin warm, the history of their enigmatic behavior. I saw in that glance a satisfaction, as if they were acknowledging the successful operation of a plan—a plan that was luminously clear to me. They had agreed, in the strength of their rapturous love, to abstain for a while from amorous dallying, out of pity for the King. It was as if they were so sure of themselves, after the Forest de la Roche Sauvage, that they could bear to be obedient.

Does the King understand they are being kind to him? Is this the source of his uneasiness?

The King cannot conceal his discontent. It is possible of course that he imagines a trick of some kind, as if the resourceful lovers were deceiving him in a new way. Or does he sense the terrible strength of a love that permits itself such denials?

In the morning, after chapel, the King and I took a walk in the courtyard. We stopped at the mews, to see a new gyrfalcon from Norway that is said to be faster than any of our hawks. Inside we found Tristan, standing in the dusky light with a hooded merlin on his wrist. The King and Tristan spoke for a few moments about the new gyrfalcon, which the falconer was training in the field beside the orchard. The King then urged Tristan to visit the Queen, who was with her companions in the women's quarters. Tristan hesitated and said he had promised to be present at the training of the new gyrfalcon, after which, if the King desired it, he would visit the Queen. The King strongly repeated his request. Tristan placed his bird on a perch, bowed his head lightly, and set off slowly for the women's quarters.

Does the King fear their abstinence, suspecting it to be the sign of a love higher than his own? Or is it that, although he cannot bear to be betrayed, he can bear even less the shame of being spared?

The King's bizarre behavior continues. Does he wish to hurl Tristan into the arms of the Queen?

Tonight as I lay in bed I heard the sound of the bar sliding back in the door of the royal bedchamber. Footsteps—unmistakably the King's—moved directly to Tristan's chamber. A knock, a sliding bar, low voices. Two sets of footsteps—the King's and Tristan's—departed from his room and entered the royal chamber. What could it mean?

I must have drifted into sleep, for when I woke I saw the light of a candle flickering on the ceiling above my drawn bed curtains. Suddenly the curtains rattled open and I saw the King's face, bending toward me. His eyes were excited and impatient. I swung my legs over the side of the bed, threw a mantle over my nakedness, and followed the King into the royal bedchamber.

In the dark, lit only by the candle, I saw Tristan lying on his back on the floor. One arm was flung out; his eyes were closed. I turned in alarm to the King, who stood over the immobile body of his nephew as if in a trance; by the light of the candle I bent over fearfully for a closer look. Tristan's eyes opened. He looked at me without surprise, smiled frankly, then sprang up, with the swift grace that has always been his, and stood before the King.

Tristan spoke in a whisper. "The Queen is sleeping soundly, my lord."

The King appeared to be waking from a dream. He turned his face toward me, while continuing to gaze at Tristan, and said in a low voice, "The Queen was having nightmares. I thought perhaps Tristan—"

Seated now at my table, I write these lines hastily. How much longer can these disturbances continue? Disorder in the bedchamber, division in the castle, unease in the kingdom. I fear for the King, fear for Tristan. They are playing a dangerous game that cannot end well. The King, feigning concern for his wife, invites Tristan into the royal bed; Tristan lies chastely on the floor. Move and countermove, trap and escape. Where will it end? Must sleep now.

I ask myself: why did the Queen and Tristan return to the castle? Is it that their idyll in the forest was born in secrecy and could not survive secrecy's end? But surely they might have fled to another forest, in another kingdom. You forget, Thomas, that the King summoned them. Why then did they obey? Can it be that, even as they betray the King, they remain loyal subjects whose deepest impulse is obedience?

Another explanation presents itself. The love of Tristan and the Queen has always flowed around and against the King. Banished from the court, alone in the forest, did they find themselves sometimes thinking of him? Were they growing a little restless, there in the forest? In order for their love to flourish—in order for them to love at all—do they perhaps need the King?

A brilliant stroke! The King has summoned the Queen and Tristan before his Council, and in the presence of his leading barons has praised them for putting slander to rest by their exemplary behavior. Since their return to court, he said, they have in all things been obedient to the royal will, and anyone guilty of words touching upon the honor of his house will be punished swiftly.

By this speech the King has accomplished two things. He has transformed the lovers' freely chosen abstinence, which galls him and provokes him at every instant, into an act of obedience to the royal will. But hidden within his praise is a second, darker, and more brilliant stratagem.

The King divines, with the keenness of a sharpened jealousy, that the Queen and Tristan are not obedient—that although they play the game of renunciation, at the hidden center of their renunciation is the opposite of self-denial: an utter abandonment of themselves to each other. For if, in the fullness of their triumphant love, they delude themselves into a concern for the King's well-being, if they take pleasure in obedience, if they savor the delights of renunciation, in truth they renounce nothing, they obey no one, they are bound to each other above all earthly and heavenly things. And because the King divines this, which they themselves have not yet divined, swept up as they are in their little drama of renunciation, the King has seized an advantage in the dangerous game all three are playing.

Baffled at every turn, outwitted time and again in his effort to find evidence of a betrayal he cannot bear to know, the King has discovered, as if by following some impulse deep in his being, the one way likely to accomplish the end he dreads and longs for.

The King watches. The court goes about its pleasures. Tristan and the Queen are the very picture of propriety. Nothing changes.

And yet I ask myself: is there not a change? It is like a summer day, a day like all other summer days, except that you feel, hidden in the heat of high afternoon, the first chill of autumn. Besides, there are signs.

I have noticed a new wariness between the Queen and Tristan. When they are together, they are no longer at ease: they avoid each other's eyes a little too carefully, stand a little farther apart than before. The King's speech before the Council has clearly taken them by surprise. They detect in it a threat that they haven't yet been able to unmask.

The Queen, especially, seems tired and somewhat strained. Each night she obediently performs her conjugal duty in the royal bed. Each day she bows her head at mass, dines at the

King's left hand, walks among her ladies. Where is Tristan? What has become of their passion in the forest? Her life is a masque, a play. Everything vital in her is hidden.

Today, as I walked in the courtyard past the kitchen and the bake house, Brangane stepped from around a corner and pressed a note into my hand. I had not spoken with her since the banishment of the Queen and Tristan. When I looked up from the note, she was gone. I was to meet her in the Queen's tower chamber after the bells tolled noon. The Queen would not be present.

In the sun-warmed chamber, aswirl with glittering dust motes, Brangane barred the door and turned to me. Her face looked worn, her eyes heavy; in the warm, agitated light, she looked as if she were growing old.

"The Queen is unhappy," she said.

"The Queen"—I hesitated, choosing my words carefully— "has many reasons for happiness."

There flashed from her a look—of disappointment, of disdain—that made me hate my courtier's smooth phrases, even as I watched her youth come rushing in.

"Why," I asked sharply, goaded by her look, "did she return to the castle?"

"The King summoned her."

"She obeys the King?"

She hesitated for only a moment. "She has always obeyed the King."

"Always?"

She looked at me boldly. "At her marriage she kneeled before the King as her lord. She left when the King banished her. She returned when he called her back."

I had forgotten Brangane's quickness. What she said was true enough, for that matter. I was turning over my reply when she said, "It was Tristan who urged her to return."

"Because they had been discovered?"

"For the sake of her honor."

I tried to imagine Tristan waking beside the Queen in the forest, seeing the King's sword.

"Her honor is now restored." Even as I spoke I regretted the barely suppressed scorn of those words, but Brangane had already leaped past them.

"I know her. I know Ysolt the Fair. I fear—" She paused.

"You fear she may do something?"

"I fear her unhappiness," she said tiredly. Then: "The King watches her."

"The King loves her."

She ignored me. "You are close to the King. You know where he goes—when he goes—"

"You're asking me to spy on the King?"

She looked at me with impatience. "I am asking you to see that no harm comes to anyone." Already she was moving toward the door.

Only after she had left did it strike me that what she was asking wasn't that I observe the King carefully, but that I report his movements to her, so that the Queen might be at liberty to—do as she liked.

At supper the King turned to me in a burst of boyish good spirits and cried, "Thomas! Why so melancholy?" I was about to answer lightly when I noticed the Queen looking at me. In that proud and sorrowing gaze I felt a confusion come over me, I could not speak, it was as if the word "melancholy" were opening inside me like a black blossom, until lowering my gaze to the edge of my plate I stared down like an awkward child, and I don't know what would have happened if the King, still in high spirits, hadn't suddenly cried out, "Tristan! A song for melancholy Thomas!" whereupon I recovered sufficiently to raise my eyes to Tristan, who was staring at the Queen.

The King, whose passion for the hunt can no longer be suppressed, has asked me to watch over the Queen in his absence. By this he means that I am to follow the Queen and Tristan everywhere. The King will leave tomorrow at daybreak and return at nightfall.

I have informed Brangane of the King's plans.

When she tried to thank me, my head felt suddenly hot, and I became filled with such rage that I could neither see nor hear. I was aware only that she had drawn her head back, as if I had struck her in the face.

Where to begin?

In the heat of the noonday sun, I sometimes like to walk in the King's garden. The white roses and red roses in their beds, the heartsease and columbine, the interlaced branches of the beech trees on the sanded paths, the leaden birdbath with its dark image of a falcon rising from the center, the arbor of purple grapes, the splash of the fountain from which water pours through the mouths of four stone leopards—all this soothes the troubled mind, soothes the body itself, which, like a tired animal, seeks out hidden and quiet places where it might lie down in the coolness of dark green shade. Here and there stand benches covered in soft turf, but I wandered into the thickest part of the garden, near the far wall. Among the fruit trees I lay down on the grass. The stone wall rose high above; through the green leaves and twisting branches I could see scarcely any sky. The King was hunting in the forest. The Queen had retired with her ladies. In the stillness of the garden I closed my eyes.

When I opened my eyes I saw the King's face bending close to mine. I could not at first account for this. The King, I thought, had come to lie down beside me in the shade of the garden, as he used to do, in the days of his boyhood, when he liked to lie on his back in the grass and ask whether, in addition to each individual tree, there was a substance named "Tree" that had a real existence, and, if so, how that "Tree" differed from the particular tree before us. Then it struck me that I must be dreaming, since the King was hunting in the forest. But already I knew that I was not dreaming, the King's face was sharp with urgency, his eyes fierce and sorrowful. He shook me roughly. "Thomas!" As I rose and began to follow him I had the sensation that the green shade, the paths, the fountain, the roses, the stillness of the hour—all were fading and dissolving behind me, like those images that stand hard and brilliant in the mind and, as the eyes open, waver and grow dim.

He led me across the courtyard to the Queen's tower, from which a narrow door opened into her walled garden.

I followed him along a sanded path shaded by a row of almond and walnut trees growing on one side. We passed a fish pond, a small herb garden of sage, hyssop, marjoram, and rue, square beds of roses and marguerites, a grove of hawthorn trees. Here and there in the garden wall I saw recesses with turf seats shaded by branches on lattice frames. Toward the northwest corner stood a tall hedge, higher than my head, with an opening shaped like an archway. As the King stepped through the opening he drew his sword. Behind him I entered the hedge, passed along the sharply turning paths of a maze with hedgerows on both sides, and came at last to a grove of fruit trees, beyond which rose the garden wall.

Under a pear tree lay Tristan and the Queen, asleep. They lay on white linen, beneath a red silk coverlet brocaded with gold lions. In the green shade they lay mouth to mouth, embracing. The coverlet was partly cast aside, revealing their naked arms and upper bodies. The Queen's breasts were pressed against Tristan's breast. What startled me was the Queen's hair, unbound, naked, wild, like some yellow eruption, pouring along her shoulder, bursting over Tristan, burning along the coverlet.

They were breathing quietly. I could not bear to look at the King's face.

The King bent toward me and whispered harshly, "We must find witnesses." He turned and strode away.

I withdrew my dagger and crept up to the sleeping pair. As I bent over Tristan, I imagined someone watching from a tree: the murder in the garden. Carefully I laid the dagger with its jeweled handle across his naked neck. Then I rose and followed the King through the hedge paths.

Why did the King leave? He left because, although he had caught them red-handed, and had every right to kill them on the spot, he had so long imagined this very scene that it must have struck him as familiar, unsurprising, perhaps a little disappointing. He left because, from the instant he saw them, he entered an unhappiness so deep that nothing could relieve him. He left because he was a just King who, although he had caught his wife and nephew lying naked under a pear tree, did not wish to condemn them to death unfairly, in the anger of the moment and in the presence of a single witness known to be his friend, for there might, even now, be an explanation that had not occurred to him and that would reveal them to be innocent. He left because he could not bear a life without the Queen, without Tristan. He left because, although he wished to return with his barons and murder the lovers in their bed, he also wished to offer them a chance to escape. He left because his heart was broken. He left because, in the first instant of seeing them there, before the knowledge of their treachery entered his heart, he had experienced a kind of awe before the beauty of Tristan, the beauty of Ysolt, two lovers under a pear tree, in a garden, out of this world.

These were my thoughts as I followed the King through the hedgerows and back across the garden to the door in the tower.

Inside the door, Modor stepped from the shadows. He had drawn his little sword, which he held high in his excitement. "You saw them!" he cried, his face savage with glee.

The King, uttering a cry, struck with his sword. The blow severed Modor's hand cleanly from his wrist. Modor gave a high, unpleasant scream and bent over violently with his bleeding stump pressed against his stomach. I looked at the little hand lying palm upward on the floor beside the fallen sword, which lay quite close to it. Modor, shrieking like a child, stumbled away into the shadows.

As he strode toward the great hall to fetch witnesses, the King told me that Modor had ridden out to the forest with the news that he had seen the Queen and Tristan go into the garden. From a ladder at the top of the garden wall the dwarf had watched them lie down under the pear tree.

When we returned to the garden in the company of four barons, we found the Queen lying alone under the tree, with the coverlet up to her neck. In terror she looked up at the six of us standing over her with drawn swords. It was evident she expected to be murdered.

The barons looked at the King. The King looked at the Queen. Without a word, he turned and headed back out of the garden.

No longer does the King leave the castle. He walks in his garden, shuts himself up alone in his tower, stares unblinking in the chapel, presides in silence at dinner beside the silent Queen. Sometimes he stands on the wall walk, looking out over the battlements. Only at meals and at morning mass is he seen with the Queen. They never look at each other.

She, for her part, spends much time in the women's quarters, embroidering among her companions, or in her tower chamber, with its window looking down upon her garden.

At night, in the royal chamber, the King takes his pleasure of the Queen. But can it be correct to say that he takes his pleasure? Is it not more accurate to say that he takes his pain? For when he lies with the Queen, does he not hear, in the bed beside her, the breath of Tristan, does he not feel, beneath his palm, the back of Tristan's hand?

Never have the King and Queen been less alone.

Having spared the Queen, the King can do nothing but bear witness to her unhappiness, her uninterrupted desire for Tristan. This form of suffering, which is unbearable, is slightly less unbearable than the suffering that would have been his if he had condemned her to death, since he is left with the hope, however delusory, that a change will come over the Queen, that in the course of time she will begin to forget Tristan.

Thus the King devotes himself to a life of suffering for the sake of a future in which he does not believe.

It is also possible that he wishes the Queen to witness his own suffering, which cannot happen if she is dead.

Is it a wonder that they can't bear to look at each other, in the light of day?

Last night I walked out into the orchard. I had not walked there for many days. The air was cool and fresh—a touch of autumn—and as I made my way along the wagon paths, under a dark sky brilliant with stars, I recalled the night when I saw Tristan and the Queen walking not far from me among the trees—walking so slowly that they were scarcely moving. I recalled the picture vividly, but for some reason I was unable to recapture the sensations that had been stirred in me then. Had they been illusory, those stirrings and wonderments? Had they perhaps been used up? I was pondering these questions when I found myself in a familiar place, not far from the fence of pointed stakes. I recognized the broad apple tree in whose branches the King and I had hidden ourselves, like boys at play.

On a sudden impulse I reached up to a branch and pulled myself into the tree. I climbed through branches heavy with ripe apples until I was nearly at the top. In one direction I could see over the palisade of stakes into the royal forest; in the other I could see, beyond the moonlit orchard stretching away, the pale, towering wall of the castle. In memory I heard the King's voice crying, "Come down, Thomas! What the devil are you doing up there?" and I was wondering how I might reply when I became aware of sounds in the near distance. Quickly I withdrew into the darkness of the leaves.

Two figures came into view, whom I recognized at once as the Queen and Brangane. I was divided between the desire to reveal myself, for I had no wish to spy on the Queen, and the desire to remain hidden, for how could I explain my presence to her, in the orchard, at night, in the trysting tree? As I held myself back, the women came up to the tree. I saw that Brangane was carrying a bundle of some kind. The Queen stood staring at the trunk as if she were imploring it to speak, while Brangane unfolded her bundle, which proved to be a quilt and coverlet. In the moon-speckled shade of the apple tree, the Queen lay down and closed her eyes. Beside her Brangane stood guard, like a crossbowman on a castle wall. They did not speak.

High among the apple branches I looked down on the sleeping Queen, who lay with her head turned slightly to one side. Her face, haughty and sorrowful in daylight, looked mild and peaceful now—the face, almost, of a sleeping child. I was struck again by the mystery of her beauty, as it streamed up at me from the foot of the tree. It came over me that I too was guarding her, as she slept her strange sleep, under the trysting tree. Only then did it all come back to me, the night when I saw them in the orchard, the wonder, the stillness, the moment when the sky was about to crack open and reveal a dazzling light.

Had she come to sleep in the open air because she was unable to sleep in the royal chamber? Had she escaped from the King, whose attentions repelled her? Perhaps she had had word from Tristan—at any moment he would leap over the wall and take her in his arms. Or had she, in her sorrow, sought out the place where she had once been happy?

I dared not move, for fear of waking her or alerting Brangane. Fortunately I am well-disciplined; as a young knight I trained my body to follow my will, and once forced myself to stand motionless in my uncle's orchard from daybreak to sunset. Time passed, or ceased altogether. I had the sensation that

I had been in the tree, guarding the Queen, not for this night only, but for many nights—for every night since the night I had seen her and Tristan walking in the moonlit orchard. I was startled, almost disappointed, when Brangane bent over and shook her awake.

She opened her eyes—I could see them opening, as if to gaze at me in my branches—then she sat up abruptly, held out her hand, and allowed Brangane to raise her to her feet.

"Quickly," Brangane said, as she gathered up the coverlet and quilt.

"He will come," the Queen said, quietly and sorrowfully.

They turned away, and I watched as they passed through the orchard and out of sight. For a long while I stayed in my tree, like a man bound in a spell. Then I climbed down and returned to the castle, even as the cocks began to crow in the courtyard.

The Queen goes out every night and waits for Tristan under the apple tree. The King cannot be ignorant of these journeys.

At this morning's service in the chapel, the Queen rose from kneeling and, growing suddenly faint, stumbled for a moment against the King. The King, who had just risen, was startled by the sudden weight of the Queen against him, and would himself have stumbled and perhaps fallen had I not been able to support him with both hands. The King and Queen recovered at once. The episode lasted the space of a moment, but in my mind I see the three of us fixed in place as in a bas relief: the Queen fallen against the King, the King fallen against his old companion, who himself leans slightly away, his left hand grasping the King's shoulder, his right hand gripping the King's back, his neck tense, his lips pulled back over bared teeth.

This night I woke from a troubling dream of Tristan—he lay wounded and bleeding under a tree—and seemed to hear a sound coming from Tristan's chamber. I sat up, listening intently. There could be no doubt: someone was stirring in Tristan's chamber. I rose, put on my robes and sword belt, and stepped from my room to Tristan's door, which was open a hand's width.

When I entered his chamber I saw in the moon-streaked darkness a figure seated on the side of the bed, between drawn-back curtains. My heart leapt—he had come!—but at once I recognized the King.

"Is it you?" he said, in a voice so sorrowful that a heaviness came over me, and I could scarcely speak.

"It is Thomas, my lord."

"Ah: Thomas. I thought—" He rose, in the dark. "I dislike empty rooms," he said. "They remind me of—" He gestured with a hand, which dropped to his side. "I sometimes come in here, at night. I don't know why. Do you remember when the three of us would ride out together? He was fifteen then. He could already cut up a buck like a man. His harp: the time he made the minstrel weep. Do you remember? I was— twenty-five. Twenty-five! God. Where has it gone? I never sleep. Do you sleep, Thomas? But of course you do. I keep thinking he'll return, to ask my forgiveness. She doesn't eat. She doesn't speak. Let me show you something."

He passed out the door and I followed him into the royal chamber. The shutters were unbarred and night brightness glowed in the room. He pulled aside the bed curtain and showed me the Queen, asleep on her side. I could scarcely see her in the darkness of the bed.

"Have you ever seen a more beautiful face?" the King asked, as he let the curtain drop back. "And yet—" Again that helpless gesture, the hand raised and falling to his side. "But I was going to show you—"

He pulled the curtain aside once more and bent over the Queen. As he gently began to draw down the coverlet, I did not know what to think. Was he going to show me the Queen's nakedness? Then I saw a glint of something; her upper body was covered to the waist. He drew up the coverlet and led me to the door.

"It's a shirt of iron. She has it from the chaplain. She wears it night and day. She is cut, bruised—all over."

"But why—"

"At first I thought she was punishing herself because she had—dishonored me. But now I believe she is punishing herself because he is gone. She removes it if I ask her to. I am tired, Thomas."

"Sleep, my lord."

"Sleep? I'm done with sleep. Sleep is for the young. Sleep no longer desires me. Good night, Thomas."

I left him standing at the door, like a knight whose task it was to guard the Queen's sleep.

I do not like that iron shirt, cutting into the Queen's flesh. Perhaps if I speak to the chaplain?

The King is mistaken about one thing: I too no longer sleep.

Today, after the tables were removed from the hall, a blind harper from Brittany played for us. I watched the King and

Queen staring fiercely at him, trying to penetrate the disguise. Even I, who saw at once it was not Tristan, studied him closely, wondering whether I had perhaps been mistaken, whether he had deceived us by changing the shape of his body.

We are all waiting for him, the shining one.

If Tristan were to return *now,* and beg the King's forgiveness, everything would be restored to him—except the Queen, except the Queen, except the Queen.

A week has passed, with little to report. The harper has left, one of the King's favorite greyhounds has died, a group of six pilgrims have taken up residence in the guest quarters for a few days, a squire accused of striking a servant girl has been given a lashing. Oswin complains that the guests will exhaust the treasury; he reports expenditures for two dozen fowls, one hundred eggs, hay for six horses. Yesterday, in the royal forest, a boar gashed the thigh of the Baron Amaury de Chastelet.

An extraordinary thing has happened.

I went to bed early yesterday evening, after listening to a minstrel's song of Charlemagne and Roland and then playing a game of chess with the King. On parting he spoke of the boar that had gored the baron, slitting him from his knee to his upper thigh; it occurred to me that the King's thoughts were beginning to return to the hunt, a hopeful sign. In my bed I fell at once into a deep sleep and did not wake until dawn. As I woke I became aware of a coldness on my neck. At first I thought it was the chill morning air, but the sensation began to resemble a pressure, a weight of cold. When I reached up to touch my neck I felt a sudden sharp pain in the palm of my hand. I sat up quickly, fully awake, and saw a streak of blood on my palm. On the coverlet lay my dagger with the jeweled handle, which I had placed on Tristan's neck under the pear tree in the Queen's garden.

He was here!—I had no doubt it was Tristan who had placed it on my neck—and before descending to the chapel I stepped into his chamber and pulled aside the bed curtain, as if I might find him sleeping there.

In the chapel, kneeling beside the King, I observed the Queen closely. And now it seemed to me that a change had come over her, that her cheeks were slightly flushed, her lips less drawn, and that I had observed these changes, without thinking about them, for the past several days.

After breakfast I sent a message to Brangane, who met me in the King's garden. On the turf bench beside the fountain of leopards I brought forth the dagger. She drew back—as though I had intended to murder her—but quickly recognized the weapon and its meaning.

"He has gone back," she then said.

Brangane revealed the stratagem to me, which was executed at precisely the time I believed I had nothing to report. The blind harper, who was not blind, was Tristan's messenger. He informed the Queen, by means of a message delivered to Brangane, that Tristan had crossed over from Lyonesse and would devise a way to enter the castle. He might easily have arranged to meet her in the orchard, but he wished to penetrate the castle itself. He and five companions disguised themselves as pilgrims and entered the castle gate; under their humble robes they wore ring mail and swords. For three days they dined among other guests in the great hall, walked in the courtyard, prayed in the chapel. Tristan revealed himself by signs to the Queen and visited her alone in her garden by day and in the orchard by night. He remained for three days and three nights; during the third night he stole into my chamber and returned my dagger. At daybreak he departed for Lyonesse, across the sea, where he lived in his ancestral castle. It was to this castle that he had fled after the night of discovery under the pear tree. There he had lived, sorrowing for his lost Queen, until at last, searching for death in the German wars and not finding it, he had plotted a return to Cornwall in the guise of a pilgrim, to pledge his undying love.

Such was Brangane's story, delivered breathlessly beside the fountain. As she spoke I saw in memory the proud youth from Lyonesse, who long ago came riding to his uncle's court in Cornwall—came riding with such easy grace that it was said he rivaled the King himself. The King had seen in that face the face of his dead sister, Blanchefleur, and I had seen the face of the young King. And in my mind, for a moment, I confused the two of them, the young Prince whom I loved and whom I had instructed in the arts of fencing and dialectic, and the young lord who ten years later came riding into Cornwall with the bearing, the elegance, the hands, the very look of my beloved and still youthful King.

When I asked Brangane why the Queen had not fled to Lyonesse with Tristan, she sat up a little straighter. "She is married to the King," she replied; in her voice I detected a note of reproach.

Tristan does not return. The Queen's face has become sharpened by unhappiness, simplified by longing; her life has contracted to the single act of waiting. It is as if she is shedding herself piece by piece, divesting herself of superfluous looks and gestures, until she has come to resemble the figure of a stone saint on a tympanum, who forever must express, in a single genuflection, the vast multiplicity of poses that constitute a lifetime. The King too is waiting, but without hope: he is waiting for the Queen to forget Tristan and turn her attention to him. Because unhappiness has made him patient, and because he is without hope, he tends to the Queen and even imagines her desires: no longer does he sleep in the royal bedchamber but has removed himself to Tristan's chamber. Sometimes he hears her return from the orchard, where she waits nightly for Tristan, despite the cold weather. Then he lights her way into her chamber, summons a servant to stoke the fire in the hearth, and wishes her a good night before returning to Tristan's chamber.

He has brought a sparrow hawk into his new quarters, where it sleeps on a wooden perch beside his bed. There is also his tame raven, which walks about on the floor or sits on the King's shoulder. Sometimes, at daybreak, the raven gives a loud squawk and flutters up onto the ledge of the window. Once I saw it sitting on top of a carved falcon on a bedpost.

"The Queen wishes to see you in the garden." These were the hushed words breathed at me by Brangane as I came upon her in the shadow of the arched doorway opening from the great hall to the steps leading down to the courtyard. I had never spoken alone with the Queen, and as I made my way to the tower that opened into the garden, I wondered what pitch of desperation had driven her to request this meeting with the King's close companion, one of the six men who had stared down at her with drawn swords as she lay under the pear tree.

Brangane was waiting for me at the tower door. She led me into the garden, along the sanded path shaded by almond and walnut trees, past the fish pond, the herb garden, the square beds of roses and marguerites, to the high hedge with its arched opening. I followed her along the maze of hedge paths, wondering if I was being led to the famous pear tree; evidently we took a different series of turns, for all at once we emerged in a small grassy plot overarched by latticework covered with vines. The Queen was seated on a yellow silk cushion on a box-shaped bench covered with turf, across from a second turf bench on which lay a white silk cushion worked with gold. She motioned me to sit down as Brangane left us to ourselves.

"I am told you may be trusted," she said, in a tone that seemed to me haughty and mistrustful. She looked at me warily, as if wondering how far she might go in usurping my loyalty to the King.

"Brangane"—I spoke carefully—"flatters me."

"No one flatters you!" she said sternly. All at once she stood up—she seemed to tower over me, like an angry father—and as I sprang to my feet I had the sensation that she was going to strike me in the face.

"Have you heard from him?" she said, with a kind of violence. "Why doesn't he come? Something is wrong." There was nothing angry in her now—only an energy of unhappiness.

"I've heard nothing," I said, startled by the change in her face, tense with longing, dangerous with sorrow.

"Something is wrong," she said again, sitting down on her bench. She looked worn and small there, like a tired child.

"If I hear anything—"

"Does he trust you?" she said abruptly, looking up at me.

I hesitated. "He has every reason to."

"Then if you hear something—anything—"

"Yes, I will let you—"

She stood up again. "Something is wrong." She said it for the third time, but remotely, as if she were no longer listening to herself. Then, turning to look at me: "Thank you for"—she thought about it—"for being a good man."

The words startled me—angered me—for it had been a long time since I was able to think of myself as a good man—but she uttered them with such force that I bowed my head in reply, even as I felt the blood beat in my neck.

I think of the change in the Queen, when she stood over me in the garden: the violence of her unhappiness, her face sharp with longing. At that moment, when I felt her passion, her features were unpleasant to look at. Is that her secret for Tristan? Is it when she *stops* being beautiful to look at that she becomes irresistible to him?

There is news of Tristan—news that must be concealed from the Queen. A fearful rumor! How long will she be spared?

I had it from a minstrel who traveled through Arundel before crossing the sea to Cornwall. He has heard that Tristan of Lyonesse has married the daughter of the Duke of Arundel. She is said to be very beautiful.

Tristan married! It is laughable. It can't possibly be true. What troubles me—what frightens me—is the name of the Duke's daughter. She is called Ysolt—Ysolt of the White Hands.

Even as I rage against the rumor, I feel the spell of that name. I imagine Tristan walking beside this second Ysolt, this Ysolt who is not Ysolt, this not-Ysolt who is Ysolt. If he cannot have Ysolt, then he will have—Ysolt. He is drawn to her beauty, but nothing in her beauty can compare with the beauty of her name: Ysolt. Tristan can never marry Ysolt, but he can surely marry Ysolt. His choice is between Ysolt and Ysolt: an Ysolt who is hidden from view, a memory-Ysolt, an Ysolt who is scarcely more than the breath of her name, and a living, laughing Ysolt, a vivid and visible Ysolt, an Ysolt who walks in the sun and casts a strong shadow. All day in exile he thinks of Ysolt, all night in his empty bed he dreams of Ysolt—and slowly, from his dream, a real Ysolt steps forth. How can he not reach out and seize her?

This rumor must not reach the Queen.

My cabin is small and dark, lit only by a lantern swinging on a hook. I steady my writing board with my hand as the shadows stretch and contract. Overhead I hear the creak of masts and stays, the howl of a high wind. So Thomas sails the sea to Lyonesse . . .

It is the King who has sent me—to confirm the rumor. Ah, Thomas, Thomas, did you really believe that such a story could fail to blow through the court like a howling wind?

The Queen, when she heard, uttered a cry that is said to have caused men-at-arms on the wall walk to turn their heads. She refused to show herself for three days. When she appeared, tightly wimpled, her face thickly lacquered with skin whiteners and vermilion coloring, her gray eyes motionless, she looked like an artful statue contrived by Odo of Chester for the pleasure of a King.

A thud from above—a rolling rumble—cry of voices. Perhaps a barrel, tumbling across the deck?

The King's decision to send me to Tristan surprised me at first, but upon reflection it seems necessary and even inevitable.

The King, for whom Tristan has become a monstrous problem, a problem that he can never solve, sees in the rumored
marriage a miraculous solution. His motive, born of despair, is
hope. Tristan married is Tristan reformed, Tristan defeated. It
is the death of Tristan's treasonable passion for the Queen. The
Queen is young, the King still vigorous; she will grieve, and
after a suitable time she will begin to heal. She will understand
that Tristan has turned from her irrevocably, that the King
alone has loved her with an unchanging passion. All this I
could read in his eagerness, his disturbing decisiveness. Already
he is prepared to forgive Tristan everything, as if Tristan's passion for the Queen were a transient, not very serious, entirely
understandable, even praiseworthy episode of his unruly youth.
He forgets that Tristan's youth was far from unruly and was
famous for loyalty and discipline. He further forgets that
Tristan's loyalty, his deep sense of honor, his purity of heart,
his knightly vow, his devotion to chivalry, his absolute and
unwavering trustworthiness, did not for a moment prevent
him from deceiving everyone at court and satisfying repeatedly
his desire for the Queen. As for the Queen, her love for Tristan
has grown more desperate with each passing day. She does not
appear to be gifted in renunciation.

On the last day, Brangane pressed into my palm a ring from
the Queen, which I am to deliver to Tristan.

The Queen fearful, the King hopeful—and I in a ship at
sea, rocked by a wind.

I write these lines in my bedchamber in Tristan's castle. It is the
day after my arrival. The chamber overlooks a cliff, high above
the green-gray sea. Through my window I can look down upon
the narrow shore and the uneven lines of waves. Far to the

right, where the cliff juts forward, I can see a blue-black forest, a line of hills like teeth.

The rumor is true. I have met Ysolt of the White Hands. She is scarcely out of girlhood, and troubling in her young loveliness. Her most striking feature is the skin of her face, which seems to glow like a bowl of translucent ivory containing a candle. Her face is made for happiness. Her eyes are melancholy.

I know who she is, this lovely bride. She is Ysolt without unruliness, without all that bursts forth and disrupts the beauty of the other Ysolt. Tristan, whose life is in terrible disarray, has wedded himself to calmness, to perfection, to innocence, to everything that cannot move him deeply.

This afternoon, when we were alone, I delivered the ring entrusted to me by the Queen. He took it—looked at me—and suddenly bent his head to his hand and kissed the ring passionately.

He does not speak of his marriage.

Evening of the next day. Not until this morning did he ask for news of the Queen. As he spoke, his entire body grew tense, as if he had asked to be lashed across the face.

A servant has spoken to one of my servants. Tristan, it is said, lies beside his wife but does not touch her. She remains a maid.

An unhappy castle! But how could it be otherwise?

Across the sea, the Queen lies awake in the royal chamber. All night long she thinks of the new bride, of Tristan asleep in the arms of his wife. In Tristan's chamber the King lies awake; he is thinking of the Queen alone in her chamber, of Tristan laughing with his bride. Here, in Tristan's castle, Tristan lies restlessly beside the beautiful Ysolt, the Ysolt who is not Ysolt, who can never be Ysolt, who by daring to bear the name Ysolt has doomed herself to lie beside him untouched, unloved, and unforgiven. Ysolt of the White Hands lies white and motionless under the coverlet. Her hands are crossed over her breasts. Her eyes remain open in the dark.

This morning I went hunting with Tristan and a small party. Deep in the forest we found ourselves alone and dismounted to rest under the shade of a tree. At once, as if we were close companions, he began to speak of the Queen. Was this Tristan?—Tristan, who keeps his deepest words to himself, as though to speak were a form of cowardice? Never, he said, has he loved anyone else. He has tried to live apart from her, has tried to form a new life—all in vain. He suffers day and night, causes suffering to others—all because of this love, a love that consumes him like a poison, a sweet poison that flows through his body. Sometimes he imagines that she has forgotten him, in the arms of the King. Then, tormented though he is by jealousy, he is further tormented by self-anger, for daring to imagine her faithlessness. He would gladly die, were it not for fear of causing her pain. He has wronged Ysolt of the White Hands, whose sorrow is nothing but his own sorrow, planted in her breast and growing in her face.

At the end of it all, trembling from the force of his unaccustomed outpouring—looking wildly at me—he sprang to his feet and drew his sword. The blade sang against the metal of the scabbard like a knife sharpened against stone. As he stood over me, holding the blade not far from my head, I felt not only no surprise that he had decided to murder me—for hadn't I heard what only the forest should hear?—but also no surprise that I should accept my death so readily, almost with gratitude.

"Thomas!" he cried, pointing the sword at his own throat. "Tell me she no longer loves me!"

Again I was struck by Tristan's flair for the dramatic, his instinct for memorable moments. It occurred to me to ask myself, as I sat there—sat at his feet, in the forest—is it perhaps the solution? Tristan dead, Tristan out of it?

I gave him the assurance he sought and, rising to my feet, returned with him to our horses.

I do not mean that Tristan's gesture was insincere. On the contrary, it sprang from the deepest part of his nature. It is simply that the heroic stance, the admirable pose, is the form most readily assumed by his passion. Tristan has always been drawn to whatever in life is high, dangerous, difficult, impossible. He must always excel, even if the only person he can exceed is himself. If he loves, he has to love more than anyone on earth has ever loved, he must love as if there were nothing else. Ceaselessly he must overcome obstacles, including the obstacle of his own rectitude.

Can his love of overcoming, his passion for reckless excelling—can this be what led him to betray his beloved King? For if he was going to betray at all, then he had to betray as deeply as possible, he had to betray down to the appalled depths of his honorable nature.

Things have taken a turn—a sudden, disturbing turn. And yet, when I consider events more calmly, was it not waiting there all along, this disaster, coiled in the heart of things like a destiny?

Yesterday, two days after our talk under the tree, Tristan and I again rode out with a hunting party. In the course of the hunt we separated into two groups. I spent the morning with the knights of my party, killing and cutting up six barren hinds and a doe, while sparing two fierce harts, for now is the close season for male deer. We fed our hounds bread dipped in warm blood. As we rode deep into the wood in pursuit of a wounded hind, one of Tristan's men called out to us from a nearby ridge. It was from him that we learned the story.

Tristan, leaving his party to follow his own path, had come upon a young knight who lay bleeding beside a stream. The knight had been set upon by four brothers, one of whom was Foulques de la Blanche Lande, a cruel lord of these parts—a man of gigantic stature and ruthless will, who rides wherever he likes, hunts in Tristan's forest, slaughters harts in the close season, and attacks whoever stands in his path. Tristan set off after the murderous band. He found them in a clearing and a desperate battle began, in the course of which Tristan slew three brothers but was wounded in the thigh by a spear hurled by Foulques de la Blanche Lande. Despite his wound, Tristan battled until the leaves were red with blood, and at last left Foulques de la Blanche Lande dead among his dead brothers. Faint from loss of blood, Tristan managed to mount his horse, which carried him in the direction of the hunt. His men led him back to the castle.

Our party returned at once to the castle, where Tristan lay in his chamber recovering from his wounds.

But the spear wound troubles us. At first it seemed a mere misfortune, an ugly wound in the upper thigh of his left leg. But the infection worsens. The physician says that the tip of the spear was dipped in poison. He has bathed the wound in white of egg and wrapped it in strips of linen. We watch the leg swell alarmingly. Tristan's face is hot and the skin of his leg is yellow. He lacks the strength to rise from his sickbed.

The physician has restricted his diet to barley water mixed with honey and, at night, the milk of crushed almonds.

It is feared he is dying.

I think of Tristan, with noble rage in his heart, setting off to do battle with Foulques de la Blanche Lande. An act of daring and courage, certainly—the sort of high deed, worthy of a minstrel's song, that makes Tristan beloved wherever he rides. And yet, in the heart of his audacity, is there not some darker and more equivocal element? Tristan, immured in a mock marriage of his own devising, tormented with longing, desperate for a way out, haunted by weeks of bliss in the Forest de la Roche Sauvage—will he not feel something terribly alluring about a fight to the death, a fight in which death might no longer refuse him?

So: Tristan wounded, Tristan dying. For it is clear he must die unless his wound can be healed.

He has asked me to send for the Queen. "You have always been true to me," he said, seizing my arm. I looked at him in amazement. He looked back at me tenderly, and again asked me to send for the Queen.

Every morning four servants carry Tristan down to the sandy strip of shore under the cliff, to wait by the sea for the Queen.

He believes that only she can save him—she who cured him of his wound in Ireland, when he went courting for the King. The drama of Tristan's waiting, the drama of his daily descent to the beach, where he lies on two quilts beneath a purple coverlet sewn with gold, his head propped by silk pillows, facing the waves, is heightened by the drama of the sails: he has so arranged it that if the Queen is on the return ship, the sail will be white, but if she remains in Cornwall, the sail will be black.

In the morning we search the horizon, our hands shading our eyes, as green waves thunder at our feet and sea spray salts our lips. In the afternoon, in Tristan's chamber, we look down at the sea stretching off to the sky; we strain our eyes to discover the precise line where sea and sky meet and where, at any moment, a sail, a white sail or a black—life or death—will appear.

How like Tristan that, even in the grip of death, he cannot forgo a taste for striking effects.

Every day he grows weaker. I think: his life has become nothing but the act of waiting. And at once I am reminded of the Queen, going out each night to the orchard, sick with longing, feverish and weary with anticipation—a life lived solely in the future, like that of a fanatical monk who has renounced this world and devotes himself entirely to the realm of heaven.

Tristan longs for the Queen, lives only for the Queen, who alone can cure him, but as he lies on the beach, searching the horizon for the white sail, death must seem not without its attractions. If she comes to his rescue, what then? Back to life, a life of bitterness and suffering, of mock marriage, of impossible separation, of unappeasable love. As he lies on the beach, deafened by the roar of the waves, does he not, in his heart of hearts, long for the black sail?

Ysolt of the White Hands, silent and melancholy, watches with him from the beach, sits with Tristan in his high chamber.

What to say? It is tempting to write no more, to abandon myself to the consolations of silence. I have grown to like the sea, the mindless fall of waves, the wheel of birds, sea-salt and wave-spray. Can it be that I am tired of human beings and their passions? But my hand moves, a force compels me to continue, as though the words I write no longer are mine, but belong to the page alone, which knows nothing, which understands nothing, which suffers nothing. So be it.

Yesterday: a day of storm and sun. Black clouds and rain all morning, then the sun streaking through in lances of light. Tristan, in his chamber, was too weak to raise his head. I sat beside him, struck by his almost boyish beauty—as if death, by eating his flesh and muscle, by ruining his hardness, were restoring his childhood. It is dangerous to have the beauty of Tristan. At twelve years old, at fourteen, he must have had to prove his strength tirelessly, to demonstrate that the lovely boy could throw a spear, kill a boar, strip a hart, thrust his sword between a man's ribs. Now he lay in his bed like a child with a fever. Ysolt of the White Hands sat in the stone window seat, looking out to sea. I could feel the thud of waves on the skin of my arms. I watched her at the window. Her young body was alert and oddly languorous—at any moment it might spring into motion or drift into deep sleep. She too was waiting—waiting for Tristan to touch her into life. Suddenly her body tightened, as if she had been struck by the flat of a sword. "A ship!" she said. Her hand in her lap was a fist.

Tristan struggled to sit up and lay back gasping. "The sail?"

His voice was soft, tender, though I saw he was trying to shout. "The sail."

She leaned her body through the open window, as though to get closer to the ship.

"Black," she said.

I saw the change in Tristan—the terrible stillness, the look, directed to me, of piercing sweetness and desolation. A dark flush burned along his cheek. I seized his hand, which did not return my pressure. He continued to gaze at me with that childlike sad doomed stare.

"Are you sure?" I shouted—someone had to shout—and shaking myself out of a trance of sorrow I released him and went to the window. On the horizon I saw a little ship. The sun was shining. The sail was white as snow.

"Tristan!" I shouted—was mine the only voice in that room?—and for a moment I hesitated. I looked at Ysolt of the White Hands. She was gazing at me bitterly, gazing at me with such hatred that I felt a sudden fear of her, as if she were a wizardess come to damn us all to hell. Her look was like a knife-thrust aimed at my eyes. I understood what she had done, and still I hesitated—hesitated as though I were bound in the spell of that look—hesitated for only a moment more before shouting, "White! Tristan! The white sail!" I found myself at the bed, gripping Tristan's hand, shouting the color of the sail long after I knew he could hear nothing.

That monstrous hesitation! Had I acted immediately, would I have saved him? And though I was startled by Ysolt's bitter look—a look I hadn't known the gentle, sad girl had inside her, growing secretly, ready to leap into her face like the revelation of a disease—it is also true that I had hesitated even before I turned to catch that look. I was taken aback—

surprised by whiteness—bewildered: yes. But isn't it also true that, far down in my mind, where no light penetrates, I wanted the sail to be black, isn't it true that the whiteness horrified me, with its promise of more love, more ruin—that, in this matter of Tristan and the Queen, I was already on the side of death?

The rest can be told quickly. The white sail grew larger, the ship made for the harbor, the Queen was ashore. She came rushing into the room, looking fierce and feverish and in disarray—looking, to my eyes, glorious and fiery, as if she were burning at the stake. She threw herself on Tristan—lay on top of him, breast to breast and mouth to mouth, though Ysolt of the White Hands stood nearby. She kissed his dead face, talked to him, tried to coax him back, as if he were teasing her, the naughty boy. No one thought of trying to pull her away. Ysolt of the White Hands said nothing. I said nothing. Brangane stood in a corner watching. I knew the Queen would never rise from that bed. She was throwing herself at death, rolling around in lovely death. There was nothing else left for her to want.

It is night now. Through my window I can hear the waves falling against the shore. The waves fall in irregular lines, in one place and then another, so that there is always the sound of the sea, louder and softer. But now and then, if one listens very carefully, one can hear something else, hidden between or within the waves, and revealed suddenly, as behind a swiftly drawn curtain: the nothing—the nothing—the nothing at all.

Three weeks have passed since my return to Cornwall. The King grieves, the court is hushed and respectful, but everyone feels the lifting of a burden. Even the King, whose grief runs deep, is not as he was before my voyage. Then, he was like a man beaten with fists, day after day, and left for dead, only to stumble to his feet and be beaten senseless again. Now he grieves with dignity, a King carrying his burden in court and chapel, a lord bearing himself well before his vassals, a public man shaping his sorrow to the gaze of crowds. His grief is deep but measured; it flows readily into the ancient forms forged by generations of mourners. It is too early to imagine the King's happiness. But it is not too early to imagine the diminution of his unhappiness.

The death of Tristan and the Queen is easier for everyone to bear than their life.

There have been changes at court. Modor has been made guardian of the King's tower, a post he holds proudly. He stands with a sharp-tipped ash spear before the chamber door, his missing hand disguised by a gauntlet of ring mail filled with strips of wool. Oswin has a new eye—a splendid eye of marble fashioned by Odo of Chester and fitted cleverly to his eye-hole. It is painted with a brilliant blue iris. Brangane has returned to Ireland; I shall miss her. Tristan's favorite falcon has been given to the chief forester.

Already there is talk at court of the daughter of the Duke of Parmenia. She is said to be very beautiful and gifted in playing the harp. Oswin is much in favor of the match. In truth, an alliance between Cornwall and Parmenia would benefit us immeasurably.

Since my return I have not been much with the King. Perhaps he has been avoiding me.

For my part, by concealing that I saw the Queen and Tristan walking in the orchard, by speaking clandestinely with the Queen's handmaid, by serving the Queen and Tristan and guarding their secret, I betrayed my King, my country, and my God. By hesitating at the window, I betrayed Tristan and the

Queen. The Queen was certainly mistaken: I am not a good man. Whether I am a wiser one is not for me to judge.

If I had it all to do over again, I cannot imagine acting otherwise.

This evening I took a walk in the orchard. The harvest is done, the smell of crushed fruit stings the nostrils like fire-smoke. I walked along the familiar wagon paths, struck into the trees, brushed past branches to which a few leaves still clung, crossed a stream. Soon those branches will be bare, the streams frozen, the paths covered with snow. But now, in late autumn, there is something bracing in the sharp night air; twigs crack underfoot, birds whistle above my head, cold stream-water trickles over stones. I like trying to become lost in the orchard, though I know it well and can rarely succeed. I had come to a stretch not immediately familiar when I became aware of a movement in the shadows not far from where I stood. Then I saw them before me on the path, the Queen and Tristan. They were leaning together, walking so slowly that they were scarcely moving. Her mantle trailed on the ground. And though I knew it was a deceiving image cast up by memory and the imps of night, though I give scant credence to ghosts, and laugh at monkish visions, though the figures were already dissolving into clumps of night shadow, I felt again, rising within me, the mystery, the tender exaltation, the fierce bliss, the serenity like fury, the sheer power of it, before which you can do nothing but bow your head. In the dark I stood there and bowed my head. When I looked up I was alone in the orchard. I turned back toward the castle.

When I entered my chamber it was dark, lit only by the light of stars through the open shutters. Immediately I became aware of a shape on the edge of the bed, beside the half-drawn curtain. A night of visions, Thomas! It struck me that little was known about the dead. Perhaps they did not vanish entirely but left behind a number of very fine skins, which stuck to things.

"Good evening, Thomas. I've been waiting for you."

"Good evening, my lord. I was taking a walk in the orchard."

"I too was out walking, in the garden. Does it help you sleep?"

"Sometimes, my lord."

"Perhaps if we were to walk together, Thomas? Perhaps we might both find sleep, wherever he's hiding."

"I should like that very much."

"Tomorrow, then."

He stood up, a massive darkness in the dark: my sad King. At the doorway he turned.

"I've been meaning to thank you, Thomas."

"I don't understand, my lord."

"For going down there. For seeing things through."

"My lord, I—" In the dark I bowed my head. I listened to his footsteps retreating toward his chamber.

Alone in the dark I felt suddenly restless. Had I not walked enough? I began to pace in the darkness, from the window to the bed and back to the window. The night air was sharp with cold. Tomorrow I would have logs placed in the hearth. Tomorrow I would walk with the King. We would walk in the garden, we would walk in the courtyard, we would tramp along every wagon path in the orchard. Two old warriors, hunting down sleep. In the meantime I was wide awake and fiercely alert. My encounter in the orchard, my words with the King, all this had unfitted me for sleep. I could think of nothing to do but pace up and down in the dark, like a man accursed, like a fool.

All at once I remembered my writing table.

I lit my candle and sat down. The feather of my quill leaped forth in the flamelight like a sword blade. My scraping knife and my lump of pumice cast two sharp shadows. My fingers tingled. No, I wasn't ready for sleep—I was ready for words. I dipped my quill in the ink of the oxhorn, shook off a drop with a single sharp dip of the wrist. I pulled the candle closer and bent over the page, my head bowed as if in prayer. I, Thomas of Cornwall, prince of parchment, lord of black ink, king of all space, summoner of souls, guardian of ghosts, friend of the pear tree and the silence of waves, companion to all those who watch in the night.

ALSO BY STEVEN MILLHAUSER

ENCHANTED NIGHT

Enchanted Night recounts the strange occurrences in a Connecticut town over one incredible summer night. A band of teenage girls breaks into homes and simply leave notes reading "We Are Your Daughters"; a young woman meets a phantom lover on the tree swing in her back yard; a beautiful mannequin steps down from her department store window; and all the dolls "no longer believed in" magically come to life. *Enchanted Night* is a remarkable piece of fiction, a compact tale of loneliness and desire that is as hypnotic and rich as the language Millhauser uses to weave it.

Fiction/Literature/0-375-70696-8

THE KNIFE THROWER AND OTHER STORIES

The Knife Thrower explores the magnificent obsessions of the unfettered imagination, as well as the darker subterranean currents that fuel them. With the panache of a magician he conducts his readers from the dark corners beneath the sunlit world to a balloonist's tour of the heavens. He transforms department stores and amusement parks into alternate universes of infinite plenitude and menace. On each page Millhauser confirms his stature as a narrative enchanter in the tradition of Nabokov, Calvino, and Borges.

Fiction/Literature/0-679-78163-3

ALSO AVAILABLE

Martin Dressler, 0-679-78127-7

Edwin Mullhouse, 0-679-76652-9

Little Kingdoms, 0-375-70143-5

VINTAGE CONTEMPORARIES
Available from your local bookstore, or call toll-free to order:
1-800-793-2665 (credit cards only).